TO BREAK A COVENANT

TO BREAK A COVENANT

ALISON AMES

PAGE STREET
PUBLISHING CO.

First published in 2021 by
Page Street Publishing Co.
27 Congress Street, Suite 105
Salem, MA 01970
www.pagestreetpublishing.com

Distributed by Macmillan, sales in Canada by The Canadian Manda Group.

25   24   23   22   21   1   2   3   4   5

ISBN-13: 978-1-64567-206-7
ISBN-10: 1-64567-206-9

Library of Congress Control Number: 2020945241

Cover and book design by Page Street Publishing Co.
Printed and bound in the United States

FOR EMMA

If you've ever seen one of those ghost-hunting TV shows, you've seen Moon Basin. Paranormal investigators have been coming here since before the Amityville hoax even hit the airwaves. There's not a show on record that hasn't done an episode here.

The bare-bones version goes like this: The coal mine came first and the town was built to sustain it. The relationship progressed symbiotically until the explosion, which left seventeen miners missing and started an underground fire that's still burning, feeding on the seams of coal. About four months after the miners disappeared, ash started raining out of the sky. It won't stop until the fire goes out, and depending on how much coal there is still left in the earth, that could be another two hundred years.

Ash blankets the Old Town now, filling the air and blocking out the sun. The air quality got so bad that the townsfolk had to move, but rather than uproot completely and go somewhere new, they simply found the edge of the ashfall and resettled beyond it. There are mining towns just like ours all across the eastern US, but that's the one thing that makes Moon Basin different.

No one ever leaves.

ONE

I sat in the graveyard waiting for Nina, drinking a slushie and sketching. It was the first day of summer vacation, and the sun was already baking the dew off the grass. My back was pressed against the pitted stone legs of an angel in the shadow of an old-money crypt, all cool marble and arching columns. There were rich people in this town once, and each of them was buried like royalty. Everyone had a statue. I was surrounded by angels and goddesses, elaborate crosses and gigantic engraved markers, but I was alone in the back half of the cemetery. No one living visited the people buried here.

I kept looking up and around. Nina never meant to scare me, but she moved fast and quiet, like a cat. I'd lost a lot of good beverages over the years when she'd popped out of nowhere like a jack-in-the-box. I took a sip and set the cup carefully next to the angel's feet. The drawing I was working on was eluding me somehow; there was a shape in my mind that I couldn't seem to get onto paper. I scratched out another attempt and started again.

"Whatcha got?"

I slammed both hands down onto the sketchbook, but I didn't jump, and I didn't scream. A rare achievement.

"One of these days I'm gonna have a heart attack," I said, picking up the cup and moving so she could sit down next to me.

1

"I'll save you." She slid the book out of my hands and looked at it. "What is this?"

"I'm not sure yet."

"I still can't believe Ms. McKeown is letting you keep an *art* dream journal over the summer," she grumbled, flipping back a few pages.

"It pays to underachieve," I said, grinning. "If you weren't so dead set on being the class of '04's valedictorian, I bet you could have one, too."

She narrowed her eyes at me and held out her hand for the slushie. I gave it to her and she returned to the sketchbook. "What is *this*?"

I looked over her shoulder. "Oh, that was a good one."

"It looks like the three of us in the desert."

"Yep," I said. "I watched *The Mummy* right before I went to sleep."

"Does that make me Rachel Weisz?" She swished her hair around as she quoted, "'I . . . am a *librarian*.'"

"Lisey's hair is bigger than yours," I said. "She'd be Rachel."

Nina nodded. "Harsh but fair." She turned a few more pages back, pausing at a jagged, scribbled circle that filled the entire page, then flipped back to the one I'd been working on. "So this is . . ."

"I don't know," I said. "In the dream I was in the woods in Old Town, and there was a shape with me, but I can't remember it, I guess? I can't make it, like, coalesce outside of my head."

She chewed on my straw for a moment and then said, "Ghost."

"Well, obviously," I said. "It's always a ghost."

She laughed. "This town is so cracked."

An understatement if there ever was one. Like calling Ted Bundy "kind of a bad guy."

"Duh," I said. "Why do you think we meet up in a graveyard all the time?"

"Because we *met* here, dork. It's the birthplace of our friendship."

"The only nine-year-olds at a funeral," I said, nodding. "They should have made us into a horror movie."

She elbowed me and got to her feet. "Let's go already. The pool isn't gonna get *less* crowded." She held out her hand and I took it, and she lifted me off the ground the same way she had on the day we met.

The whole town came to my father's funeral. The men sweated in suits and ties and the women wore too-short cocktail dresses that they tried to make somber with veils and hats. The whole thing took less than an hour. My mother's wrists were still bandaged.

Afterward we drove to the cemetery, separate cars all trailing the hearse. There wasn't enough room for everyone to stand around the coffin. I pressed my back against the Kildare tomb, the marble only slightly cooler than the heavy air, watching the crowd. My mother was crying. I squeezed her hand and felt her fingers flex lightly in mine, the most motion she could summon. I wasn't bored, exactly, but I couldn't keep my mind on my father, supposedly in the box in front of us. I leaned my head back against the dead Kildares and watched a cloud sail in front of the sun.

After the crypt had been closed and Reverend Parker had

said his piece, there was a mad dash to be the first to speak to my mother. People kept clasping her arms. "Oops—sorry, June, I'm so sorry, are you all right? I mean, not—I know you're not—sorry, sorry—"

"He was such a good man, just *such* a good man—"

"I have a book that absolutely *saved* me when I lost Daniel, I'll send it to you—"

In the crush of people trying to comfort her, I slipped away.

The cemetery was massive. I made two or three confused turns before I found myself in a completely deserted section of graveyard. It was the older part of the cemetery, where they put all the bodies they brought over from Old Moon Basin, and there was a sort of shambling, winding-down air to it that put me on edge. I sat down on the ledge running around a smaller mausoleum, my back against the robes of the least forbidding-looking angel, and surveyed the area cautiously. It was still hot, and the cloud I had watched had long since passed the sun, but I felt like I was sitting in shadow.

As I sat there staring at the crumbling gravestones, my head began to swim. My vision started to go white around the edges and I could feel my heart leaping in my chest, a swooping, hollow sensation that made me gasp for air. The gravestones tilted, drawing me toward them. I gripped the stone beneath me, breathing shallowly, and suddenly a small sweet face appeared in front of me. For one paralyzing moment, I was sure it was one of the angels, climbed down from its marble pedestal to grab me, to *get* me, and I was drawing breath to scream when it spoke.

"You look weird," she said. "Are you okay?"

"You look weird," I snapped, instinctively defensive, angry at myself for being scared. I wanted to get up and walk away but I didn't trust my body just then. I pressed farther back into the angel's robes.

The girl plopped down on the ground in front of me, folding her legs into a pretzel. "Okay," she said.

I kept my eyes fixed on the gravestone ahead—Myrna Walters. I tried to breathe evenly and waited for her to leave.

"Is the funeral for your family?"

I didn't speak.

"I know it is," she said. "My dad said we should go."

She flicked a pebble at me. It hit my shoulder with a soft *thwip* and fell into my lap. I whipped it back at her, harder than I meant to. "What's it to you?"

She shrugged, rubbing at her arm where I'd hit her. "I just thought you looked sad, is all. Sorry." She pushed herself up off the ground. "Hope you feel better."

Her hair swung around her shoulders as she turned to leave. Something twanged in my chest, my heart clenched and unclenched, and I blurted out, "Wait."

She looked back at me, popped her hip, and folded her arms. She raised her eyebrows.

"I'm sorry," I said. "I am sad. I'm sorry."

She sat back down. "I'm Nina."

"Clem." We sat there in silence for a while, and finally I said, "My dad died."

Nina nodded. "That's what my dad said. He wouldn't tell me how."

I didn't know then either. I didn't know until Danny Nelson told me on the last day of eighth grade and I punched him in the face.

"My mom wouldn't tell me either. But she was in the hospital for a while after." I studied the weeds growing up around the base of the stone I was sitting on. "I stayed at the motel."

Three days alone there, lying on the scratchy coverlet while the air conditioner poured cold across my skin. Anson and Sherlene Perry came by in the mornings with food, bottles of water. They disconnected the cable so I couldn't watch the news, gave me a stack of movies. I watched *The Last Unicorn* seven times. I floated in the pool. I waited for my mother to come and get me.

Nina pursed her lips. "Was it fun?"

"I guess. The vending machine has orange soda." My dress was scratchy, and it stuck to my back in the heat. "Why did your dad say you had to come?"

She looked a little embarrassed when she said, "He saw you at the motel. He works there."

I thought about the man that I'd seen refilling the ice machine, skimming the pool. He'd smiled at me.

"He thinks my mom is dead," she said. Her face was doll smooth, totally blank.

"What?" It took a moment to settle in my brain, and then I asked, "Why?"

"She drove off the road. They only found her car. We had a funeral, too."

"How come they couldn't find her?"

"I don't know." She tucked her hair behind her ear and tilted her head so that the dark wing of it swept out across her back.

"That's really sad," I said. At least I knew where my dad was. At least I could visit him.

"I was little." She looked down, but not before I saw the glint of tears in her eyes. She pushed some dirt around with the toe of her shoe, making a tiny hill and then flattening it again.

After a minute, she looked back up at me. "He said you looked like you needed a friend."

I wanted to try for nonchalance, to impress this blunt, lanky girl with the kind eyes, but I've never been wired for cool. I closed my eyes and thanked her father silently. "I guess I do," I said, swallowing the lump in my throat.

She smiled then, and I felt the shadow recede. "Do you wanna leave?"

I looked over my shoulder, back toward the main part of the cemetery. The crowd was starting to disperse. "I think we have to do the—the after thing," I said reluctantly. "Back at the house."

She stood up and held out her hand.

"We'll go together, then."

Paranormal America, Episode 1
Unused Footage

(An elderly man sits in a rocking chair in what appears to be his living room. Seated across from him is a young woman holding a clipboard. The boom mic is visible in the top right corner of the frame.)

KEITH JEPSON: Oh, a'course I remember when the mine blew up. I knew Vinnie Freeman. Fine man. Fine man. A shame he didn't manage to get that wife of his pregnant before he died. We coulda used another Freeman in this town. And a'course she left after the whole kerfuffle. Should have been an example for that other'un.

SIOBHAN SINCLAIR: You're referring to Mellie Harington. *(She glances at the camera.)* The wife of the miner believed to have caused the explosion.

JEPSON: Oh, ayuh. Loony bird. Wa'nt her fault, poor thing, but she sure did make for good newspaper. Guess she rather'd Sidney be crazy than admit he got a bunch of good men killed 'cause he was stealin' from the mine.

SINCLAIR: Did you ever experience—then or now—any of the paranormal phenomena that other residents of the town reported? I understand that you and your wife didn't want to move to "the new Basin" even after the ash started falling.

(JEPSON purses his lips and blows a weak raspberry. He waves a hand.)

JEPSON: We never. Irma sometimes slept-walked, I guess, but she did that before the mine blew up.

(His eyes flick upward, staring at something above the camera.)

JEPSON: I never had any kind of . . . what do you say. Paranormal. Nothin' like that. We just didn't want to leave our house.

SINCLAIR: And what about now? Do you still believe you're unaffected by whatever presence exists here?

JEPSON: We built that house, y'know. From the ground up.

SINCLAIR: Sir—

JEPSON: Wa'nt fair of the gov'ment to make us leave. We're citizens. We have rights.

SINCLAIR: I understand. If we could just—

JEPSON: What business is it of theirs, a person wants to die in his own home?

SINCLAIR: —just go back to—

JEPSON: We tried to sue, y'know. Don't remember if I told you that. Lawyer said we didn't have a case. Because it was for our welfare.

SINCLAIR: Sir—

JEPSON: Now I'm gonna die in this goddamn trailer.

(SINCLAIR *looks at the camera and makes a slashing motion at her neck. A hand closes over the lens, and then there is darkness.*)

TWO

My mom was a surgeon—the Basin's only surgeon—before my dad died. Then she went into the mine, and the tendons in her wrists got cut so deep they couldn't be repaired. She got carpal tunnel gloves and a job at the grocery store, and the two of us got a different life.

Less than a month after the funeral, we moved into a two-bedroom trailer in a park so close to the end of High Grange Road that it didn't even have a name. We were shuffling down the ramp of the moving truck, holding my mattress, when I saw Nina in the common yard. I flashed her a smile as I fought to keep my grip, afraid to put the full weight of the mattress onto my mother's damaged arms. We wrestled the mattress inside and came back out, and I paused for a second while my mom ducked back into the truck.

"Are you moving in?" Nina asked.

I nodded and she beamed. The trailer she had come out of was directly across from ours, sunflowers blooming cheerily around its front stoop.

"You should come over for dinner tonight," she said. "You and your mom. My dad will make something really nice. Have you ever had real Mexican food?"

"My mom works tonight," I said, my heart sinking. "Overnight."

"Well, you should definitely come over, then. Sleepover! Or I can come to your house."

"Um—"

"Come on," she urged, taking both of my hands in hers. "It'll be fun."

I promised I'd ask and she disappeared back inside her trailer. As my mom and I continued moving our stuff in, I caught her peeking out her bedroom window, which looked directly into mine. She gave a tiny wave, and her face looked worried. I could tell she was afraid she'd been too pushy. I smiled at her through the windows and waved back, trying to put her at ease. When my mother left for work that night, I followed her out, then crossed the yard to the sunflower stoop. The door swung open before I could knock.

"Yay!" Nina cried, clapping her hands together. She turned and yelled something in Spanish and a man's voice replied. She turned back to me and grinned. "Come on in."

Her father came out of the kitchen, a blue towel slung over his shoulder. He was smaller than I'd thought he was when I'd seen him at the motel, but he had Nina's eyes, and he smiled at me as he took my hand.

"I'm sorry about your father," he said. "I'm Nina's dad. You can call me Paul."

Over dinner he told us stories about his job, the strange things he'd found, the people he'd met. The time he'd been snowed in a few winters ago. At one point I laughed so hard I coughed a grain of rice out of my nose and froze, completely mortified, until the two of them started howling with mirth. I felt more and more at ease as the evening passed, and time went by so quickly that I was surprised when Paul finally pushed back his chair and stood.

"I have to go to sleep, girls," he said, collecting our plates. "Mr. Perry wants me at work bright and early tomorrow."

"When is the pool open again?" Nina asked.

"End of the school year," he answered, patting her head as he walked toward his bedroom. "Night, girls. Sleep tight. Love you."

Nina made a face at me and then broke into a smile.

"Did you bring PJs?" She stood, shoving her chair back. "I have some super-cute ones that're too small for me now. C'mon."

The pajamas fit after I rolled the cuffs a few times. They were perfectly worn in, and wearing them made me feel like I belonged there, in the trailer with the sunflower stoop. We sat on Nina's bed, watched horror movies on her tiny bedroom TV and talked, chewing on gummy bears and shrieking with laughter at all the bad special effects. After a long time, as the moonlight glowed around the edges of her curtains, we fell asleep next to each other, holding hands.

Everyone in town warned Paul about getting a pet. Kim, who owned the liquor store, told him about the schnauzer puppy that disappeared out of her front yard. One of the waitresses at the diner moved away after her dog Snaps went rabid. Everyone old enough to be a parent here had a dead pet story, and that's why none of their kids had any.

A cat won't last, they told him. Get her a snake. Get her a fish. Something cold-blooded. But Nina wanted something soft and warm that she could hold, and Paul wanted her to be happy, so Toast came home.

"You can't let him outside," Paul said with his hand resting on the carrier, making eye contact with each of us in turn. "It's not safe."

The coyotes of Moon Basin hunt up in the hills, but they come down into town during the new moon when everything is pitch-black and quiet. They move without a sound, walking up and down the streets, pausing to look in people's windows. No one's ever seen them kill anything, but any animal that gets outside at night, it's not there the next morning. Or it's there, but it's chewed open, and it's clear it didn't die quick.

I didn't feel Toast get up from between us and jump down off the bed. I'm a light sleeper. I know Nina blamed me, even though she tried not to. I imagine he prowled through the trailer before he saw the window above the kitchen sink. It was slightly ajar, as it often was, but on that night there was the very beginning of a tear in the screen that had gone unnoticed by the three of us. Toast leaped up onto the counter, put his nose to the window. He wriggled through the hole, still such a tiny cat, and then he was gone.

We found him on the side of High Grange Road with his feet chewed off.

Nina threw up and I held her hair, and then we sat on the gravel and held each other and cried. We buried him in the field right then, scraping out the grave with our bare hands, dirt caking the tear tracks on our faces. Nina said a prayer in

Spanish, and I repeated the words as best I could. Paul looked sad and small at dinner that night. He put his hand on Nina's very briefly before he said, "I'm so sorry, mijita."

"It's not *your* fault," she said, her meaning clear.

Paul's voice sharpened as he replied, "There is nothing wrong with Moon Basin. What happened to Toast was an accident."

Her chin jutted out the way it did when she felt accused. "People in other towns have cats."

"I know."

"And those cats don't die."

He looked even smaller then. He rested his hands on the edge of the table, staring down at his splayed fingers. "I know," he said again, quieter. "I'm sorry. I shouldn't have let you get a cat. I should have listened."

I was trying very hard not to cry, staring into my plate, thinking about Toast and how if we had never met him, he would be alive somewhere else.

"Maybe in a few months, when we're a little bit less sad, we can think about getting something that lives in a cage, so it can't get out."

"I don't want a cage," Nina said sullenly, stabbing her fork at individual kernels of corn. "That's mean."

"Well, that's a good point," he said, almost pleading with her. "That's very kind of you to think about."

Stab, stab.

"So, okay. No cage. We'll just keep hanging out, the two of us. But someday when you're older, after you graduate from college and move somewhere else, you can have all the cats you want." He smiled at her. "As long as you promise to come and visit your papa."

There was a long silence before she laid the fork down. At last she looked up at him.

"Well, duh," she said, and that was that.

Later, when she thought I was asleep, I heard her crying. I reached across the Toast-sized gap between us and took her hand.

Grave Encounters, Episode 12
Unused Footage

(A girl wearing a corseted dress crouches in the middle of a fallow field. Her black hair is drawn into spiky pigtails. Her hands, when she lifts the mic, are gloved in fishnet.)

BATTY: Are you getting it? Can you see it if I'm crouching?

DAWSON BROWNE, *from off-screen*: Your skirt's kind of in the way, can you just—?

(BATTY shifts her weight, pulling the skirt back to reveal the small dead animal lying in front of her.)

BROWNE: Yeah, better. It's still kind of hard to tell what it is, though. I wish we had something to, like, hold it up with.

BATTY: I mean, I'll grab it.

BROWNE: Batty, Christ, don't be weird.

(She bares her teeth at the camera and looks back down at the animal.)

BATTY: Maybe we can start without me in the shot. Like a real close-up zoom of it and then you pan out to show I'm here.

(The camera zooms in on the little corpse, revealing it to be a rabbit with its spine torn out. Its eyes have burst.)

BROWNE: That's better. You can really see it now.

BATTY, *now off-screen*: Okay, good.

(The camera begins zooming slowly in and out as BATTY talks.)

BATTY, *intermittently off-screen*: I do think it's bullshit they won't let us go in there, though. I mean, what is even the *point*, right? If you're gonna have this big haunted reputation, you have to let people actually *experience* your shit. I'm going to talk to that sheriff again, I think. He seems like a pushover. I mean, we *paid* to come here. This is our *job*. He should be grateful people are still interested in this shitbox.

(She looks into the lens, unaware that the camera is zoomed in so far that the shot is just her nose and black-lipsticked mouth. She grins.)

BATTY: You think we'll ever get an actual sighting?

BROWNE: Not if you keep dressing like an eighth grader playing Ouija.

BATTY: Ah, fuck you, Dawson, you prick. Who gets the ratings?

(The camera swings around to face BROWNE. He gives it the middle finger with both hands.)

BROWNE: My camera work, is who. Look how you're holding that thing.

(The picture jitters and swoops down to the dead rabbit, focusing on its punctured eyeball.)

BATTY: Ugh. So gross. Love it.

BROWNE: You know, if you press the zoom button, you don't have to actually put the camera lens *into* the disgusting dead animal—

BATTY: Fine, hotshot. Show me which one the zoom is. Is it this—

(End of footage.)

THREE

For years Nina and I were a snake consuming its own tail: a perfect circle, a closed loop. We sat at lunch together, just the two of us, heads bowed over books and pens and friendship bracelets, tangled together with so much embroidery floss. We weren't mean, exactly. We were just . . . enough. Enough for each other. We filled up our lives and there wasn't room for anyone else.

We were in the park on the east side of town, lying on our backs on the merry-go-round. Nina was tall enough that her feet touched the ground, so she was kicking us around in a slow circle. There was no one else in the park. It was too hot to be outdoors, and everyone was either at the pool or inside with the shades drawn and the air conditioner blasting.

"Hey, can I ask you something?"

"Yeah," I said.

"Do you like anyone at school?"

The merry-go-round creaked gently, a rhythmic, rusty whine that came at regular intervals, and all around us was the sound of insects buzzing.

"Do you?" I countered, stalling. I had known for a little over a year—since I was maybe twelve—that I liked girls, but I hadn't figured out how to tell Nina. I didn't want her to think I had a crush on her. I didn't want anything to change between us.

"I don't think so," she said. "Now you."

I took a deep breath.

"I don't think there's any girls at school that would like me," I said. "So I guess there's nobody that I like."

She was quiet for a moment. I closed my eyes against the sun, looking at the pink backs of my eyelids, counting my breaths.

"I bet there's gonna be a girl who will like you," she said after another minute. "Only girls?"

"Yeah," I said. "Why, what about you?"

"I dunno," she said. "I guess we'll see."

I put my hand up over my head and grabbed Nina's wrist, felt her clasp mine. The soft scudding of her foot in the playground wood chips lulled me, and the slow spin of the merry-go-round swung me gently down into sleep.

I don't know how long we were asleep, but when I sat upright and clanged my head on one of the bars, the sun had moved considerably. I yelped, then collapsed back onto the hot metal. Nina propped herself up on an elbow and leaned over me.

"Nicely done. Ten out of ten."

I rolled my eyes at her.

"You're gonna have a sunburn," she said.

I stretched out my arm, looked at my skin, and winced. "Probably." I shuffled onto my stomach, pressed myself up to sit against the peeling blue-painted bar. "Why didn't we go to the pool again?"

"You'd still burn at the pool. The problem is the sun."

"I remember sunscreen better when we're going to swim."

Nina shrugged. "Whatever. I'm hungry. Let's go to the Half Moon. We can get you some aloe at the drugstore."

She shimmied under the bar and stood, shaking her hair out

over her shoulders and tucking it behind her ears. I slithered out behind her. Before we had taken more than three steps, Nina stopped short. I practically climbed up her back, sleep-dazed as I was, not watching where she was going. She pulled me around next to her, almost roughly, and jerked her chin to our right. I followed her gaze out across the grass to a maple tree.

"What?"

She sighed and yanked my arm, moving me, and then I saw the fan of blond hair. There was a girl pressed against the trunk of the maple, her hair a massive, cloudlike curtain that fell over her shoulders and most of her back. She was clutching the tree hard, like she was drowning and it was a life raft. I couldn't see her face, but it felt somehow like she was looking right at me.

"Hey!" Nina called.

The girl flinched. She seemed to shrink, to recede farther into her cloud of hair, but she didn't move away.

Nina waved. "Hey! Are you okay?"

She tugged my arm and we started walking toward the tree slowly, like we were trying to catch an animal.

"Is she in our grade?" I asked in a whisper. "I don't remember ever seeing her before. Like, ever."

"I don't either," Nina whispered. "Maybe she's home-schooled?"

She stepped away from the tree as we got closer, but she kept her hand on the trunk. Her slender fingers splayed across the bark, digging in ever so slightly. She barely glanced at me before shifting her gaze to Nina.

"Hi," she said. Her voice was thin, almost reedy.

"Hey," Nina said again, matching her volume, and I echoed her.

"Hey."

We stood there for a moment, watching each other. She was wearing jean shorts that she had cut off herself, the uneven legs fraying well above her bony knees. Her hair was almost white, her skin practically translucent. I don't think either of us had ever seen a girl that totally colorless. Her eyelashes were white too, long and thick, and it gave her a staring, wide-eyed look that fell just short of unsettling.

"Were you watching us?" Nina managed to make this sound like a real question, rather than an accusation.

The girl lifted one shoulder, dropped it again.

"For how long?"

Blink-blink of the snowy lashes.

"You could have just come over, you know," offered Nina. "We don't bite."

The girl looked at me, like she wanted me to confirm whether or not this was true. I smiled limply at her. I wasn't sure what Nina was doing.

"I'm Nina," she said, raising her eyebrows expectantly.

"Elise," said the girl. "Lisey."

Nina put out her hand, her skin even darker against Lisey's, and they shook. Lisey turned her strange eyes on me and I said, "Clem." I took her hand, her clammy fingers sliding past mine.

"Do you wanna come get cheese fries?" Nina asked her, throwing me for a loop. I shot a look at her, like, *What the what?*, and she gave me one back that I couldn't quite decipher. I felt prickly and possessive and annoyed by both of those feelings. She was adopting this girl like she had adopted me, and I didn't like being in the same category as this pale, frail creature.

Lisey shook her head.

"No," she said, in case we hadn't gotten it.

Surge of triumph. Prickle of shame for feeling said triumph.

Nina shrugged and turned to go, and I was about to follow her when Lisey said, "Wait."

We looked at her. She placed a finger to her lips and then pointed beyond us, into the scrubby field with the spray-painted baseball diamond.

"What?"

"The bird," she whispered. "Do you see it?"

"The crow?" I was liking this less and less by the moment. "Um, yeah. It's a crow."

The glossy bird was hopping around, fluttering its wings every so often. It was almost the size of a hawk.

"I'm trying to tame it," she said, still using that hushed tone. "It startled when you hit your head"—she darted a glance at me—"but it didn't go far. I think it likes me."

I widened my eyes at Nina, trying to convey how much I thought we should leave. She gave me what I can only describe as her *sorry-you're-on-the-rollercoaster-now* look and crouched down next to Lisey, who was arranging a little pile of peanuts on the ground.

"Why?" Nina asked. "Why tame it?"

"They're important." Lisey's voice was almost reverent. "They can go between worlds."

"What?"

"This one and the next one. Where dead people are. The king of the gods has one who sits on his shoulder and tells him what he needs to know because the spirits whisper it to him. They remember faces, and they teach each other. If you hurt one of the flock, that crow tells all the others about you and then they know who you are. So if I make friends with one, that one will bring others to see me. They're smart. And they protect their families."

She pressed her lips shut, as if surprised she'd said so much.

Nina shifted down more fully onto the ground and poked at the peanuts thoughtfully. "I like that. Family has your back." She looked up at Lisey and grinned. "You can sic 'em on anyone who messes with us."

Lisey blushed all the way from the neckline of her shirt to the tips of her ears. On such a pale face it was startling, and for some reason it made me soften toward her. She had no camouflage, no natural defenses.

"I don't think I can, like, make them do my *bidding*," she said with a hint of a smile in her voice. "I'm not a *supervillain*."

"Well, maybe you can work up to it."

I could feel the longing radiating off of her, this tadpole of a girl. I recognized it. I thought about Nina finding me, pressing past my defenses. She saw something in me that made her want me around; she sensed that I was lonely. She was little and her dad told her to be nice to me, I know, but. Standing there, watching Lisey flick peanut halves toward the crow, I understood the impulse. We could make ourselves a home for this girl.

I sat down next to her.

"Okay," I said, snagging a peanut and popping it into my mouth. "If he doesn't eat one in the next fifteen minutes, we're going to the diner."

"He's gonna eat one."

"Bet he won't."

"He will."

He ate one, in the end. She had to flick it all the way over to him; he refused to move any closer to us, shifting from one foot to the other as he eyed the food. As we walked away, leaving the little pile of nuts behind us, I heard the flutter of wings and the cackle of a delighted crow.

FOUR

I was lying on the floor of the living room listening to Patsy Cline. My mother came in about halfway through "Seven Lonely Days," stooped to pat my head, and disappeared into her bedroom. The record spun out soon after that, and I turned the player off rather than flip it over. I was dozing a little bit when Nina came in like a hurricane.

"Clem!"

I looked up at her. From that angle she seemed even taller than her nearly six feet, hair twisted up on top of her head, Nirvana T-shirt barely skimming the waist of her cutoffs.

"God, you sleep a lot," she said.

"Yeah, but not *well.* I take it where I can get it."

She rolled her eyes and dropped a sheaf of paper at my feet. "PSATs, baby."

"Ugh, why? They don't even count until next year."

"You're not gonna get into an Ivy with that attitude." She flopped down beside me, pulling a gigantic book out of her bag. "Here. Practice tests."

"You know it's, like, the third day of summer break, right?"

"You know that means I gave you, like, two whole days off, right?"

"I wanna sit in the park and eat snow cones," I said, closing my eyes. "I don't want to do anything that requires thought. It's too hot."

She put something on my forehead.

"Is that an eraser?"

"Yes." She placed a pen under my nose, horizontally across my lip like a mustache. "It's important to get a head start on this, Clem. So you can either study with me, or I can sit here and stack things on your head until you decide to study with me. Either way you end up studying, so the sooner we start, the sooner you can get a snow cone. Eh?"

She was wiggling her eyebrows. I could tell with my eyes shut. I rolled onto my stomach, propping myself on my forearms to look at her. "I'm not getting into an Ivy regardless of the PSATs. So I don't really see the point in wasting my time."

"Of course you are. Now that you're doing better with math—"

"Nina. I don't want to go to college."

She looked at me then, genuinely surprised. She almost laughed a little. "What?"

"I don't. I can't afford it, and I don't . . ." I waved my hand halfheartedly. "I don't know, I just don't want to."

"Clem. We've been talking about going to school together since sixth grade. Even Lisey wants to at least move away with us."

"I know, and I don't—I don't want us to be apart, but—"

"But what?"

"But I don't know! I just—now that it's more real, I . . ." I couldn't figure out how to finish the sentence.

She folded her arms and looked at me. "So, what. You're just not gonna go to college."

"I don't know yet, Neen. I didn't say I'm definitely not going.

I just—"

"You just don't want to go with me."

"What? Why are you being so—"

"I thought we had a plan, Clem." She was talking too loud, her voice high like she was about to start crying. "I thought we were going to leave together, go out into the world and *do* something—"

A tear slipped down her cheek and she swiped it away.

"Whatever. Fine. Stay here forever. I just thought we wanted the same thing."

We did want the same thing. We wanted to stay together. But it needled me that she was so set on this one specific thing—this idea that we had to *leave*. She always had such a clear vision of the future that I never needed my own, but for the first time, I didn't agree with it.

"Well, why don't you go to a state school?"

"Great, perfect, so you're going to have me ruin my future—"

"Wow, it would *ruin* your *future* to stay in the Basin? It would *ruin* your future to not have to pay fucking tuition at—"

"Scholarships, Clem, don't be obtuse—"

"I don't have the grades for scholarships," I snapped. "I don't play a sport. I am academically average at best. There is literally nothing about me that would compel anyone to give me a free ride, let alone an Ivy, except maybe the fact that my dad got yanked into a thresher and shredded like cheese when I was a kid. What do you think, do you think that'll do it?"

She sank back onto the floor like I'd slapped her.

"Good things don't happen to people who leave town, Nina," I said, staring at the floor, trying to will the anger away.

"What are you even *talking* about? Are you really trying to blame the *Basin*—"

"What do you think happened to your mom?"

As soon as it left my mouth, I knew I'd gone too far. We didn't talk about Nina's mom. We didn't talk about the people who disappeared. I knew better. The *I'm sorry* I needed to say lodged behind my lips and I couldn't get it out. Nina's mouth crimped into a tight flat line and she wouldn't look at me.

"Okay, well," she said, her inflection indicating that she hadn't really meant for anything to come after those words. "I'll just—"

She pushed herself to her feet. Her face was flushed and her eyes were still glittery. She kicked the book across the floor to me. "In case you change your mind."

Then she turned on her heel and left the trailer, shutting the door quietly so as not to wake my mother. I balled up one of the sheets of paper and threw it hard at the wall. It bounced off and fell behind the TV. I flopped back onto the floor.

After about half an hour of staring at the ceiling, I kicked my feet into sandals and banged out of the house. I wanted to go to the cemetery, but if Nina decided to look for me that was the first place she'd go. I walked for a while with the sun beating down on me, sweat rolling down my face, and gradually I realized I was heading for the bridge.

The Moon Basin River Bridge is high and arched and made of stone, shrouded by willow trees that have been dying slowly for years. It's a narrow footpath, worn smooth and treacherous, and the sides are low enough that you could easily fall over them. Or jump if you wanted.

It was cool in the shade of the willows and I settled down on my back, hiking my shirt up to let my skin touch the stone. I lay there, feeling my way through my anger, watching the light shift as the wind swayed the willow branches ever so slightly. I could feel my sweat puddling under me.

I had reacted too strongly. I knew that. I wasn't signing a blood oath to leave the Basin by taking the PSATs. And even if I was, what exactly was keeping me here? Was I actually against leaving, or . . .

The possibility that I might actually believe the shit Moon Basin sold the tourists had never occurred to me, but it had bubbled up from inside me like it had been there all along. *Good things don't happen to people who leave.* Was that thought really my own?

It was natural to believe the Basin was haunted. It was just part of us. Some towns were lobster towns; we were a ghost town. Ghost tourism, ghost key chains. *I went to Moon Basin and all I brought back was this T-shirt (OR WAS IT???).* It was our industry. It sustained us. But there weren't lobsters holding anyone captive up in Maine somewhere. This couldn't be the reason I didn't want to leave. It *couldn't.* Moon Basin was haunted, but it wasn't *evil.*

Right?

I tried to calm down and organize my thoughts. Be rational. What would it really look like to leave the Basin?

Maybe after I'd worked at the radio station long enough Cecil would give me a raise. I'd make enough money so that my mom could work less, and I'd see her more. I could move to the city, meet someone, bring her home. Or maybe I'd move to Connecticut with Nina when she got into Yale. Her in law school, me doing—something. They had community radio at Yale, probably. Maybe I could be a swimming instructor, a lifeguard at the beach, knifing through the waves to rescue chubby toddlers who'd floated out of their parents' grasp. I could drive a cab. I could get serious about art and apply to school somewhere, a correspondence course, maybe.

I closed my eyes, putting my arm over my face. It all seemed so theoretical, so impossible, and I didn't know why. I didn't want to think about it. I just wanted to let things happen. If I woke up one morning and decided I wanted to leave after all, I could figure my way out from there. It just seemed stupid to do all this preparation for something I didn't know I'd want—if I'd even be *able to do*—when the time for it actually came.

I felt the presence before I moved my arm. The dappled light changed, becoming a solid heaviness above my eyes, and I spoke without looking. "I'm sorry I was such a dick." My words were muffled on my own skin. I pulled my arm away from my face and opened my eyes. "Oh, hi. Shit. I thought you were someone else."

The girl standing above me blinked her huge dark eyes. My body registered that she was pretty before my brain did, and I scrambled upright as I tried to formulate another sentence.

She smiled, teeth brilliant against her deep black skin. "As far as apologies go, that one is a little weak. Direct, but not very . . ." She flourished her arm. "Elegant."

I wriggled my way around as gracefully as I could until I was sitting with my back against the low stone wall that bordered the bridge. "Ah. You think I should go with 'penis,' then."

She snorted a laugh. "Member."

"Fuck stick," I said solemnly, and she dissolved into giggles.

"There it is," she said, taking a breath. She drew herself up, and all of a sudden, a high, fluty English-accented voice was coming out of her mouth. "I do apologize for being such a terrible fuck stick when last we spoke."

I laughed. "That might be enough to earn forgiveness, actually."

She sat down next to me. "What did you do?"

I made a face and shrugged. "I was a fuck stick."

"Well, yeah, but. Specifically."

She tilted her head like she really cared about the answer, like we were already friends. The way she talked, it was like we'd picked back up in the middle of a conversation, and it made me feel like maybe I could trust her.

I decided to roll with it. "I yelled at my best friend because she wanted us to study for the PSATs today and I don't want to go to college."

She arched an eyebrow. "At all?"

I folded my arms. "Maybe not. And it's none of your business," I added, keeping us both in line. Just because it felt like we were friends didn't mean we actually were. Yet.

"Sorry," she said, not looking at all sorry. "It's just surprising."

I didn't say anything. Who was she to be surprised? She didn't know me.

"I just moved here," she said. "Yesterday." She was making an offering, letting me know she understood I didn't want to talk about me anymore.

"Cool." I was still a little pissed, but more at myself for sharing in the first place. She was brand new in town; I couldn't fault her for trying to make friends.

"My name's Piper."

She looked so hopeful. I relented. "Clem."

"Clem?"

"Short for Clémence."

"Mercy."

I glanced at her. "Yeah. My dad was French."

"It's pretty." She stretched her legs out and pointed her toes, flexing her calves. She looked strong, like maybe she was a runner or something. She cracked her neck and looked at me. "I want to go to college. You have to go to college to go to law school."

"That's true," I said, hoping my annoyance was obvious. I wondered if I should just get up and leave, but I didn't think I could be that mean. Maybe I could bore her into leaving.

"My mom's a lawyer," she offered after a minute. "I sort of don't have a choice."

"I hope she doesn't think she's gonna get any work here."

"She does tax law."

"Oh," I said.

"Also, she's still in Boston. My parents are divorced. Are you saying there's not any crime here?" There was a playful edge to her voice.

"I'm saying there's no crime lawyers here," I said, a little more nicely.

"How does that work?"

"I don't know. There's never been, like, a trial. I guess maybe people just plead guilty if they get arrested. Sheriff Nelson's not exactly known for being chill."

She laughed a little rumbly laugh in her chest. I felt myself softening toward her again.

"So why are you here?" I asked. *Why would anyone move here* is what I meant.

She pulled her foot up close to her, resting her chin on her knee. "My dad's an engineer. The town council wanted him to come and check out the mine and make sure everything is stable."

"Why?"

"What do you mean, why?"

"I don't know," I said, bemused. "I guess I mean, why now? Like, are we in danger?"

"Jesus, I hope not," she said.

I laughed. It was a stupid question; the mine was closed off for a reason. I should have asked if we were in more danger than usual.

"I don't know," she said. "How long has it been since the explosion? Maybe the city just figured it was time."

"Since '64, I think," I said. "Did he tell you the whole story?"

"Just a little," she said. "It sounds wicked, though. I'm dying to learn more."

"Well, the museum's in the motel," I said. "Anson Perry will talk your ear off if you let him."

"Might take him up on that."

"So it's a short-term thing, then?"

"I guess it depends on how big the mine is."

I nodded. No one really knew how big the mine was anymore. The company maps only showed the original tunnels, and even before the explosion, the miners were branching out into new areas. It was honestly surprising they'd only hired one guy to check out the entire thing. Then again, the sheriff was very, very serious about keeping people out.

"I get a haunted summer vacation, at the very least," she said.

"We could show you around if you want." I was surprised by the words, by the fact that I'd said them at all. I still wasn't even totally sure if I liked this girl. There was something about her, though, something that felt almost familiar, and it made me feel like I wanted her around. I sucked my lips against my teeth, creating a vacuum seal as I tried not to take the invitation back.

She looked at me with some trepidation. "Are your friends gonna be mad you invited a weird stranger to hang out with you?"

"Nah," I said, pushing myself up off the bridge, trying to convince myself as much as her. "Nina will probably like you more than me right now. College dreams and all."

She laughed. "Is it just the two of you?"

"And Lisey," I answered. "She's . . . well, we love her. She's a little—" I waved my hand like sparkles were coming out of my fingers. "You'll see."

"She sounds delightful," Piper said as she stood up, and she sounded sincere.

"I should probably try and patch things up with Nina," I said. The sun was getting lower in the sky, blue giving way to tendrils of orange bleeding into pinky-purple dusk. Old Town was west of us, so the sun set through the ash, and it was always gorgeous. "Do you live nearby?"

"In town," she said. "The big yellow house right on the edge near—"

"Near the gas station." I nodded. "Cool. Maybe we'll come by tomorrow?"

"Sure," she said.

We walked together through the cornfield, and then we went our separate ways.

I knocked on Nina's door when I got home and no one answered, so I crossed the yard to our place and let myself in. The smell of butter and tortillas frying hit my nose immediately, and my heart squeezed.

"Migas," I said, and Nina came out of the kitchen holding a spatula.

"Migas," she said. "I'm sorry."

"No, I'm sorry." I hugged her. "I was so out of line. I was being shitty."

"Well, I was being pushy," she said, brushing a strand of hair out of her face. "So we're even."

"I'll hang out with you while you study next weekend," I offered. "Maybe I'll even learn something."

She narrowed her eyes. "Don't be cute. I'm not ready to joke about it."

It stung like a paper cut, but I knew she was right. I couldn't just skip past the hurt feelings. We were both still a little tender, and that was okay. We were still us.

"I met someone today," I said, following her back into the kitchen and sliding into a chair.

She gave a little yelp. "A *someone* someone?"

"No, no. At least, I don't think so. She is really pretty, though. But I don't think so."

She made a face and turned back to the stove.

"I told her she could hang out with us."

"She *must* be pretty."

"Shut up."

"What if I object?"

I felt a brief pang of worry. "Do you?"

She took the pan off the burner. "Nah. But I'm just saying."

"You didn't ask me if I wanted to be friends with Lisey," I reminded her. "And look how well that worked."

She scooped a mound of eggs into a bowl, topped it with cheese, and handed it to me. "True." She sat down across from me with her own bowl. "Four is a nice round number."

"Square," I said through a mouthful. She rolled her eyes.

"Did she just move here?"

"Yeah, her dad is doing something with the mine. Making sure it doesn't collapse or something."

She put her fork down. "Is that a possibility?"

"Apparently."

Nina grimaced. "Well, I hope he's really good at his job, then."

She was mostly joking, but I felt the tug of anxiety under her words. She could ignore it when people said the mine was dangerous because it was haunted—she didn't believe in ghosts. But she had no choice but to believe in actual, physical danger.

"It'll be fine," I said. "You can ask him about it tomorrow, when we hang out with her."

Her eyebrows arched wickedly. "I hope she can handle it."

We finished our dinner and Nina left, saying she needed to spend some time with her dad. I washed dishes and thought about the mine stretching out underneath the town like some long, twisted creature, looking up at us, waiting for something. When I finally fell asleep I didn't dream, which felt like a blessing.

When Nina showed up at my door the next morning she was holding a plastic container filled with cookies.

"You're really amping up the new-friend hazing," I remarked as we set off toward Lisey's. "I truly don't know if she'll be able to handle it."

She gave me a tiny sideways glare and then hip-checked me gently into a mailbox. It was too hot to talk; we walked in silence as the sun rose higher in the sky, and by the time we got to Lisey's we were both drenched in sweat. I scooped up a bunch of little pebbles and started throwing them at the side of the house.

"One of these days you're gonna break that window," Nina said.

"Listen, I never know when her parents are home, and we don't have an hour to talk to Mrs. Bossert about crystals today."

"The mystical properties of the yoni egg demand a lengthy explanation, Clem." Nina smirked and leaned against the fence. After a few more rocks pinged off the glass, the window slid up and Lisey's hair floated out, followed by her face.

"Hi!" she said, sounding surprised.

"Hey," I called, trying to keep my voice down. "Come out."

She flashed a hand—five minutes—and pulled her head back inside.

Three minutes later her front door swung open and she emerged, halfway through a pink shirt, her white belly glowing in the sun.

"Hey," she said through the fabric. Her hair crackled with static as she pulled her head through the hole. "What's up?"

"New friend," said Nina ominously. "Maybe."

"Definitely," I corrected. "Probably."

"Ooh," said Lisey. "Let me get my whistle."

She darted back inside, returning a moment later with the little silver tube clutched in her hand. "Okay." She shoved it into her fanny pack. "Rock and roll."

"Cookies and birds," I said. "How can she resist us?"

FIVE

I was the one who knocked on the door, since I was the only one she'd actually ever met. A man answered, tall and professorial, wire-rimmed glasses sliding down his nose.

"Hi, there," he said, leaning against the door. His smile was as big and gorgeous as Piper's. "I'm sorry, are you . . ." He waved a hand. "Selling cookies?"

"Dad!" Piper yelled, skidding down the stairs in her socks. "Not Girl Scouts. Not Girl Scouts. Friends of Piper, teenage friends of Piper, please don't be weird—"

He laughed and opened the door wider, ushering us in. The house was still full of boxes, but the mantel above the fireplace was already covered in framed pictures of Piper. There was a half-finished Muppets puzzle spread out on the floor next to a heap of what looked like video equipment, cords spiraling every which way. It smelled like new paint and cedar.

"Sorry about that," Piper's dad said. "I didn't think she'd have met friends so soon after the move. Clearly I underestimated you, cub." He chucked her under the chin, which she allowed with good humor, and then tugged at the end of one of her braids. She slapped his hand away gently. "So what are you all doing today?"

There was a slightly-too-long silence before Nina finally spoke. "I actually . . . I actually did bring cookies."

39

She lifted the container like she was toasting him with it. He looked at us, then at Piper, and then burst out laughing.

"Oh, good," he said, getting himself under control. "I hate being wrong."

He stuck out a hand, and Nina shook it with the one that wasn't holding the cookies.

"Carlisle Wharton."

"Nina, Clem, Lisey," she said, gesturing at each of us. "Moon Basin doesn't have a Girl Scouts chapter, so you got the next best thing."

"Damn," he said with feeling. "I should have stocked up."

"On that note," said Piper, taking the cookies from Nina and setting them on the little table standing next to the door, "let's get out of here."

"Back by six, please, my precious daughter whom I love so much." Carlisle leaned against the doorjamb and waved at us. He pitched his voice up a few octaves. "'Bye, Dad, you're the best, I totally love you! I'll be home on time and I definitely won't get into any trouble!'"

"That's not what I sound like," Piper called over her shoulder. "But I love you anyway."

"Your dad is adorable," Nina said as we turned onto the road. "He gives me, like, Giles vibes. You know, from Buffy?"

"Must be the glasses," Piper said. "He's useless with any kind of filing system. He'd be a *terrible* librarian. I guess he's sort of like my Giles, though. He'd definitely try to help me save the world."

"Well, that's what counts."

We walked down the road a ways, the sun getting higher in the sky, and after about ten minutes Lisey stopped.

"Do you wanna see something cool?"

Piper nodded. Lisey unzipped her fanny pack and pulled out a little folded square of wax paper, unfolded it, and set it on the ground. Sitting in the middle of the opened flaps was a lump of raw meat. Her hand dipped back into the fanny pack and came up with the whistle, which she put to her lips. She looked at us, her eyes dancing, and then she blew three high, piercing notes one after another, *ree-ree-ree*. Piper winced, but she looked interested. Lisey put the whistle back in her bag and tipped her head back, looking west.

"They're coming," she said.

We'd seen her do it before, and we'd learned over the years how smart crows were, but it never failed to give me a little thrill of fear and awe. I looked in the direction she was facing, tried to hear the beating of wings.

Three crows swooped down out of the sky, alighted at Lisey's feet, and immediately started pecking at the meat.

"Whoa," Piper said, looking at them. "Did you do that?"

"Yeah." Lisey was beaming. "They like me. They know me."

"Sometimes they give her stuff," Nina added. "Presents."

"What is a crow gonna give you?"

"Oh, it depends," she said, crouching about a foot away from the birds. "Sometimes little pebbles, feathers, bones. Bottle caps, glass."

"So, trash." Piper was smiling when she said it, though, and I could tell she was impressed.

"Gift trash." Lisey giggled. One of the crows flapped its wings and she stretched out a hand to it. It hopped closer to her and cocked its head. "They don't eat out of my hand, but I think they would. It's just not really something crows do."

"Are there more?"

"Oh, yeah, lots. It just depends on how many are within range. Most of the flock hangs out near my house."

Piper whistled. One of the crows looked at her and screeched.

"It likes you!"

Once they'd finished their meal, the crows hopped around for a bit, looking for more food. Lisey made little cooing sounds at them, letting them flutter around her, and then she stood. "Where are we going today?"

The three of us turned to Piper.

She raised her eyebrows. "I'm gonna pick? I've lived here all of three days."

"What have you seen so far?" I asked.

"Not much. The bridge. The grocery store. Uh, the park, a little, when we drove in." She looked up. "Actually, you know what I haven't seen?" She grinned and her dimples popped. She looked like she was getting ready to tag one of us and run away, like a kid about to go to the amusement park. "The haunted part."

"There it is," said Nina. "Took you long enough."

The sun was directly above us as we walked into the gray fog that shrouded the first Moon Basin. Somehow it felt less oppressive than usual. We tromped past the Sugar Bowl, the dried-out ravine on the very edge of Old Town. The water stopped running there decades ago; the ground got too hot from all the underground fires and just evaporated it all over time. Everyone called it the Sugar Bowl because the ash from the mine drifted down into it. It looked like clumpy gray sugar, piled there at the bottom of the wash. Lisey scuttled down as we walked by to retrieve an empty schnapps bottle someone had left.

"Just because it's Old Town doesn't mean littering is okay," she grumbled as she climbed back to us. She held the bottle as we walked on, the open top making the slightest, hollowest wailing sound as her arm swung back and forth.

"It used to be, like, *so* cool to dare people to roll down there," Nina told Piper. "Like, only the coolest, bravest kids would do it."

"Yeah, because people kept breaking all their bones on the way down," I said.

"Only the cool people," she said serenely, and held out her hand so Piper could high-five her.

The air got closer and grayer as we moved deeper into town. We walked through empty streets, past abandoned houses, and Piper kept breaking away from us to look closer at everything.

"Oh, *hell* yes," Piper said as we came into the town commons. "This is so cool. It looks exactly the same as the one in town. Look at the gazebo!"

Maybe because I was looking at it with fresh eyes, new-in-town eyes, as Piper marveled over everything, but I felt strangely fond of Old Town that day. It didn't feel haunted, or if it did, it felt haunted by something friendly.

"They pretty much made the new town a carbon copy of this one," I said. "Left out some of the cool shit, though."

"Like what?" Piper asked.

"The bathhouse," Nina said.

"Like an old-fashioned one? Can we go?" Piper's voice crackled with excitement.

"Yeah, everything's locked up, but we can at least look around the outside. The vines and stuff are so cool."

Her excitement was catching, and I couldn't help but grin.

The natatorium was perfect—creepy, overgrown, but beautiful. Its glass panes still had a dull shine. It would be a perfect first-time Old Town experience even without going inside.

As we approached it, I could see something was off. The dark stone of the front wall was marred by an even darker void, a jagged hole in the window.

"A bird must have flown in there," Lisey said, peering through. "How sad."

"There aren't any birds in Old Town," Nina said, running her gaze over the ground. "Move."

A thrill coursed through me as I realized what she meant to do. She hefted a good-size rock up out of the earth, shucked off her T-shirt, and wrapped it around the stone. Then she stepped up to the window, shoulder blades flexing smoothly under her undershirt, and tapped the whole package around the edges of the hole like she was cracking an egg. Piper caught my eye and looked away. The only sound was the glass breaking, the soft music of the shards hitting the dusty floor inside. Nina kept tapping methodically until the window was gone.

"Ta-da," she said with a flourish, rolling the stone out of its cocoon and putting her shirt back on. "It was broken when we got here."

"Not technically untrue," Piper said, eyebrows arching. "Wicked."

Without waiting another moment, Piper planted a hand inside the window frame, the other on the wall outside, and hoisted herself carefully through the hole.

"Bunch of birds about to be in here now," she said with a grin. "Fly on in."

Nina was so excited she practically dove through the window.

"Come on." She turned back to us and held out a hand. Lisey took it and wafted herself over the threshold, and I followed.

It was dark inside, but there was enough light filtering in from the skylights, even blanketed with ash, that we could see faintly. We stood there looking around, letting our eyes adjust. It was cooler inside, although the air was stale and musty. The window hadn't been broken long enough—or wide enough—to let much fresh air in.

The natatorium was built to look massive on the inside. The whole building seemed to soar up from the ground, converging high above us between the rows of skylights. There were windows everywhere. The muffled quality of the light gave the whole place a dreamy, not-quite-there feeling, like the building was underwater. It seemed blue, somehow, a bluish green that suffused my vision as I looked around. In the center of the building was the pool—empty, of course, but waiting for the ceiling to collapse into it one day. For now it was surprisingly clean inside, no debris obscuring the stripes of blue tile.

"Look," said Nina, her voice bouncing around the space. "Diving board." She trotted over to it and climbed on, bobbing gently.

"If that breaks, you're gonna splat," Lisey said nervously.

Nina took pity on her and backed off the board.

"I love it," Piper murmured, head tilted to look up as she paced the length of the building. "Why didn't they rebuild this?"

"I don't know," I said. "Probably too expensive. It can't be cheap to build something like this."

She nodded, turning slowly in a circle as she moved forward. "Makes sense. It's like something that should be in a castle. How many pools do you think there are when they're all full?" She trailed her fingers through the dust on the wall. "It looks like more than it is, I bet. Like those little ones flow into each other. See where the naiad is?" She trotted over to the statue, her steps echoing. "God, this is lovely," she said, her voice rapturous. "Like a Degas."

She sank onto the rim of the pool, took a handful of her braids in her hand, and mimed wringing them out, mirroring the little nymph. Then she lay back on the edge of the pool, her hair spilling out of her hands and onto the floor.

"It's so romantic here. Gothic romantic, I guess. Like, it might be haunted, but by someone who died of a broken heart."

"In the pool?"

"Like Virginia Woolf. Just let herself sink."

"Or they were *murdered*," Lisey intoned dramatically. "By their *lover*."

Piper made a high warbling sound, a ghostlike moan that rebounded on itself as it bounced off the walls and back to us, layering and building until it sounded like a flock of mourning doves. She rolled off the edge of the wall down the gentle slope into the empty pool.

"Did anyone ever die in here?" she asked. "Like, has anyone ever seen a ghost here? This would be a great place to haunt."

"Not that I've heard about," Nina said.

"Anson would know," I said. "One of these days when we go to the real pool we can ask him."

"Cool." Piper held up one hand, like she was shielding her eyes from the sun. "The water was probably so blue."

We watched her, not saying anything. After a little while she rolled over again and pressed herself to her feet, walked over to the deep end of the pool. She held out a hand and I seized it and pulled her up and out, her toes kicking one-two off the wall as she pushed herself upward. We lay there for a moment on our backs. Her hand was still clasped in mine.

"Reminds me of poor old Gatsby," she said, getting back to her feet. "I'm gonna go explore some more."

I looked up at the high, arching ceiling disappearing into the gloom. "I bet it would be nice to have the record player in here. Something with a cello."

Lisey hummed deep in her chest and lay down next to me, hooking my pinky with hers. Nina stepped out of the shallow pool and folded herself down next to us.

"I like her," she said, leaning back on her hands.

"Me too," Lisey said. "She's so cool."

"Aw, you guys." Piper's voice was loud enough that she could have been right next to us. I bolted upright, whipping my head around, but I couldn't see her.

"What the—"

Her laugh echoed around the room. "This is awesome."

"Where are you?" Lisey asked, sitting up. "Can you see us?"

"Up here."

We tilted our heads back to see her, peeking over the balcony of the upper floor.

"Oh my God," Lisey squealed. "How did you get up there?"

"I flew," Piper said with a dramatic flourish. "C'mon, Lise. Stairs."

"So unsafe!" Lisey put her hands over her eyes, as if to shield herself.

"I didn't even see the balcony!" Nina said, scrambling to her feet and looking around. "How creepy. People could just watch you swimming?"

"Come down before Nina finds the stairs," I called up to Piper.

She grinned, then hoisted herself up onto the edge of the balcony. "Be right there."

Lisey shrieked, a little high-pitched yelp of terror that was just shy of a real scream. "Get down!"

Piper blew her a kiss and then rolled herself backward off the railing, turquoise shoelaces winking in the dim light as her feet disappeared.

I lurched to my feet. "Piper?"

She bounded out of the darkness at the edge of the main room, smacking into Nina, who had almost reached her. "I love this place!"

"What are you, a gymnast?" Nina asked, grabbing her shoulders to better inspect her.

Piper laughed and bent away from her, down into a backbend. She kicked her feet up neatly, just missing Nina's nose, planted them on the ground behind her, and straightened gracefully back to standing.

"Cheerleader," she said solemnly. "Can you believe it?"

Encounters from Beyond, Episode 19
Unused Footage

(Town sheriff MARSHALL NELSON leans against his desk. He is agitated, fidgeting alternately with his gun, his badge, and his hat.)

NELSON: Look, no one goes in the mine. It's the town council's orders and it's my orders, and there's not a television crew in the world could change my mind, all right? Look, this is—this is off the record, all right? Turn that off. *(The picture shakes and swings down to a lower angle. NELSON's legs and torso are still visible.)*

NELSON: When I was still a deputy—maybe, oh, ten, twelve years ago—the sheriff let a crew in. They convinced him.

JUDD LONGIN, *from off-screen*: That would have been the *Grave Encounters* crew, yes?

NELSON: Sure. I guess. They—they were down there for six *days*. We sent in people to search for 'em after the second day, and they just . . . weren't there. Like '64 all over again. Their van just sittin' in the motel lot. Then a few days later, the little girl, the one with the pigtails—

LONGIN, *still off-screen*: Batty.

NELSON: Son, would you just—that girl came tearing into the town commons like her hair was on fire. She led us to the rest of them, but they weren't—they weren't right. It was like they were tuned to a different frequency. Far as I know they never got better. The city gave them . . . a lot of money. A lot of money, a lot of papers to sign. Turned out it didn't even matter. They said all their footage was just darkness and static, you'd hear a word every so often but it wasn't anything good. The mayor jumped the gun, I guess, but it doesn't matter. The point is, no one goes in the mine, okay? It's not good. It gets . . . it gets in your head. Too long down there and you get confused.

(NELSON removes his hat and begins worrying the brim.)

NELSON: If it were up to me, I wouldn't let you people into Old Town at all, but it's not, so you get to have your little adventures. But even the town council isn't so desperate for money that they're willing to overlook the . . . the way the mine is.

(He sets the hat on his desk and rests one hand on the butt of his gun, almost caressing it, as if it comforts him.)

NELSON: I still have dreams about it sometimes. The tunnels, they look empty, but they're not. They *react.* It's not physical, but it's there.

LONGIN: What is?

NELSON: I don't know. Look, if you want to ask me about it, start rolling again and I'll give you the standard bullshit answer, okay? This isn't show and tell. If you go down there, we won't come in after you.

LONGIN: What if we sign a waiver?

NELSON: What? No—fuck—you're not listening. This isn't a game, all right? I am telling you this for your own good. There is no waiver in the *world* that could convince me that you understand the danger here.

LONGIN: Sir—

NELSON: If I see you starting to mobilize over there, I will arrest you. I will confiscate your footage and your equipment and I will not reimburse you for it, and you will never know how much of a debt you owe me. But if you sneak in, if you go behind my back and you go down there, *we will not look for you.* I don't know how to make this clearer to you, son. I won't risk my people for yours. You going down there, all it will do is wake it up, and then—

(NELSON shifts. His face comes into frame and he looks at the camera.)

NELSON: Are you still filming? What the fuck—

(NELSON lunges for the camera. The picture swings, a scuffling sound, darkness.)

SiX

It was Saturday morning. The four of us hadn't spent more than a day apart in the two weeks since Piper moved to town. We were sprawled on the floor of Piper's living room eating cereal, half watching some animated show about a raccoon.

"Why is the keyboard magic?" Piper asked through a mouthful of cornflakes. Nina made a muffled sound, *i-unno*, as she chewed. Lisey was braiding Nina's hair, unbraiding, rebraiding. She kept taking locks about an inch wide and pulling gently, all the way from root to tip, her long pale fingers disappearing into the bright henna-red mass. It gave me shivers to watch. The only time I ever wished my hair was longer was when Lisey was doing Nina's hair, that gentle pulling, like following a thread. I mashed my cereal down, waiting for it to get soggy. Nina swallowed and kicked me in the ankle.

"That's so gross," she said. "Just eat it."

"The marshmallows get fluffy if you leave it alone," I said. This was an argument we'd had before, and it was more a comforting ritual than an actual debate.

"Slimy," she corrected. "They get slimy."

"I say potato . . ." Lisey singsonged, twirling a strand of Nina's hair.

The sound of the front door jangling open made us all look up.

"Hi, girls," Carlisle said, setting down a battered leather bag. "Happy Saturday."

"Hi, Carlisle," we replied, already returning our focus to the television.

"Hi, Dad." Piper got to her feet. "What's up, is the mine collapsing?"

He laughed. "Not yet."

"Do you know why the town council thinks it's going to?" Nina turned around to look at him. Lisey started running her hands through her own hair, looking for split ends.

"I think they're just trying to be safe," he said. "The fact that the fire's still not out means those seams of coal go pretty deep into the ground, so the possibility of the earth shifting isn't out of the question."

"Creepy," Piper said.

Carlisle waggled a hand, *kind of*. "It's less about immediate danger, really more a question of next steps," he said. "Filling it in, reinforcing the tunnels, things like that. They want me to recommend some different approaches."

"Is there a way to tell, like, how much coal is left?" Nina asked. "Like, how much longer the fire will burn?"

"Not without excavating it. Just have to keep checking every so often."

"Hmm," Piper said. "Weird."

He looked around at all of us then, taking in the rumpled pajamas, the tangled hair. "Big plans today?"

"Nah," said Nina. "This, probably. Maybe go to the pool."

"Do you girls want to go down into the mine with me? I only came home to replace the batteries in the probes. I have to go back as soon as they're charged, but if you don't have anything to do, I don't know, it might be fun." He spread his hands, shrugged a little bit.

"Is that allowed?" Piper asked. "I thought the whole thing was—"

"Yeah, it's super illegal," Nina said. "The sheriff is really intense about it."

"Well, you'd be with me, and it's an educational outing," Carlisle said. "But also, I won't tell if you won't." He grinned, his expression almost heartbreakingly eager.

Nina and I looked at each other. None of us had ever been into the mine. Lisey had walked there in her sleep as a toddler and almost fallen in, so she was vehemently opposed to going anywhere near it. She was avoiding eye contact right now, keeping her face turned toward the floor. I could see her hands shake as she pulled them through her hair.

We stared at each other for a beat too long, and Carlisle started to say, "Never mind—"

"Sure, Dad. That would be cool." Piper flicked a look at each of us in turn. She wanted to go, it was clear, but she also didn't know the things we knew. Nina and I both looked at Lisey. After a long moment I saw her chin dip in the tiniest nod.

"Yeah," I said, still watching her. "Cool."

We retreated to Piper's room to get dressed. Every time I saw it, the room looked a little more like her. She didn't decorate much because she didn't know how long she'd be in Moon Basin, but little by little she was claiming the space. There were pictures of her old cheerleading squad tucked into the edge of her mirror, and there was a sewing kit on her bed I'd never seen before. It looked like she was hemming fabric for curtains. It made me happy; I wanted her to settle in. I wanted her to stay.

"Can we wear flip-flops?" Nina yelled down the stairs, holding hers to her chest.

"Absolutely not," Carlisle yelled back.

"Ugh," she muttered, pulling a pair of battered sneakers out of her bag. "Too hot for these."

"Well, you don't want to fall in," I said, half paying attention. I was watching Lisey, trying to gauge her mood. She still hadn't spoken.

"Fall in," Nina said. "We're going in. On purpose."

"Yeah, but we're *climbing* in," I reminded her. "Not slipping off the ladder halfway down and breaking our ankles."

"Ugh," she said again, twisting her hair up on top of her head.

"I can't believe you guys have never been down there." Piper handed her a hair tie.

"Well, we—" I glanced at Lisey, unsure if she was willing to share.

"I walked there in my sleep when I was really little," Lisey said. "Almost fell in."

"Jesus."

"Yeah. It was like a magnet pulled me there. My mom ran halfway across town with no shoes on and she barely caught me."

"That is . . . creepy as hell," Piper said.

"The whole thing is creepy," I said. "I know we didn't tell you a whole lot about it, but it's . . . not totally safe to be down there. Not just from, like, a physical standpoint, but sort of a mental one. I mean, people think it's haunted for a reason."

"Well, let's not get carried away—" Nina started.

"The sheriff doesn't even let the ghost hunters go down there anymore," I said. "The last crew that went in got really messed up." I thought about the scars on my mother's wrists. "People just react to it . . . strangely."

"God, are you sure you want to do this?" Piper's brow creased with concern as she looked from me to Lisey. "I didn't realize you had, like, *history* with it—"

"Yeah," Lisey said. A small, brave smile crossed her face. "We're together. It'll be fine."

I squeezed her shoulder. "Remember, you're not allowed to talk to anything down there," I said, trying to lighten the mood. "No ghost friends."

Nina pursed her lips. "If you start making ghost friends, Lise, I'm leaving you in there. 'Cask of Amontillado' style."

Lisey crossed her eyes. "Seal me in," she croaked in a deep, ominous voice. "The ghosts will keep me company and we will drink all the Amontillado, which I'm pretty sure is wine . . ." She reached for Nina, warbling in the back of her throat. "You will hear us in the night. . . ."

Nina threw one of the flip-flops at her.

Piper bumped a drawer shut with her hip and leaned against the dresser. "So you guys really believe the stuff people say about this place? In ghosts and shit?"

"Yes," Lisey said, at the same exact time that Nina said, "No."

All three of them looked at me.

"Yes and no," I said.

Piper snorted. "Very diplomatic."

"I believe in what I can see and touch." Nina tucked an errant strand of hair behind her ear and folded her arms. "I know that's unpopular around here, but there it is."

"I believe what I feel," Lisey said.

"I . . . don't know what I believe." I tugged at the hem of my shirt. "I definitely believe in *something*, though. I don't think Moon Basin is the same as other towns."

"What does your dad think?" Lisey asked. "He's the only one who's been down in the mine in years. Has he seen anything?"

Piper laughed. "He definitely doesn't believe in ghosts."

"Still, though." Lisey leaned toward her. "He hasn't even heard anything or felt anything?"

Piper looked at her, eyebrows raised. "Should he have?"

Lisey blushed. "No, I don't—I just mean—I think most of the people that have ever gone down there have experienced *something*. So I just wondered."

"Well, he's probably not 'open to it' the way you are." Piper grinned as she lilted along the words. "I think the whole being-a-scientist thing keeps him on this side of reality."

"Rude," Lisey said. "It's not my fault I was conceived at Burning Man."

"Guys!" Carlisle yelled up the stairs. "It's not a fashion show! Let's roll!"

We drove out to Old Town. Carlisle's equipment rattled around in the trunk. Piper sat up front, fiddling with the radio dial as the signal faded out. Nothing really worked under the heaviest parts of the ashfall. Cecil was on, reading horoscopes, but his voice flickered and then died altogether as we navigated into the grayness of the old Basin. I fiddled with the door lock, popping the little stick in and out of the window ledge. I couldn't tell what I was feeling. The blue leached out of the sky as I watched, my head tipped back, and after a few more minutes Carlisle stopped the car.

I opened the door and immediately a wave of humidity rolled in, slicking my skin in sweat. We followed Carlisle into the fog, all of us in a scraggly line behind him. My shirt stuck to my back, and I wished for the air-conditioned vacuum of Piper's living room. We trudged forward, all silently regretting coming, and then Carlisle threw out an arm. There, in the ground in front of him, was a tiny orange flag on a wire.

"It always sneaks up on me," he said with a laugh.

He unsnapped the helmet from its place on his belt, put it on his head, and flicked on the light mounted in front.

"There are stairs cut into the walls." He pointed the beam into the hole in the ground. Ash floated in the light like dust motes, twirling lazily. He knelt on the ground, then backed his feet over the edge, climbing down until only his torso was visible.

"There are thirty steps," he continued, looking at each of us in turn. "Wait until I'm all the way down before the next one of you goes."

We stood there looking at each other, listening to Carlisle's footsteps echo up to us. It was very quiet in Old Town. No birds, no wildlife, no traffic. Nothing to create the sounds of life you're so used to hearing that you only notice their absence. When Carlisle called up out of the mine the sound was flat and muffled, like a handclap in a dark room.

"Come on down!"

Piper shrugged and wriggled over the edge of the hole. Nina and Lisey and I watched her get swallowed into the dark mouth of the tunnel, and a few minutes later her voice floated up.

"Clear!"

Lisey went down then, eyes big as she disappeared from view, and then Nina. Then it was my turn.

I climbed down into the mine. The daylight faded almost

immediately, like a curtain dropping as soon as my head got below the lip of the tunnel. I counted as I descended, keeping my eyes turned up toward the dwindling light above me. I pressed myself hard into the wall, nails scratching into the dirt, toes reaching for each step, brushing against the wall every time I extended a foot.

I was about halfway down when I realized the light was gone altogether, and immediately I felt a needling panic in the base of my skull. The walls of the mine shaft began to close in around me, pressing against my back, squeezing the air from my lungs. I took small, shallow breaths, flattening myself against the warm earth as I tried to push myself down faster, and I was gasping by the time my searching foot met the floor of the mine. My knees buckled as I released my death grip on the wall and I stumbled. Nina touched my arm, her face questioning. I smiled weakly at her, nodded, tried to slow my heart rate. Carlisle clapped his hands.

"Here we go." He handed Piper a massive flashlight. "Stay close. The tunnels branch out."

I had thought the light was gone when I was still on the ladder, the dark, small space sucking the air out of me, but as I looked around me I almost wanted to climb back up. The bottom of the mine was so much worse, so much hungrier. The darkness was penetrating, alive, and utterly opaque. The flashlight beams only reached about three feet in front of us, ash swirling and clouding the air. Recognition shivered through me. It felt like town during a new moon. I thought about coyotes dragging dead men up out of these tunnels.

We moved forward slowly into the mine along the main tunnel. It curved out and back, and the darkness seemed to be crawling toward us, swallowing our advancing light. The ground was flat, mostly, and as we moved, my fear settled a little. It was swelteringly hot. Beads of sweat crawled down my face, trickling onto my neck, and I swiped my arm over my forehead, trying to keep my eyes clear. Ash smudged along my skin, sticking to the dampness. I could see electric lights, or something that looked like electric lights, up in the ceiling where wooden beams ran across in an arch to hold the shaft up.

"Why aren't the lights on?" I asked.

"No way to light 'em," Carlisle called over his shoulder. He reached up to the ceiling, stabbed a small, thin metal sliver up into the earth, and moved forward, looking at the flat black device in his hand.

"Okay, so what are you doing?" Piper asked. She trotted up alongside him in the dim light.

"So these are probes that measure the PSI of the earth." Carlisle handed her a metal spike. "Basically, as long as they stay consistent, we're in good shape. It's when the pressure starts to drop that we have to be concerned, because that could mean that the earth is collapsing somewhere else, causing the rest to spread out. . . ."

Lisey paced herself back next to me, letting Piper and her dad get a little farther ahead. "It feels bad down here," she said under her breath. "Like it's hungry."

It was true. There was all around us a sense of wanting, of *craving*. I felt like I did when Danny Nelson and his minions leered at us from across the street. Slightly nauseous, ashamed, afraid I was somehow responsible. Part of me wanted to press my body flat against the earth and see what happened, but the other part—the underneath part, the animal part—said the ground was soft and fragile, like rotting cloth, and couldn't be trusted.

"I feel like it can see us," I said, trying to keep my voice as quiet as possible.

"What can?"

I almost shrieked as Nina's face appeared just inches from ours. "Jesus, Neen!" I hissed. "Don't sneak!"

"Are you anthropomorphizing inanimate objects again?" she asked, walking backward so she could face us. Lisey sped up and ducked past her to Carlisle and Piper. Nina looked at me and raised her eyebrows. I gave her my best *I don't know* shrug and she frowned, but she dropped it. She turned back around and called out, "Where are we, Mr. Wharton? In relation to town?"

"Under the edge of the graveyard," he said, squinting at the little device in his hand. He dug in a pocket of his bag with the other hand. "Here."

Nina took the tattered piece of paper from him and opened it to reveal a crude, hand-drawn map of the Basin. Scrawled across it were wide, nonsensical loops and whorls, dead ends and sharp turns.

"The mine?" I asked, taking it from her. The lines seemed strange, unbalanced, but I didn't know how to dig a coal mine. Maybe you followed the coal, and maybe sometimes the coal went in—I peered closer—something that really, really looked like a perfect spiral.

"I didn't realize any of the tunnels were under the graveyard," I said, an inexplicable shudder working through me. "Uck."

Nina shot me a look. "You love that cemetery."

"That's what I'm saying. I don't like knowing the mine is underneath it."

Piper called to her dad, who had moved ahead of us while we looked at the map. "Why don't you just tell them to fill it in?"

"It could make things worse," Carlisle said. "There are a lot of things that can go wrong, and as you would say, cub, it's *wicked* expensive."

She laughed. "So what *is* the plan, then?"

"That I haven't decided." He looked at us over his shoulder and winked. "Obviously, I'm very glad to have this job, but most towns like this, people leave. *Actually* leave, not just move a few miles over. There's not a lot of precedent for a project like this."

The tunnel widened into a larger clearing—not much larger, though. There was room enough for us to squeeze in and still be able to move around a little bit. Carlisle clamped a pair of headphones over his ears and started waving another flat black box around.

"What's he doing now?" Nina asked.

"EMF readings?" Lisey guessed. "For ghosts?"

Carlisle saw us looking at the box and held it up so we could see. "Fancy metal detector," he almost yelled. "Large deposits of metal could cause problems later!"

He stopped a few feet away from us, peering at his tablet. The little room got smaller and hotter every time I took a breath. I backed away, and my foot caught on something that rattled. I crouched, eyes on Carlisle, hand extended behind me, until my fingertips brushed over one of the little metal probes. I closed my hand around it and straightened back up, squeezing the point of it into my palm. As I focused on the way it felt in my hand, my breathing slowed. The jagged edges of my brain started to think about smoothing themselves out. I turned my attention back to Carlisle.

He was still staring at the box, but something about him was different. He moved the box away from him, back toward his body, away, back again. In the glow of his light, propped at the base of the wall, his eyes were feverish, glittery. His gaze was fixed intently on the earth, but he was somewhere else. His face was empty. He stepped closer to the wall, scratched at it with his nail. My heart beat painfully in my chest, the heat making me confused and tired. The thought *Should we have worn masks?* curled through my mind and vanished. I felt another bead of sweat make its way down the back of my neck and I wiped at it, rubbing my hand on my shorts.

The four of us stood there watching him, barely breathing, as he leaned closer. I felt something metallic and sour in the back of my throat, a creeping dread that mounted as he moved toward the wall. I wanted to reach out, to say something to stop him, turn him away, make the terrible blank focus of his eyes and his slackened face snap back to something I recognized. I couldn't move.

"Dad," Piper said, her voice loud and urgent. Carlisle turned around sharply, yanking the headphones off. His eyes did something strange; his face almost—almost *shivered* back into place. One second he was gone, and the next he was there, blinking at us in the dim light, a smudge of dirt on his cheek.

"Did someone say something?"

He looked at all of us standing there, breathing hard. I forced myself to unclench my fists.

"Is something wrong?"

"You were majorly zoning out," Piper said. "Like, *gazing* at the wall. Very embarrassing for you."

He laughed. "What can I say? Sedimentary composition, it

drives me wild. Ooh, wait, hang on. It rocks my world."

"*Dad*," Piper said, but she was grinning. "Can we go? It's hot."

"Weaklings, all of you." He pulled out a tiny notebook and scribbled down a few words, holding the pen cap between his teeth, then shoved everything back into his pack. He wound the headphone cord up carefully, cradling the EMF reader inside, and stowed that away, too. Then he turned to look at us. "You know, not everyone gets to come down here. You shouldn't . . . take it . . . for granite."

He looked exactly like Piper when he smiled, right down to the dimples.

The walk back to the entrance seemed longer than the walk in. I was anxious for fresh air, for light. There was a faint glow in the distance and it wouldn't come closer, no matter how fast I walked. Finally I realized I was trotting ahead of everyone else like an impatient puppy. I willed myself to slow down, shortening my stride, until I was almost back in line with them. The last hundred yards felt like an eternity, but the light was getting closer, and by the time we got to the ladder I was panting.

"Me first." I launched myself up without waiting for permission. I clawed my way out of the ground like the end of *The Shawshank Redemption*, panting and clammy, and flopped onto my back. Nina was right behind me. She sat down next to me.

"Doing okay?"

"Mmm." I stared up into the gauzy gray of the sky.

"Small space."

"Yeah."

She flicked at the leg of my shorts. "Did you cut yourself?"

"What?"

I looked down. There was a dark smear of blood on my leg

where I'd wiped my hand earlier. I looked down at my hands and realized my right hand was stained as well, gray smears of ash mingling with streaks of red.

"What the—" I squinted at my palm, trying to find the source. "I didn't think I did, but—" I turned my hand over and over, searching for a break in the skin. I sat up.

"Wait," Nina said. "Your neck."

"My *neck?*"

I touched the back of my neck gingerly with my fingertips, and they came away wet with blood. "Oh, ew," I moaned. "What the hell?"

She licked the side of her hand and rubbed at the back of my neck. "You're not bleeding from here, either."

"Wait, I'm not?"

"Not that I can see. Did you hit your head? Could you be bleeding, like, in your hair?"

I ran my hands over my head, trying to feel for an injury. My hair was limp with sweat, which made it difficult to determine, but it also gave me a thought. "In the mine," I said, still patting along my head, "I kept thinking I was sweating a lot. I kept feeling drops roll down my neck and I just assumed they were sweat, so I wiped them off—"

I tugged at my shorts. Nina made a face. "Maybe it just looks like blood. Maybe it's some kind of gross mine water, or rust, like, it has a really high concentration of minerals or something in it to make it red."

"Yeah," I said, scratching at the back of my neck. I looked at the black-red stripe under each fingernail. "Yeah, probably."

She knocked the toe of her sneaker against mine. "It's okay, Clem. Stop worrying."

"Did you feel strange in there? I felt so strange. Like I couldn't breathe."

"I didn't love it," she admitted. "It made me feel kind of cloudy. In my head. I think that was just being so hot, though."

Lisey's head popped up out of the ground like a whack-a-mole.

"Hi, guys," she said, and hoisted herself out. Piper came out a little quicker, not as panicked as I was, but clearly ready to go home. She pulled me up off the ground, and Nina unfolded herself up to join us. We stood there in that warm, grasping air and waited. Carlisle didn't appear. Nina bumped my hand, locked her pinky with mine, and looked at me. Her eyebrow lifted just a bit before she took a step forward, back toward the hole in the ground.

"Mr. Wharton!" she yelled. "Is everything okay?"

There was a muffled sound that might have been an answer. Piper leaned over the edge and screamed louder. "Dad!"

It was impossible to see into the mine shaft, but I thought I could hear the scraping of feet on stone. We leaned closer, listening, willing our eyes to see farther, and then there was the beam of a flashlight shining right at us.

Carlisle practically jumped out of the hole, appearing so quickly that Piper jerked backward and stumbled, almost falling.

"Sorry, cub," he said, steadying her. "Had to get a few last readings right near the entrance."

"God, Dad." She punched him on the shoulder. "Creepy much?"

He laughed, and we piled back into the car. He flipped the visor down, catching the keys neatly as they fell out, and started the ignition. The radio blared on for a second, as if it had forgotten where we were, and then faded back into static.

"So." His voice was compressed as he turned his head back, making what seemed like a ten-point turn to get us out of the woods. "What did you girls think?"

"Very cool." Piper's voice was full of genuine enthusiasm, and as Carlisle looked forward again, I saw him smile.

"It was different than I expected," I said. "I've only ever seen it in the TV shows. It was like it was bigger and smaller than I thought it would be at the same time."

"Ah, the TV shows."

Nina rolled down her window and surfed her hand through the air. Ash swirled into the car. I saw the white flick of a deer's tail as it vanished into the gloom.

"I wish you'd lived here when they were filming," I said. "We might have actually made it into an episode."

He chuckled. The woods were growing lighter, more alive looking. I could feel my heartbeat growing steadier as we put the mine behind us.

"Well, maybe they'll come back."

Lisey scoffed. "They've pretty much seen everything there is to see in Moon Basin by now."

"Yeah," mused Nina. "We missed our shot."

"Maybe not. You never know. Right, girls?"

It was weirdly ominous, but it felt like a dad thing to say. Never say never, reach for the stars, maybe someday you'll be on a TV show about ghosts. You know.

When we got back to Piper's, I scrubbed at the blood until my hands were bright red and raw, and still I could see it grimed under my nails. Finally I gave up and walked into Piper's bedroom, drying my hands on my shirt.

"Look," I said, holding out my hand. Nina glared at me but

I plowed on. "This is blood, I'm pretty sure. It was dripping on me down there. All down my neck. It's still there, I bet." I turned around to show them. "The whole time I thought I was sweating, but—" I turned back around and shrugged. "I know it might be something else, but it really looks like blood."

Lisey got up from her chair and pressed her nose into the back of my neck, at the base of my skull. "It smells like blood." She wrinkled her nose as she sat back down.

Piper's eyes were wary.

"Wow, ew, Lise," Nina said. "Get right in there."

"You didn't just cut yourself or something?" Piper asked.

"I checked," I said. "So did Nina."

"That still doesn't mean it's blood," Nina argued. "It just means it smells like it. Metallic, right? Like I said, it could be some kind of mineral concentration."

"Only dripping on me and none of you?" I said.

"That's possible!"

"I guess," Piper said doubtfully. She looked at me hard. "What did it feel like in there for you?"

"It was bad," I admitted. "I felt like the walls were breathing and it was taking my air. Like it was smothering me. It made me feel hazy."

"I felt that, too!" Lisey sat up straighter. "The walls, I mean. They felt alive."

"What else did you feel, Lise?" I asked gently.

She shrugged as she answered. "It wasn't really bad or good. It was kind of like being in someone else's head. I knew I was me, and my thoughts were there, but there was something else there, too."

All three of us looked at Nina.

"What?" she said. "I'm telling you guys, it was just hot down there. You were hot."

"Nina." I raised my eyebrows at her. "You really didn't feel anything strange?"

"*This* is strange," she muttered. I leaned back in my chair and folded my arms, waiting. She took the moment to stab a straw into a juice box. "It made me a little nervous," she said at last. "Cagey, you know? The farther we went in, the more freaked out I got that we weren't going to be able to get back out. But that doesn't mean anything. That's just being in a small, enclosed space."

"Even though we were with Carlisle? He knew how to get us out."

Her eyes flashed. "You asked how I felt. I'm telling you how I felt."

"But you don't think it was for any reason except being underground."

"I certainly don't think it was because of *ghosts*, and even if you believe that, none of this makes sense. Why would there be blood down there? Lisey? Anyone? The explosion was decades ago. They never found any bodies, and even if there somehow was one down there, it wouldn't be *bleeding*. And the last I checked, ghosts don't bleed, and also, they *aren't real*."

"We shouldn't have gone down there," Lisey murmured, almost in singsong. "Too hard to get back."

"Lisey, I love you, but cut that shit out," Nina said. "I know you get bad vibes and I fully understand that, but it's just an empty space. It can't hurt us."

Unless we let it, my brain said. The thought was gone as quickly as it came.

Ghoul Boys, Episode 28
Unused Footage

(Interior shot: the lobby of the Moon Basin Motel. In the far corner, the edge of the reception desk is visible; there is a book of crosswords on it and occasionally a hand sneaks into frame to add another word. In the foreground, there is a large glass case containing a tattered journal, propped open on a book stand. The case is obscured slightly by SHANE RYAN, who is adjusting his hair using the display on the video camera. Behind him ANSON PERRY, the proprietor of the Moon Basin Motel, is unfolding a large sheet of paper. RYAN straightens up, satisfied.)

RYAN: Thank you again for agreeing to come on the show, Mr. Perry.

PERRY: Of course. You guys are the real heroes, you know. You're getting the story out there when most people won't.

RYAN: Well, we try.

(PERRY tacks the paper to a small bulletin board and motions for RYAN to bring the camera closer. The picture zooms slowly in, cutting off the top of PERRY's head. In the corner of the screen a small red battery icon begins to flash.)

PERRY: This is the frequency of any paranormal occurrences, plotted over time. Here's 1964, the year of the explosion.

RYAN: Very high.

PERRY: Pretty steady for a year or so, then it drops. Now, mind you, the low points here aren't *nothing*. They're just more standard fare—voices, noises, strange dreams, you know. Kind of a baseline. I don't know of a single person in town who's never heard *anything*. Even people who say they haven't, you get a couple drinks in 'em, they'll spill the beans. Some people are so *embarrassed* about it. Like it isn't something spectacular. I mean, come on. Anyway, like I said. Low points, but still, you know, higher than the average town.

RYAN: Sure.

PERRY: Here's the next big spike, when the town council had an assessor come to see if there was any way the fire could be put out. Lot of dead animals that time. They said it was the teens, the Satanists, but I know better. Then it goes back down again. All these red dots are deaths—

RYAN: Are the deaths connected to the mine?

PERRY: Well, no. Not necessarily. But they're sudden or unexplained or both. Accidents, suicides, stuff like that.

RYAN: Ah.

PERRY: We're in a lull right now, I think. We did have a death recently—a freak thing, farm accident, just real tragic— but besides that it's been pretty calm. I keep my ear to the ground, you know, taking the temperature every so often. See who's waking up their husband when they wander out at night.

RYAN: So what is the conclusion you're drawing here?

PERRY: Well, it seems to ramp up every time someone goes down in the mine. I don't know why. But there's always a little ripple effect afterward, like after an ambulance goes through a big city and all the cars crash into each other.

RYAN: Have you ever been caught in one of these . . . these ripples?

(PERRY opens his mouth and then pauses. His face goes slack, his eyes seeming to sink deeper into his skull. Before he can answer, SHERLENE PERRY speaks from out of frame.)

S. PERRY: Anse. "Very sad turnout," five letters.

(PERRY's face regains its animation and he turns to her, RYAN's question seemingly forgotten.)

PERRY: "Death."

S. PERRY: Needs to start with an N.

PERRY: Hmm. "No one."

S. PERRY, *clicking her tongue*: That *is* sad.

(RYAN clears his throat. There is a series of soft beeps and then the picture cuts out.)

SEVEN

Anson Perry was, to put it mildly, thrilled as fuck to welcome us to the unofficial Moon Basin Museum. It had apparently been a slow season thus far. He insisted on giving us the VIP tour, gesturing wildly with his cane, and he was almost twenty minutes into his spiel before any of us could get a word in.

"Mr. Perry?" I finally asked. "Can we ask you some questions about the mine?"

He looked at me, jarred out of his recitation by my interruption. It took him a moment to answer. "Sure," he said. "What's up?"

"You collect people's stories, right?" My fingers strayed toward a tiny figurine at the edge of the miniature Moon Basin replica. "Like, paranormal experiences they've had?"

"That's right," he said. "I'm kind of the town historian."

"Can you tell us about them?"

He shifted his gaze to Lisey, who was chewing on the end of a lock of her hair. "What do you mean?"

"What type of things happened?" she asked. "What did they see?"

"Some of them didn't see anything," he said, scratching at his beard. "Some just heard things or dreamed them. Come with me."

He led us behind the front counter, past the rows of keys into the little office and through another door into what appeared to be their private apartment. It was surprisingly ghost-free, and I guessed Sherlene had probably limited his decor permissions to the museum. There was one framed photo of him with the host of *Paranormal America* hanging on the wall, but everything else was macramé art and little planters shaped like birds. The orchid-scented air freshener was undercut by a slight hint of chlorine, and I could hear the slap of water. The pool was right out the window.

"I didn't realize you lived here," I said, looking around. "How cool."

He either ignored me or didn't hear me, focused as he was on wrestling with one of those folding, sliding-track doors. He managed to get it open enough to pull out a cardboard box, which he let fall onto the carpet with a dull thump.

"Don't open that one yet," he said, a little out of breath, and dove back in.

By the time he was satisfied, he'd maneuvered two other boxes out into the living room. Something about them made me nervous; I could almost feel the texture of rotting cardboard under my fingers. I shoved my hands into my pockets and found two tiny people I'd lifted from the replica town commons.

"This is every episode of every show that's ever come to Moon Basin," Anson said, opening the first box. "And a lot of bonus content, stuff that got cut, you know. I like to have the crews send them after they air."

The box was full of tapes and CDs, all neatly stacked and labeled.

"When was the last time there was a show here?" Piper asked.

Anson pursed his lips and sat back on his heels. "Geez, I dunno. It's been a while, that's for sure. Would it have been that girl with the pigtails . . . ?" He trailed off, eyes unfocused as he tried to remember.

"No, it was *Haunted Lives*, remember?" Nina looked at me. "The creepy twin hosts? They interviewed Lisey?"

"That's right," I said, surprised I'd forgotten. "Didn't one of the crows—?"

"Pecked Caro Ramsey right in the head," Lisey said solemnly. "She deserved it."

Nina smothered a laugh with her hands. "Please, Mr. Perry, tell me that's in the bonus footage."

Anson was still half inside his own head, and he didn't answer right away. "*Grave Encounters* was the girl with the pigtails. The little goth girl. I don't know if they ever sent me a tape. I don't think they aired an episode, actually." His face darkened for a moment before he shook his head. "Huh. Well. You're right about *Haunted Lives*, I think. Gosh, can you believe it's been almost four years?"

"When was the last time someone actually went down there?" Piper asked, her tone a little sharper than before.

"County assessor," he said promptly. "Maybe seven years ago? After the goth girl. That's when the sheriff shut it down for good." He looked at Piper, eyebrows knitted. "Your father's going down there this summer, though."

"Yes," she said.

"Gonna stir things up."

She started to say something, but he held up a hand.

"I've been watching this town a long time. Whenever someone goes down in that mine it ripples out and touches every single person here. I've felt it and I wager you all have, too."

It was almost like he could see the cloud of anxiety hanging over my head. I had badgered everyone into coming to the museum to see if I could get some answers about the blood, and I was way more on edge than I was comfortable admitting.

"Well, did you *feel it* this morning?" Nina challenged, scorn in her voice. "Because we were in there."

I flinched. I hadn't planned on telling Anson we'd been down there. I really didn't want word getting out that we'd gone in.

Anson sat bolt upright. "In the mine? You were?"

"Yeah," I said, glaring at her. "Just a little over an hour ago."

"Wow," he sighed. "I have so many questions. Wow. Did—"

"Has anyone ever seen blood down there?" Nina interrupted.

That pulled him up short. He held up a finger and then dove into one of the unopened boxes, digging until he came up with a notebook bound in red leather. He held it out to Nina.

"That's a list of everything that everyone has ever said they experienced, either in the mine or out of it. Off the top of my head I don't recall anyone ever saying blood, but—" He shrugged. "Could have been a throwaway remark, and I jotted it down and forgot about it."

Nina opened the notebook and began paging through.

"Have you ever experienced anything, Mr. Perry?" Lisey asked. "Personally?"

His face dimmed and his eyes shuttered. "Not personally," he said. "Not anything concrete. Sometimes I have nightmares, but I don't remember them."

"Sounds like a blessing," Nina muttered.

I poked her in the side. She looked at me and I mouthed, *Be nice.*

"Can I ask you to do me a favor?" He looked at each of us in turn. "Can I ask you to document anything that seems out of the ordinary over the next—mm, let's just say till the end of summer. And can you ask your dad—I'm so sorry, I've forgotten his name—"

"Carlisle," Piper said.

"Yes, yes, can you ask Carlisle to describe his experience down there? I have a recorder you can give him; hang on—"

He got to his feet faster than I would have thought possible, levering himself up with his cane, and disappeared into the back of the apartment.

Nina flipped another page. "'Coyote prints in living room,'" she read. "Lock your windows. 'Baby monitor playing Satanic music.' Radio interference."

"'Awoken by sensation of drowning,'" I read over her shoulder. "'Dark figure in bedroom.'"

"All of this can be explained." She closed the book and tucked it back into the box. "You'll see."

Anson returned with a tape player clutched in one hand, which he thrust at Piper.

"There's a brand-new tape in there. Six hours. I can get you more if he needs it."

"I don't really know what he'll have to say," she said, voice tinged with doubt. She took the tape player hesitantly, like he was going to snap something at her *Pretty Woman*–style.

"Maybe it'll be helpful for him." Lisey put a hand on Piper's arm. "Like taking notes, only out loud."

"True." Piper turned it over in her hands and tapped on the little clear window with a fingernail. "I'll give it to him and I'll tell him what you're looking for, but no promises."

"Thank you," Anson said, eyes shining.

Nina pushed herself to her feet. "We've taken a lot of your time."

"No, no, I'm happy to—"

"We really appreciate your help," she said, voice firm.

We were almost to the office door when he said, "Wait! Hang on. You should take these tapes." He stabbed at the boxes with his cane.

"Why?"

"To see if anything sounds familiar," he said.

EiGHT

"I hate every single one of these people," Nina said two hours later. The stack of videos outside the box had finally grown bigger than the jumbled pile left inside it. "I hate Moon Basin, and ghosts, and television, and—"

"Shhh," Lisey said, shuffling toward the screen. The tape she'd just put in was starting. "Look."

It didn't start with video: just a still frame of someone in shadow, in profile.

"I think I'm cursed," a female voice said over the image. The recording was staticky. "I must be, because Sidney was. He told me what was happening to him."

The silhouette disappeared, the frame cutting neatly into a small, cluttered office. A young woman sat at a desk, looking directly at the camera. "Mellie Harington's psychiatrist recorded her sessions," the young woman said. "Doctor-patient privilege is waived after death. What we're hearing here is a woman at the end of her rope, desperate for help, with nowhere to turn."

"Gag," Nina said. The office faded out; the silhouette returned. Closed captions scrawled across the bottom of the screen as the audio played.

"He said it made his head funny," Mellie's voice said. "Being down there. Like the air wasn't right, like it was contaminated. He didn't feel like himself, didn't feel right. He said he could hear whispering sometimes and—sometimes—now that he's gone, I hear it, too. Whispering all the time, crawling into my head. A rustling sound. Do you know what it told him? It told him to put me in there. He went down and all he could hear was *Bring her bring her bring her* . . . It's funny . . ."

She trailed off. The silence crackled.

"What's funny?" a male voice asked. The psychiatrist, I guessed.

Mellie laughed. "It says the same thing to me."

The screen filled with snow.

"Holy what the hell," Piper said. "Is that all? Is there more?"

She scrambled toward the box. I stared at the screen, imagining that sad voice coming out of the mouth of the smiling dark-haired woman whose picture hung in the lobby of the motel. Had Mellie dreamed of the mine? Had she heard breathing somewhere behind her, drawing closer?

"Maybe the show still has her tapes," I suggested. "The copies, I mean. Would they have kept them?"

I clicked the remote, drawing the video back to the young woman in the office and pausing. Then I started fast-forwarding, wondering if anything had been recorded after the static.

"I can't imagine they were cheap," Nina mused. "Getting a doctor to release medical records to a TV show? They probably paid too much to throw them out."

"Guys." I hit the Pause button. "Look." It was a frame that listed a point of contact. P.O. box, phone number. Ghost hotline, tell us your secrets. Nadia al-Jamil, paranormal reporter. We left a message from Nina's home phone, hoping that someone would eventually check the mailbox.

"Now what?" Nina asked, stretching out across the floor.

"I can't watch another one of those tapes. I'm sorry, I can't."

"No, I think I'm done, too," I said. My head felt water-logged, stuffed with faces and voices and a dark pulsating sound that kept getting louder. I wasn't afraid; I repeated it to myself. I wasn't afraid. But I was uneasy. I felt like my bones were too big for my skin, like a collection of pick-up-sticks in a thin paper bag, like silk over broken glass. I felt *wrong*. I felt, I realized, like I had in the mine. I squeezed my eyes shut and shook my head, trying to will the feeling away.

"I'm starving." Piper shoved the box of tapes away from her and stretched. "We haven't eaten since breakfast."

"Lisey," Nina said from her corpselike sprawl. "Ice pops. In the freezer. Save us."

Lisey rolled her eyes and bounced up off her chair, returning a moment later clutching an armful of neon-colored tubes. She handed two to each of us.

"If we each eat, like, twelve of these, it counts as dinner." Piper gnawed at the plastic wrapper.

"I have chicken," Nina said around her own ice pop. "I will make chicken. I just have to get off the floor."

"Ice pop dinner," Lisey said. "Band name."

I extended my tube toward her and we clinked.

"So how much do you know about Mellie?" Piper asked.

Nina looked at me. I shook my head. "You're the one with the good grades."

She sighed. "Mellie was married to one of the miners. Sidney. He was, like, a union guy. Or an anti-union guy. I can't remember. Either way, it wasn't going well for him, so he started robbing the company. I guess you can blast extra coal out of the seams if you wedge explosives into the right cracks. So he did that, and one day he must have used too much, because that was the day of the explosion."

"Okay," Piper said.

I chewed open my second ice pop, felt the cold blueness of it in my throat.

"So everyone vanished," Nina continued. "Died, obviously, but they never found their bodies. And everyone was like, okay, clearly the one guy is responsible, even if we can't prove it. So the whole time they were building the new town everyone was harassing Mellie absolutely to shit. They never left her alone."

Piper held up a hand. "Sorry, hang on. Everyone just sort of glossed over the fact that—how many?—seventeen guys were just missing?"

"Most people think the coyotes dragged them out," I said.

"Which is bananas," Lisey chimed in. "And also doesn't explain why they couldn't find any collapsed sections of tunnel."

Piper rubbed her temples like she was getting a headache. "And why did they think it was him? Harington?"

Nina opened her mouth, wrinkled her brow, and closed it again. "I think he was pro-union. Because he was just, like, constantly talking about how they weren't being paid enough. Like, all over town. Everyone knew he was really pissed off with the company."

"Okay," Piper said. "So everyone thinks he's a thief, the explosion happens and the miners vanish, and then everyone gangs up on Mellie."

"They didn't at first," Lisey said. "But she stopped sleeping, and she started telling everyone that Sidney was visiting her at night. She started saying it wasn't his fault. The other widows thought it was disrespectful."

"So then she was alone." Piper looked down at her lap.

"And she kept seeing him," Lisey said. "And no one believed her, and no one listened to her."

"They found her in the river," I added. "They don't know if she sleepwalked there or if she went in on purpose."

"Jesus," Piper said. "How awful."

"Do you think Nadia will have the tapes?" I asked, leaning against the couch. *She probably won't even call back*, I thought, and then hated myself for thinking it.

Nina started the process of rolling over, talking as she did. "I hope so, but even if she doesn't, maybe she can tell us about them. I wonder where the originals are." She stood up, chewing on the half-empty tube. "Do you think the psychiatrist was here in town?"

"No way," Lisey said. "I bet she went to the city."

"That makes sense," I said.

"Because you know everyone here looked at her like they look at me."

"Aw, Lise," Piper said.

Lisey shook her head. "No, it's okay. It's just sad to think about her all alone, you know? At least I have you guys, even if you don't necessarily believe like I do."

Nina pointed the ice pop wrapper at her. "On that note, it's time for me to see a man about a chicken."

GhostWatch, Episode 53
Unused Footage

(PHILLIP "FISH" FICINSKI stands outside a gas station next to a display of propane canisters. He looks nervous. GLEN CAREY stands beside him with a mic, sweating profusely.)

CAREY: Thank you for speaking with me, Phillip.

FICINSKI: Fish.

CAREY: Fish, of course. Sorry. Thank you for speaking with me, Fish.

(FISH shrugs and shoves his hands into his pockets. He appears to be regretting this decision.)

CAREY: So tell me what's been going on.

FISH: Man, I don't—can I just tell you this shit and then you don't put me on the show? Like, can I just give you information and not have my face—

CAREY: We can blur your face.

FISH: I'm the only person who works here.

CAREY, *with some aggravation*: We can edit out the background.

FISH: I still—

CAREY: Kid, I don't even know if what you have is worth airing, okay? I have a lot of shit to get done here in a very limited time, so either we roll on this or we say bye-bye.

FISH: Fine. Fine. Obviously you know the general story, right?

CAREY: Yes.

FISH: So you know no one's been down there since *Grave Encounters*.

CAREY: Yes.

FISH: They hired some guy this year to go in. He's, like, checking all the tunnels out to make sure they're stable. He's been down there once a day since the beginning of summer.

(CAREY is about to speak, but then FISH continues, looking almost surprised at himself as the words pour out.)

FISH: I was, like, twelve when that girl came out of the mine. Batty. I was obsessed with her. I would hang around the motel trying to get her attention. I didn't really have any stories of my own, but I'd heard things, you know? I could have told her some interesting stuff.

CAREY: Sure.

FISH: I was there when she came out. I was in the commons skating, trying to land a kickflip, and all of a sudden I hear this *screaming*. Like nothing I've ever heard before. It was unreal. You know when your balls just like, *whoop*, just retract into your body? That's what happened. Sorry, can I say "balls," or—

CAREY, *wearily*: Just keep going.

FISH: She runs into the commons and she sees me, and she grabs me like she's drowning. She's covered in blood and ash and, like, chalk, she had these weird stripes on her face, and she just won't stop screaming. She's saying, like, "I can hear them," or something.

CAREY: I don't mean to be, um. I—has anything happened recently? The man who called us made it sound like—

FISH: No, yeah, sorry. I just remember what it was like back when people were still going in there on, like, a regular basis. So I can tell that it's happening again.

CAREY: What's happening?

FISH: The mine is doing stuff again. Usually people have

nightmares, they sleepwalk, um, a lot of people see things—

CAREY: What's happening specifically?

FISH: Sorry. Yeah. Um, there's a waitress at the Half Moon, that's the diner, she tried to take her baby down there when he was first born. He's older now, obviously, but I was in there last week talking to her, and she got this look on her face like she was listening, like, trying to hear something really quiet. And then she said, "I wonder if Sammy would like to see the mine," in this really weird voice.

CAREY: Weird how?

FISH: Flat, kind of. Like a robot. She was wiping the counter down, and she just kept wiping this one spot over and over, and her eyes sort of glazed over, and then she said it again: "I wonder if Sammy would like to see the mine." And then she kind of came back into herself and got this *terrified* look on her face. She dropped the rag and took off her apron and left. Like, walked out of the diner. I'm pretty sure she hasn't been back since.

CAREY, *looking at his watch*: Interesting. Has anything happened that's, mm, more concise?

(FISH sighs. He seems to understand he is not holding CAREY's attention.)

FISH: I keep dreaming I'm buried alive. Does that work?

CAREY: Sure. Thank you for your time.

(CAREY waits until FISH has gone back inside the gas station, then turns back to the camera.)

CAREY: Man. If the rest of them are like this, we're gonna get fucking canceled, dude.

(Sound of laughter from cameraman. End of footage.)

NINE

I was alone in Old Town, in the woods, and the ash was thick, choking, stinging my throat. Something was wrong. The trees were impossibly tall. They stretched up and away into the white-gray sky and I couldn't see where they ended. I sensed that they were meeting up there, twining around each other into a dark canopy, and the thought filled my head with cloudy, viscous poison. I was walking forward, one foot in front of the other, and I realized I didn't want to. I realized I couldn't stop. Dread, cold and hollow, curled around my bones, climbing my spine, burrowing at the base of my skull. A small black point of light opened in the distance and I peered toward it. Something like a whimper escaped me and my head pulsed with pain. It was the mine. I tried to stop, but my wretched feet carried me forward. The hungry mouth of the mine yawned. I could see the canopy of crooked trees now, just overhead, and I realized they weren't trees at all, but the ceiling of a mine shaft. I swallowed a scream and then another as a small white hand floated out of the darkness before me.

"Clem," said a voice—the voice of something whose lungs and throat were clotted with dirt and ash, whose vocal cords were going soft and liquid after too many days somewhere down there in the earth.

The fingers of the hand opened and closed almost experimentally, mechanically, and they had too many joints somehow. I watched them flexing, hypnotized, and I was still walking closer. The hand was beckoning me, drawing me down into the mine, and this time the voice came much closer, and I felt something warm and rotting breathing on me.

"Clem," it said again, and then the darkness of the mine was all around me.

I woke up drenched in sweat, my hands clenched tightly on the sheets. I rolled over and looked at Nina. Her eyes were moving back and forth under her lids, teeth chattering behind closed lips. She was perfectly still aside from these two things. I didn't want to wake her but the sight chilled me so deeply, filled me with such dread, that I climbed out of bed and crept into my mother's empty room. I stopped just short of locking the door and fell into her bed, burrowing under the blankets like I had when I was little. When I woke up again, it was daylight and I could smell waffles.

"Where'd you go?" Nina asked, looking up as I shuffled into the living room. She was wearing my pajama pants, comically short on her, and a hoodie of hers I'd borrowed approximately three years earlier. She had an open magazine on her lap, glossy palm trees, shiny-toothed smiles.

"You were talking in your sleep." I was lying, but she used to do it a lot, so it wasn't coming out of nowhere.

"Shit," she said. "Did I say anything good?"

"Nah." I walked into the kitchen, trying to settle into the normalcy of toaster waffles. "At one point it almost sounded like 'pineapple soufflé,' though."

"Mm," she said, "sounds delicious."

We ate breakfast and the shadow of the dream receded, and by the time my mom walked in I felt normal again.

"Hi, girls." She dumped her keys onto the table by the door.

"Hi, Mom," I said. "How was work?"

She just shook her head and ripped open the Velcro tabs on her shoes.

"Do you two mind going outside?" she asked. I could see the faint brackets around her mouth that meant she was in the grip of a bad headache.

"Of course not," Nina said. "Get some sleep."

We sat in the yard bouncing a tennis ball back and forth, drinking apple juice, watching the sun climb higher in the sky. We still hadn't heard back from Nadia.

I missed the tennis ball by a hair and it bounced off the trailer, rolling back across the yard and under Nina's stoop.

"I'm not getting it," she said around her straw. Her hair straggled out of her ponytail, the tendrils limp in the heat. "I have sunstroke."

I sucked down the last of my juice. "Pool?"

"Pool."

We changed in her trailer and started walking down the road. We couldn't cut through the field because the corn was fully ripe, fat ears crowding the little path that we used so often. So we went the long way, past the bus stop, down the long spoke of the road toward town. The motel was out on an adjacent spoke, off the highway, the crescent of its neon moon visible over the hills just as you saw the sign for the exit.

As soon as we hit the blacktop and headed out of town, we saw a van parked in front of the doors. The NO in NO VACANCY was flashing above it in slow, strobing motion, and I wondered if anyone ever swerved onto the exit only to see the NO flash up a second too late.

I could hear shouts and splashing as we got closer, and my head gave a single hollow thud. Crowds weren't my favorite thing, especially when they were made up mainly of shrieking, overheated children.

The silhouettes of the people unloading the van wavered in the heat, shimmering and resolving as we drew closer. They were shaking out yards of cable, clipping mic packs to their belt loops. One of them drew out a long, thin metal tube, and I knew at once it was a microphone.

"Holy shit," I said, nudging Nina. "Hunters."

"Speak of the devil," she murmured. "Anson's been busy."

"You think he called them?"

"I think he called them the day Piper and her dad got here."

"I wonder why he didn't mention it to her," I said. We had slowed our walk considerably, trying to stay out of their immediate surroundings.

"Probably gonna try and sell them the audio of Carlisle, if Piper gets it," Nina said.

It was cynical, but I didn't disagree.

"Here we go," she said as we drew closer. "God, I'm so not in the mood." She looked idly at her nails as we hit the parking lot, our flip-flops scuffing against the asphalt. The people were wearing black T-shirts emblazoned with the word GHOSTWATCH.

"Embarrassing," I said under my breath, and Nina huffed a laugh.

"Ladies!" one of them said, striding over to us. He was wearing cargo shorts and a beret, for some reason, and sweat was already beading at his temples. "How are you on this fine day?"

Nina just looked at him and kept walking. I didn't want to be rude, so I did the high school-jock nod and hoped it would suffice.

"My name is Glen," he continued, walking alongside us. "I'm here with *GhostWatch*. Have you heard of us?"

I could see the cameraman following our movement, the Handycam at his side tracking us as he pretended to examine a shrub.

"No," Nina said flatly.

He seemed to think she was going to say more, but when nothing was forthcoming and we kept walking, he quickened his pace and leaped in front of us. "Can I just ask for a minute of your time, ladies, a quick minute to talk about—"

"Excuse me," I said, pushing past him. Nina jostled him on the other side.

"Do you have any comment about the recent paranormal occurrences here?" he yelled after us. "The sightings in the mine?"

I stopped. I couldn't help it. Nina groaned as I pivoted back to Glen. "Don't encourage him."

He jogged up to us, fumbling with the mic pack at his belt. "There have been reports recently that town residents are seeing things in the mine again."

"No one goes into the mine," Nina said, annoyed. "So I guess you heard wrong."

I thought about Carlisle for a second, a brief glimpse of an idea before it skittered away. "Yeah," I echoed. "No one goes in there. It's not safe."

He jammed the mic toward my face. "Why isn't it safe?"

"Didn't you do your research, Glen?"

"Of course we did our research. But a local perspective is always—"

Nina put her hand over the mic and pushed it away.

Glen lost whatever composure he'd had left. "What about the voices?" he yelled.

We froze, taken aback by the outburst. "What?" I asked.

"The voices," he said, still too loud. "Locals are hearing voices again. The most frequent occurrences since the town was relocated."

"Who told you that?" I asked.

"We don't reveal our sources. We were told that—"

"Who told you?" Nina demanded.

"—that a local woman was hearing voices telling her to go into the mine. Another young man said—"

"This is bullshit, we're out of here." Nina grabbed my hand and pulled me toward the motel. She turned back to Glen with a look of disgust on her face. "You're a parasite."

Then we were through the sliding door into the cool air-conditioned lobby. I paused as we walked toward the pool to glance at Mellie, frozen there on the wall, and then we were back outside and the heat rolled over us, carrying the sound of too many voices. Nina unslung her towel from around her neck and walked toward the pool, stepping out of her shorts as she moved. She dropped the towel in a heap on top of them. In another step she was in the pool, water closing over her head as she sank with barely a ripple. I threw my own towel on top of hers, peeling off my shorts and top and then sitting down on the edge of the pool. My feet looked paler underwater, rippling under the surface.

Nina surfaced, her hair plastered to her back and shoulders, eyelashes beaded with water. "C'mon," she said. "It's not gonna get any colder."

She wrapped one of her long-fingered hands around my ankle and pulled gently until I pushed myself off the edge and slipped in. The cool water closed over me like silk, resting heavy on my eyelids, pulling itself through my hair. I folded my legs, pushing upward against the water, forcing myself into a seated position at the bottom of the pool. I felt the cold all around me, felt it filling my ears and muffling my thoughts, and then someone kicked me in the head. I jerked and yelped and gulped a mouthful of chlorine, shooting to the surface even as I hacked my lungs out.

"Sorry," the little kid said when I splashed up, gasping. He smiled at me, displaying an unnerving lack of front teeth, and paddled his little kickboard away.

"Ow," I mumbled, rubbing my head. I coughed up a little more water, my throat burning.

Nina watched me. I could tell she was trying not to smile.

"Oh, shut up." I pushed a little wave at her. "I could have drowned."

"I'd save you from drowning."

"Unless it was a little kid that drowned me. Then you'd be too busy laughing."

She grinned and propped herself on the edge of the pool, her elbows holding her above the water as she leaned back and looked around. I pressed myself against the wall next to her, keeping everything below my chin submerged. We looked out across the pool, the crush of bodies and floaties and a beach ball that kept getting bounced out of the water, a different kid scrambling to retrieve it each time.

"Not bad," she said.

"Not bad," I echoed.

She kicked her feet up out of the water and we looked at her pink-painted toenails way down there at the end of her legs. She tipped her head back, letting her wet hair puddle on the concrete behind her.

Suddenly we were in shadow, and I looked up to see Danny Nelson leering down at us.

"Nina," he said, grinning unpleasantly. "You're looking ripe."

"Sit and spin, Danny," she said without looking up. "Stop blocking the sun."

"I'll sit anywhere you want, mamacita."

Nina rolled her eyes and slid underwater, surfacing a moment later to clamber out of the pool. I climbed out behind her and started picking up our stuff. She moved up close to Danny, wringing out her hair, and looked down at him. Danny's not as tall as she is and he hates it, so she tries to remind him whenever possible. She cocked her hip and folded her arms, waiting for him to speak.

"Hey, it's cool," he said, holding his hands up. "Just trying to be friendly."

She sighed. It was a long sigh, a beleaguered one, and I could tell she was deciding whether or not he was worth the effort. Finally she reached out, put her hand on his face—it covered the whole thing, like a starfish—and pushed him gently out of our way.

"Let's go, Clem." She stepped back into her sandals. "See you, Danny."

Paul came out of the stairwell into the lobby just as the doors opened for us, carrying a tank that looked like something out of *Ghostbusters*.

"Room 217 again," he said.

"Ghosts," Nina singsonged.

"The curse of the haunted air conditioner." He laughed. "See you at home."

"Bye, Papa. Don't work too hard."

The ghost hunters were still in the parking lot. Nina strode up to Glen and tapped his arm. He flinched and she smiled.

"Listen, I was rude before," she said in her sweetest voice. "We're all just under so much stress because of all the haunting. You know how it is. Let me make it up to you, okay? There's a kid in there who's definitely had some wild paranormal encounters."

She saw she had his attention, lowered her voice to just above a whisper, and continued, "He's like, five eight or so, green swim trunks, his name's Danny, and you should definitely interview him. Like, don't let him get away, because he could *make* your show."

We made it far enough away that we could barely hear them rushing all their equipment into the hotel. Then we burst out laughing.

"Very elegant," I said after a minute. "Much less violent than your usual Danny solutions."

She shrugged. "I'm tired of having to explain to his dad that I'm not playing hard to get."

"Fair."

We walked across the center of town, onto the spoke directly opposite the highway—technically, the spoke that led to Old Town—and headed for the SuperStop. The gas station was a weird community hub; there were always at least a few kids skateboarding in the parking lot or sitting in the bed of a pickup truck while they shotgunned beers. It had two pumps, one of which was cash only, and a sign in the window that said NOT HAUNTED. They put that up after the third time a ghost hunter accidentally broke the security camera with a boom mic, hoping it would keep the (admittedly very tiny) store clear. It had mixed results—show a ghost hunter a sign that says NOT HAUNTED and you're essentially begging them to assume it's a lie—but at least they only take the handheld cameras in there now. We pushed through the shrubs lining the parking lot and crossed the black-top, which was hot enough that it felt vaguely sticky. There was a little kid trying to do a wheelie in the shade of the metal canopy as Sheryl Crow played tinnily from the overhead speaker.

"Hey, Fish," Nina yelled as we jangled through the door. Fish was nineteen and totally in love with Nina. She let him give us free slushies and trusted him not to report us truant when we showed up on school days, but he was a dropout, so that was as far as he was getting with her. "How's it hangin'?"

"Same old, Terrazos." He always talked real slow, his words pulled long and soft like taffy. "You here for a job?"

"Wouldn't you love that," she said, sashaying back to the slushie machine. She cranked the handle down, filled two cups, and handed me one, cherry-red and sticky. I sucked in a mouthful, crushing the ice into the roof of my mouth. Nina bared her pink-slicked teeth at me in a sweet, feral smile.

Fish cleared his throat. "You hear about Rennie?"

"Rennie? From the diner? No, what happened?" Nina asked.

"She quit," he said. "A few days ago. She walked out. I was there."

"Weird," Nina said. "Why?"

Fish leaned across the counter, completely oblivious to me. I picked up a lip balm and put it down.

"You probably don't remember," he said. "But a while back—when I was pretty young—she went away for a while. To an institution."

"Fish, you're only, like, two years older than us," Nina said. "Whatever. Go on."

"I heard my parents talking about it once. They said she was hearing stuff. They said she tried to take Sammy into the mine."

"Her *kid*?"

"Yeah," he said. "Fucked up, right?"

"Why would she do that?"

My mouth was dry. I closed my hand around a pair of tweezers.

"I don't know," he said. "But I think she's gonna go away again. I think she's hearing whatever she heard back then."

Fish's throat worked. Nina raised an eyebrow. I slipped the tweezers into my pocket.

"You sound like you really believe that," she said.

He flushed and folded his arms. "Why wouldn't I?"

"Why would you?" she said.

"I've been hearing things, too." He leaned farther over the counter. I moved my hand away from the gum. "In my head."

"Some people call that 'having a thought.'"

"Don't be an asshole. Have you ever had anything like that happen?" Suddenly he was looking at me, his face too close to mine. "Have *you*?"

I shook my head, not to say no, but to try and clear it. He looked nervous, almost defensive, like he wanted us to validate what he was feeling. He wanted stories that would prove he wasn't alone. "You're the one who talked to Glen," I said slowly. "You told him about the voices."

Nina slapped her hand down onto the counter. "Oh, goddamn it, Fish—"

"Look, Nina, just because you don't believe in it doesn't mean it's not real," he snapped, eyes flashing. "It doesn't mean it can't hurt you."

Nina rolled her eyes. "Thanks for that, I'll log that away. I hope you at least made him give you a free T-shirt."

Then her cold hand was in mine, pulling me, and we were walking out of the gas station into sunlight. She waited until we were past the drugstore and then looked at me, chewing on her straw.

"Little miss stress-klepto," she said as she held out her hand expectantly.

I could feel myself blushing as I placed the tweezers in her palm.

"You gotta work on this," she said. "Not everyone is as enthralled by me as Fish."

She turned and walked back toward the SuperStop. I stood there sucking on my straw, letting the tiny crystals of ice slide down my throat and paint my insides cool and calm and red. The shoplifting was a nervous habit I'd tried and failed to break. Half the time I didn't even realize I was doing it. I felt a bright flare of panic every time I found something new in one of my pockets, but I didn't know how to stop.

I thought about Rennie, trying to take her baby into the mine. I thought about Sidney trying to take Mellie down there. I thought about the way Carlisle's face had gone flat and lifeless as he listened to the silence in the tunnels, and I was walking before I'd consciously made the decision to go back. I slammed open the door just as Nina was turning away from the counter and demanded, "What did you hear?"

Fish looked up at me, eyes narrowed. "I heard you're still shoplifting."

"No," I said impatiently. "The voices. What did you hear?"

He darted a glance at Nina. "Um—well. It's not always words. Mostly it's just like . . . this really strong urge to go into the mine. And then sometimes it kind of sounds like—" He laughed, rubbing the back of his neck. "I don't know, man. I know how it sounds. I just feel *off* lately, you know?"

"Yeah, totally," Nina said, the sarcastic inflection too subtle for him to pick up on. I felt a twinge of pity for him.

"Has it happened before?" I asked. I wanted to understand why he was scared now, why he felt like something was different from the shadow of the mine we all lived in every day.

He flushed and ducked his head. "I've had dreams. They're worse now, though, and they happen more often. Last week I woke up on the floor."

I nodded, thinking about Lisey walking all the way to the mine in her sleep. I could feel Nina trying to push me out the door with the force of her gaze alone.

"I'm not the only one," he said. "I've heard a lot of people say things are weird the past few days. I don't know if we're all feeling the same thing, but—" He shrugged. "I hear it," he said simply. "That's all I know."

"I believe you," I said. It surprised me, but I felt the truth of it as I said it. I'd been down there. I'd felt the strange wrongness of it, the way it seemed to crawl into my head. It didn't feel like a stretch to think that others were being affected.

He gave me a halfhearted smile and turned to reorganize the lighters.

I looked back through the glass door as we left. He was still standing at the counter, his back slightly hunched. As I watched, he ran a hand through his hair and then blotted his eyes with the sleeve of his T-shirt.

"I can't believe he was my first kiss," Nina muttered as we walked deeper into town.

"You were, like, five," I said. "I don't know if that counts."

"Well, it counts enough that he's still obsessed with me," she said.

"Don't be shitty," I said.

She sighed and hooked her cup into the trash can outside the grocery store. "You're right. I'm just wound up 'cause no one will shut up about the mine."

"Why are you so upset about it?" I asked, looking at her out of the corner of my eye. We turned onto the spoke of the wheel that led toward the park and the library.

She sighed. "Because it's not real, Clem."

"Okay, but . . . it's always like this," I said, puzzled. I pulled at the sleeve of the T-shirt I was wearing. "It's like, our whole thing. I'm literally wearing a *Paranormal America* shirt right now."

Nina was always a skeptic, even when we were kids. I remember watching the Moon Basin episode of *Haunted America*, cringing as the camera panned past an empty wheelchair in the corner of an old hospital room. All Nina said was, "Why would the hospital be haunted? The *hospital* didn't explode," and kept eating her tangerine. She was always an island in a sea of believers, but it hadn't ever upset her the way it seemed to now. I didn't know what had changed.

Nina sighed and looked around, trying to decide where she wanted to go. "Can we just walk for a bit? I don't really feel like going home."

"Yeah, I don't care." We veered onto a side street and walked side by side, and after a few minutes she spoke again.

"Do you remember that game, Bloody Mary?"

"Stand in front of the mirror, say her name three times," I said. "Right?"

"And then she comes through the mirror and kills you," Nina finished.

"Okay."

"The last few weeks," she said, staring into the distance, "have felt like being at a never-ending party where everyone is screaming because someone saw Bloody Mary, and none of them ever stops screaming long enough to notice that no one is getting killed by Bloody Mary. It takes on a life of its own, it spreads, and then it doesn't matter if it's true or not."

She turned and plunged off the road. I wasn't sure where she was going, literally or conversationally, but I stayed right behind her.

"We're all always involved in this, like, shared reality, this *deception.*" She grunted as she clambered over a low wooden fence. "'Moon Basin is haunted.' But there's an unspoken agreement—at least I thought there was—that we don't actually *believe* it."

"I think this is private property . . . ?" I said weakly. One of the frayed threads of my shorts caught on the splintered wood as I shimmied over the fence.

She kept talking like she hadn't heard me. "It feels like everyone who was in on that agreement made some new arrangement. Like, 'normally we just play along, but now for some reason we're gonna actually straight-up fuckin' believe in ghosts.' Someone at the party started screaming, and now everyone is. Look at those trees over there."

Momentarily thrown by the abrupt change of topic, I looked out to where she was pointing. A little stand of trees grew in the distance, green leaves fluttering in the wind. She took off toward it without waiting to see if I would follow.

"Lisey believes it," I said as I drew even with her.

"I know," she sighed. "And I love her, and I love that *about* her. I don't know why this is so different."

"Maybe because she's not scared," I said.

The field was fallow, maybe for an off-season, maybe for a fall crop. We made our way across the rutted ground, the dry dirt crumbling into our flip-flops, and the trees never seemed to draw closer. Nina seemed determined to reach them. She'd stopped talking, eyes fixed ahead, walking with purpose. I could feel sweat trickling down my back, soaking the waistband of my shorts. I wanted to see what was drawing her forward, and my curiosity outweighed the concern I felt about potentially trespassing on someone's land, but her intense focus was making me anxious. I wanted her to say something, to look at me, to come back just for a second.

"I'm gonna burn," I said, holding my arm out toward her.

"You always burn." She didn't turn around.

We walked for maybe half an hour across the field, and there was nothing in sight. No house that we could see, nothing at all except the trees in the distance. Slowly, slowly they grew bigger, and I started to hear a strange rushing sound.

"That's wind," Nina said, speeding up. "In the leaves."

The fence circled around again, jutting out before us like a line of crooked teeth. The side near the road had been maintained, at least a little—it was standing, for one thing. This side was a collection of stakes hammered into the ground, scattered beams in between them in various stages of decay.

"This is strange." Nina crouched down to roll one of the fallen posts over. "Ugh. Wet." She stood up, wiped her hand on her shorts, and stepped over the crumbling line. "See? Now we're out."

"Or on someone else's land," I said, but I didn't believe it.

"Yeah, well, if whoever is maintaining this fence owns this land, I'd say we're not gonna see them out here anytime soon."

She took my hand and we walked toward the trees.

The copse was a freestanding spike in the middle of the field, which was marbled with tufts of grass and the occasional tall thistle. There were maybe six or seven trees in all, but something about the place made it seem like there were a lot more. As we drew closer I could see that they were tall, but they couldn't have been as tall as they looked. Nothing about them seemed normal, and yet they were comforting somehow. They made sense to me, even as they defied basic, rational understanding. We made our way toward these strange trees, and even though we had never been here, it felt familiar as we walked into their shade.

It was like we had come through a door into a green, sun-dappled space that had been created for us. The light fell in splashes and stripes across the grass, which was thick and lush, protected from the wind and heat that had decimated the field outside. There was a fucking butterfly perched on a flower, opening and closing its wings. It looked like a painting, or a scene from *Bambi* in a universe where his mom doesn't get murdered. It took my breath away. As I stood there I could feel something changing, shifting inside my head. Pressure I hadn't known existed was ebbing away. I looked at Nina.

"Do you feel that? In your head?"

She looked uncomfortable, but after a second she nodded. "It's like a radio station. When you finally get it perfectly clear after miles of static."

"I wonder why," I said. I was afraid to mention the mine so soon after she'd calmed down, but a part of me wondered if it was somehow emitting something, *rays* or something, and these trees were shielding us.

"It feels like we were supposed to find it," she said.

Without consulting one another, we moved toward the center of the little space and sat down, then flopped onto our backs to look up. I could just make out the blue of the sky beyond the leaves as they moved gently in the wind, the flashes of green-blue-green like a school of fish darting by above us. I turned my head to look at her and found she was looking back. Her eyelashes flickered and she smiled, her slightly crooked front teeth catching her lip like they always did.

"I like it in here," she whispered after a long silence, and she reached out and wrapped her hand around my wrist.

TEN

It was early but already oppressively hot. The air shimmered and rippled, insects whirring in the trees all around us as we walked through town. It had been a little over a week since we went into the mine, and things were starting to feel more normal. Lisey jumped onto Piper's back and instead of bucking her off, Piper grabbed her legs tight and took off running, Lisey screaming her head off, both of them laughing like hyenas. Piper didn't put her down until we reached the fence and then we stood there, the four of us, looking past it at the trees.

"You sure it's okay?" Piper arched her eyebrow at the fence.

"I swear," Nina answered. "I don't know why, but—you'll feel it when we're in there. It's safe."

Lisey was humming like a tuning fork. "It does feel good," she agreed, her voice faraway. "Let's go." Without waiting for us, she put one hand on the rail and one on the post and vaulted her skinny body into the field.

Piper whistled. "Girl got ups." She slung herself over the fence. "If we get arrested, you owe me dinner."

"Yeah, yeah," Nina said.

The sun rose as we crossed the field, crickets ricocheting off our legs as they tried to get out of our way.

"My dad's been having nightmares," Piper said abruptly. She

was trying to sound casual but there was a catch in her voice, and she didn't look at us.

"About the mine?" Lisey asked.

"I don't know. I just hear him talking at night." She shoved her hands into her pockets. "Have you guys been feeling anything weird?"

I elbowed Nina before she could say something dismissive. I could see the worry etched onto Piper's face.

"Everyone always feels a little bit weird here." Lisey's voice was gentle. "That's sort of the way the Basin works."

"So you don't think it's anything, you know—" Piper waved her hand. "Anything more than that? I just keep thinking about all those tapes we watched. Shit, I need to give him that damn recorder. I keep forgetting."

"It's . . . possible that there are more people having nightmares lately," I said, trying to find the least concerning wording. "Since the beginning of the summer."

"Since he's been going into the mine, you mean," Piper said.

"It's just on everyone's mind," Nina said. "People know he's going down there, they get paranoid and think about it more, and it bleeds into their dreams."

"Yeah." I smiled at Nina, thanking her for being tactful. "He's probably just got it on the brain because he's down there so much, you know? I'd keep an eye on him, but it's probably nothing to get freaked out about."

"I guess so," Piper said. "You're probably right. I've definitely been thinking about it a lot, too, and I don't even have to work down there, so I guess it makes sense."

Lisey squeezed her shoulder. "You're officially one of us now. You and your dad both."

Piper gave her a small smile. Lisey grinned and said, "Now let's go already. I wanna see this magic meadow." She looped her arm through Piper's and pulled her along.

I felt a flicker of unease as we got closer to the trees. I couldn't see the little opening that led to the clearing, and I started to panic. What if it was different? An image sprang unbidden into my mind: the clearing dead and barren, blackened with rot, filled with ash. Or—an even worse idea, one that chilled my blood—what if it wasn't there at all? What if we came through the trees and all we saw was the other side of that empty field? I held my breath as we walked in. Nina reached out and took my hand, and I knew she was scared, too.

"Oh my God," Piper said softly from ahead of us. I couldn't read her tone. My stomach clenched as we pushed forward through the arching tree trunks. I heard the rustling of the leaves and my heart stretched and blossomed like a flower toward the sun.

"It's still here," Nina said, and the relief in her voice loosened the knot in my own throat. I squeezed her hand and let go, watching Piper and Lisey. Lisey was walking in a slow, careful arc around the edges of the clearing, hair glinting as she tried to see everything at once. She looked like a baby deer learning to walk, exploring the world. Piper stood motionless in the little entrance arch, eyes filled with tears.

"Pipes," I said. "Are you okay?"

She blinked and the tears spilled over her lashes, and then she gave me a heartbreaking, brilliant smile. Her voice trembled as she spoke. "It's exactly like you described it. I feel like—like I've been standing in a shadow, and I just stepped into the sun. My head feels so *clear*." She turned in a circle, taking it all in. "I guess everyone really does feel weird in the Basin."

Lisey walked over to us with an armful of flowers. "It's like something out of time. Like a rock in the middle of a river."

"In the Basin, but not actually part of it," I murmured.

Lisey beamed at me. "Exactly. It's been waiting for us."

How to explain it: the wide-open plummeting terror of love. We lay there, loose-limbed in the sun, watching Lisey stringing daisies. Nina rolled over and grabbed her wrist and Piper's. She put Lisey's hand in mine, crushing the tiny flowers between our tangled fingers, and we all fumbled for each other until we were lying there on our stomachs, a tiny circle linked by clasped hands, heads bowed together. After a minute, Nina took her hand out of mine and held her palm out to us. She untangled her other hand from Piper's and pulled something out of her shirt pocket, showed it to us glinting between her first two fingers.

"It's a blade," she said, and she placed it on her palm. "From one of those craft knives. I thought—I thought maybe—like in the movies?"

She ducked her head. I picked the blade off her palm.

"Blood brothers?" I said, half joking.

But she jerked her head up and looked me right in the eyes. "Sisters."

She handed me the knife, the tiniest sliver of brightness pinched between my fingers. I pressed the blade into her left palm, too softly, thinking about all the tendons and muscles just beneath the skin. My fingers shook and slipped and the blade fell into her hand. It didn't even scratch her. I steeled myself, picked it up again and pressed hard and suddenly she sucked in her breath and up came the blood, welling bright and hot in the sun, filling the cup of her palm, dripping into the grass. I cut Piper next, not as deep, both palms, and Lisey, too, and then my left.

Something new sizzled into my veins and I smiled huge at Nina. She took the blade and my right hand and clasped them both into her right hand. I felt the shock, the sharpness, Nina's blood and my blood, and we all took each other's hands, Lisey on my left and Piper on hers, arms crisscrossed over and under each other. I felt my edges soften and disappear. I felt us blurring into something strong and solid and for the first time since we'd gone into the mine, I felt wholly, perfectly safe.

We all let go at the same time, without knowing how or why. I don't know how long we sat there like that, intertwined, but the sunlight had shifted. Nina wiped her palms in the grass and we all followed suit, dark handprints against the green. I was glowing, humming, every inch of me alive. I felt Lisey, her gentle strangeness, I felt Piper's sharp strong wit, and Nina. I could always feel Nina, even before, but that day I felt I could see clear down to the depths of her soul like looking into still water. I felt all of us inside me, together, and I knew the others could feel it, too, and there was nothing to say. We lay there in the grass looking up at the sky, waiting for the bleeding to stop, and finally Nina sat up and brushed the grass out of her hair and looked at us.

"Slushie?"

The Unexplainable with Reagan Walker, Episode 50
Unused Footage

(REAGAN WALKER sits opposite an elderly woman in a crowded living room. She moves a decorative pillow out from behind her while the woman settles into her chair, puts on a pair of small round glasses, and reaches for the cup of tea on the table beside her.)

MARLENA RIOS: One night I was asleep, you know, around midnight, and I woke up real sudden. Like someone shook me, only Lee was working overnight so it wouldn'ta been him. Anyway, I woke up and looked around, and there wasn't anything I could see or hear so I tried to go back to sleep but I just couldn't. I felt so uneasy, like my heart wouldn't quit racing . . . so finally I got up and—I don't know why, you know? There was no reason for it. I went to the window and I put my hand on the cord and I was—I was just frozen, I don't know, like a part of me wanted to open it and the other part of me knew I shouldn't. I opened the blinds and there was—there was a pair of eyes, a pair of glowing yellow eyes, as close as—as close as you are now. Like whatever it was had its face pressed up right against the glass. And I could see—I swear to you, I know how this sounds, but I could see—below the eyes, the lips were pulling back into a smile, just a gash under the eyes that kept widening, and I was still frozen, and I—I knew that if I didn't look away I would go insane. I just—my mind would snap, and I knew I couldn't look away because if I did it would be in the room with me, I would turn and those eyes would be right there, that smile—

(RIOS stops talking abruptly, breathing hard. The teacup rattles against the saucer as she tries to raise it to her lips. Her hand is shaking too badly for her to be able to take a sip.)

WALKER: Take a moment if you need one. Do you need some water? Should we go outside?

(RIOS shakes her head. She takes a careful, trembling sip of her tea and sets the cup down. She looks at the camera.)

WALKER: What happened next?

RIOS: I was holding my breath, and I guess—I swooned a little bit. I didn't faint but I sort of stumbled, and my vision went, and I stood back up so fast—to not let it out of my sight—but it was gone. Or—it wasn't right there anymore. I could see two little lights out in the distance and I heard the coyotes calling, and I said oh, Marlena, you goose, it's a coyote, a trick of the moon and a coyote, but . . . I don't know. I see those eyes in my dreams still.

WALKER: And what happens in those dreams?

RIOS: I can't look away. I don't dare. Those eyes, they get bigger and bigger and I see that smile starting to slash open and I wake up all sweaty.

(RIOS laughs, a loud, startlingly genuine sound.)

RIOS: Don't put that in. Say I wake up with perfect hair. Lord, I haven't talked about this in such a long time. It's like picking a scab. Oh, don't put that in either, what is wrong with me! Let's take a break now. Do you want a slice of lemon cake?

ELEVEN

". . . and that was their latest single," I finished.
I looked down at my promo sheet. "Moon Basin Community Radio is supported by listeners like you and our local small-business sponsors like SuperStop. If you need a car wash, a slushie, or some plain old fossil fuel, there's only one place in Moon Basin you can go—SuperStop. On the corner of Priory and Motton. Open eight a.m. to ten p.m., and if you come by another time, you'll just have to come back. SuperStop."

I turned up the fader on my other turntable, clicked off the mic, and looked at Cecil. "There's literally only one place they can go, Cecil. There's only one gas station."

"That's the joke," he said, pulling on his coat. "Are you okay to lock up?" He asked this every time, even though I'd been doing it for almost a year.

"Yeah." I waved at him as I rolled my chair over to my crate. "Tell Carlos I say hi."

He beamed. "Of course." He shouldered his bag and strode toward the door, stopping only briefly to look back at me. "Leave right at ten, Clem."

I nodded, already sliding a record out of its sleeve. *Bye*, I mouthed as I clicked the mic back on.

I spun out the next hour on autopilot: a few riotous punk songs, a few of the Top 40 for me and the tweens, and then down into something gentle and lush. A good way to fall asleep, if I said so myself.

I pushed myself up from the desk at a quarter to ten, going through the little closing checklist as quickly as possible. A photobooth strip of Nina, Lisey, and I watched me from the corner of my monitor as I put all the records back in their homes, wound down the faders, flipped the big main light switch in the utility closet. We'd done our damnedest to get all of us into every single frame, faces squished together, just a hideous blob of teeth and eyes unless you looked at it closely. Lisey didn't even look like a person; she was just a lens flare in the corner, a blur of light. I loved it.

I locked the big double doors and shook them, and then I walked into the field. I did a lazy vault over the low stone wall that bordered the graveyard, putting my butt down and swinging my legs up and over so my shoes didn't touch. There was no fence around the graveyard, just the wall, and as long as people didn't take advantage of that, I guessed it would stay that way. There were so many places in Moon Basin to fuck or smoke weed or whatever that fencing the graveyard just seemed silly.

As I wound through the stones, the moonlight silvering their letters, I thought about the mine. I knew it didn't reach this far into the New Basin, but suddenly the idea that I was about to step into a hole and fall straight down into a tunnel was the only thought in my brain.

"Shit," I whispered aloud. I walked a little quicker, looking down, putting my feet one in front of the other, and thanking the moon silently for being out. It wasn't quite full, but it was enough to see. *It wouldn't be if you fell into the mine*, a traitorous voice said inside my head. I pushed it aside and kept walking, almost breaking into a trot. I was almost to the other side of the graveyard, the other end of the low stone wall, when I heard a loud, sharp crack like the snap of a bone. A shriek burst out of me and I dropped to the ground without realizing I'd done it. My hands clasped over my mouth, I peered around the edge of the grave marker I was next to.

There was a deer standing in the middle of the cemetery, head raised, ears alert. At first I thought it had made the sound—stepped on a branch or something—but then I realized it, too, was listening. I sat there in silence watching it, and little by little its ears lost their panicked set. It was lowering its head to the grass when it jerked upright, nose to the north, and then exploded into a run.

I didn't look to see what had scared it. I pushed myself up off the ground and ran, arms pumping, head down. I jumped over the wall of the graveyard like a hurdler, praying that whatever had been out there liked deer more than it liked high schoolers. I didn't stop running until I was halfway down High Grange Road, the packed-down gravel glowing white as a strip of bone through the dark meat of the fields around it. I smelled rain on the wind, but the sky was clear and I could see all the way back across the field. The light atop the station blinked calmly. The fear drained out of me, leaving only a deep, aching tiredness in its place. I walked the rest of the way home, my feet crunching on the road in a quiet rhythm.

I let myself in quietly, even though the car wasn't out front. There's no reason to be loud when you live alone, or so close to it that it makes no difference. I locked the door, located the kettle in the little pantry, and put on some water for tea. I sat down at the kitchen table, pried off my shoes, and kicked them under my chair. The remote was sitting in the center of the table. I grabbed it and flipped the TV on, wanting some noise in the house.

An old black-and-white movie was on. We didn't get many channels this far out, or on our limited cable plan. The lead actress was pretty, dark-haired and stern. She was frowning at a man—he'd disappointed her, no doubt. I clicked the volume up a few notches, enough for the murmur of voices to fill the room, and then I got up and made my cup of tea. When I came back around the counter the dark-haired woman and the disappointing man were kissing. I put the tea on the coffee table and curled into the corner of the couch. I thought, *I'll just put my head down for a moment.*

The knock on the door woke me from a dream about the mine, one of the recurring ones I'd been cycling through that week. I was suffocating, choking to death on dirt and ash, trapped in the tunnels as they caved in around me, and then— diverging from the usual course of the dream—there was a loud, distant thud that sliced through the terror.

I opened my eyes.

Two more loud thuds, and then the tap of a waiting foot. I raised my head and saw Nina curled up in the armchair. The TV was off, the remote on the floor where she'd dropped it.

"When did you get in here?" I asked, rolling off the couch. "Was that you?"

She groaned but didn't move. The thumping sound came again and I realized someone was knocking on the door. The foot-tapping increased to a fever pitch. I threw the door open. Piper ducked past me, nervous energy vibrating off of her.

"Is there coffee?"

"Piper, I was *asleep*. What's going on?"

She was already clattering around the kitchen, yanking open cabinets. "Let me caffeinate."

"I'm not sure you need to caffeinate more." I flopped back onto the couch, cocooned myself in the afghan, and watched her spoon coffee grounds into the machine.

"What's happening?" Nina sat up, rubbing her eyes with the heels of her hands. "Oh God, my neck hurts so bad."

She got out of the chair, slithered under the afghan next to me, and promptly fell back asleep. Piper clicked the coffeemaker on and walked over to us, sitting down cross-legged on the floor.

"So," I said, prompting her.

She shook her head. "Just wait. Lisey's on her way."

Something in her tone, her eyes—the sentence was flat and final and somehow frightening. It sent chills through me. "Piper, what is going on?"

The coffeemaker chimed. She got to her feet.

"Neen," I said.

"Mm."

"You're drooling on my arm."

"Mm."

"Don't make me kick you off the couch."

"Try it."

"There's my girl," I said. "Feisty."

Piper rolled her eyes at us as she returned from the kitchen with her cup. She sat down once more, hands wrapped around her mug, and stared into her coffee. The door opened then and Lisey drifted in.

"Hi," she said, kicking her shoes into the corner. She collapsed onto the floor next to Piper like a rag doll and looked at us. "So what's up?"

Piper's mouth twisted. "It's my dad."

"Oh no," I said. "What . . . what happened?"

She scratched at the handle of the mug with her thumb-nail, some tiny imperfection making a little ticking sound. "I know you guys don't know him really well," she started. "I—it's hard—okay."

She set the cup aside and took a deep breath, shaking her head as she let it out.

"I'm named after a plane," she said. "The Piper Cub. My dad's idea."

Another breath.

"He used to fly. My mom always said she didn't think he could love anything more than flying until I was born. He took me up in the Cub for the first time when I was barely two. He taught me how to take apart its engine when I was ten. That plane was like his other child.

"He crashed a few years ago. He couldn't fix it. He tried for months. He slept in the garage with it. What I'm saying is that I've seen him . . . obsessed."

She cleared her throat and took a sip of coffee.

"He was still my dad when that was happening. He still talked to me. He was still *there*."

Something cold ticked against the inside of my skull, behind my eyes.

"Something's wrong with him." She wiped her eyes with the back of her hand and then looked up at us. "It's like he's eroding. When I talk to him he responds, but it's like talking to someone who's on the phone with someone else. He's listening enough to know when he needs to say something back, but he can't tell me what we were talking about even five minutes ago. Last night when we were eating dinner, I asked if he remembered working on the plane together and he looked at me like—" She spread her hands. "Like he'd never even heard of a Piper Cub."

Piper pulled her knees to her chest and wrapped her arms around them. "He's just—he's *wrong* somehow. It's like there's something wearing him."

A shudder rippled through me. I thought of something inside Carlisle's skin, maneuvering him through the world, and my stomach heaved.

"And he won't stop talking about the mine. His *plans* for it. This morning when I left he was sitting on the porch and I think he was just staring at a Polaroid of a tunnel."

"Maybe we should go talk to him," Lisey said. She was rubbing Piper's back gently, trying to soothe her. "It might be—mm . . ." She bit her lip. "Maybe he just needs to talk to someone who's from here."

Piper sighed. The corner of her mouth pulled sideways like she wanted to cry. "Please don't judge me when you see the house."

Witness, Episode 75
Unused Footage

(A close-up of LORNA KILGRAVE, seen from the shoulders up. Her lipstick feathers gently away from her mouth and she blinks too often, as if trying to convince herself she is awake.)

KILGRAVE: It was the strangest thing. I was in the kitchen. I was mixing batter. I think I was making biscuits? Biscuits or a cake, I suppose, I don't make much else. I was looking out the window above the sink and I saw just a jet of fire, it just shot up into the air above the Creighton's—that was the grocery store, I'm sorry—and I dropped the bowl and it shattered. My glass mixing bowl. Cut my feet something terrible, I didn't even realize until later. I called the sheriff and I said Merle, you better get over toward the store because I believe something is on fire over there. I didn't realize it was out beyond the store. It was so tall, I thought—I thought it had to be close. Anyway, I turned away from the window to start picking up the glass and I swear to you, I swear on my life, I saw a man in the kitchen, in the corner of the room. I almost thought it was Gerald, but he wasn't ever home that early. He was next to the pantry door, there's a little nook there and he was in shadow, but I blinked and when I looked again, he was gone. Then there was just this overwhelming smell of smoke, oh, it was horrible, like burning hair, it hurt my eyes!

(She looks at something behind the camera.)

KILGRAVE: Mm? Oh, yes. Mellie and I used to laugh about it, you know—how much that husband of hers looked like Gerald. And once I smelled that smoke, I knew. I knew something was wrong in the mine, and I knew that man was involved.

TWELVE

The house was quiet and still and blazing hot. It almost didn't feel any different than outside.

"Oh my God," Nina murmured as we walked in. "Is the *heat* on?"

"Yes," Piper said, closing the door. "It makes the cold spots more apparent."

"Cold spots, like when a ghost shows up?" I asked. We'd watched enough tapes by that point to qualify as experts.

"Yeah. I don't know why they make it cold, but I guess they do. Hence these." She flicked a fingernail against a small digital thermometer sitting on the table in the hallway. There were at least four more that I could see around the room. Boxes were strewn everywhere, like Carlisle had given up on unpacking, and wires and cords were strung every which way. Thermometers sat on the mantelpiece, on the floor in the corners, next to the TV in its little cabinet. There were coffee grounds scattered across the floor in the kitchen and what looked like a line of salt separating it from the rest of the house. A long silver microphone was propped on the table next to another thermometer, wired into a little box with a flashing green light. The basement door had been taken off its hinges and there was a video camera on a tripod perched on the top stair, pointing into the main part of the house.

"It takes energy for them to manifest," said Lisey. "They pull the energy from the room and it makes it cold."

Piper looked around nervously. "He's going to see that we were here. So just try to look like you're interested, like I'm showing off. The audio on the cameras only triggers if the temperature drops."

"Cameras, plural?" Nina asked. "I see that one, but—" She pointed at the basement door.

"Plural," Piper said grimly. "Come on."

We followed her deeper into the house. She pointed out cameras as we passed by—guest bathroom, living room, laundry room—and showed us the best way to slip around their fields of focus. There was a fine layer of grit on almost every surface; I ran a fingertip across a bookshelf and realized it was dirt. There were gaping holes in the walls, too, like Carlisle had tried to mount whatever equipment he was using without checking for studs first. It gave the house an unhinged feeling that put me on high alert. We moved upstairs, feet crunching on the same mixture of salt and coffee and dirt, and into a guest room. A bell on the door jangled as Lisey pushed it open.

"Why is there a hole?" Lisey asked, poking her finger through the space below the handle.

"He took the locks off all the doors," Piper said. "All except his study."

Lisey shivered, pulling her hand away and tucking it into her pocket. I turned back to the room just as Piper said, "Clem, wait, *wait*—" and something grabbed my ankle. I went down hard, windmilling my arms, and as I fell there was a blinding flash and a sound like an explosion.

"What the fuck?" I said from the floor, blinking the spots

away. Piper reached down and hauled me off the carpet.

"Trip wire," she said. "And terrifying old-timey camera."

I looked down. The wire was still quivering. "Why would a ghost be able to trip a wire?"

"They're in every room. And there are other cameras rigged to the thermometers in case the temperature drops. In addition to the ones that are always on."

"Holy shit," Nina said, looking at the camera.

"Yeah," I grumbled, rubbing my shin. "That's gonna be a great shot of the inside of my nose."

Piper almost smiled, but the hollowness didn't leave her eyes. She led us upstairs and down the hall to a closed door. "His office," she said. "He keeps it locked, but he left the key out last night and I took it."

She opened the door and all three of us gasped. Lisey gagged, recoiling, and I hugged her against me even as my own stomach rolled.

"The smell," Nina whispered. "How—"

"It's him," Piper said. "That's what he smells like now."

How long had it been since we'd last seen Carlisle? It had barely been two weeks since we went into the mine with him, barely a month since they'd moved to town. My skin was crawling, writhing under the surface with terror. As one, we moved into the office. The overhead light was burned out, which was maybe a blessing, considering what was revealed by the light of the television monitors. There were ten of them, covering the entire wall, each with multiple views of the same tunnels, different angles, infrared, night vision. In the glow I could see empty cans, dirty plates, food wrappers. There was dried blood on one of the screens, a clear fingerprint in the lower corner.

There was dirt—and ash—everywhere.

"It's like he brings it home with him," Piper whispered. "The mine. Like it's becoming part of him. I think—" She swallowed hard. "I think he's been in here the past few nights. Not sleeping, just . . . watching."

"Why?" I murmured, moving toward the monitors. I didn't want to, but I couldn't stop. "Why is he doing this?"

I lifted a piece of paper off the desk. It was covered in spidery handwriting. I could only make out the words *in the house*; the rest of the page was taken up by jagged scratches, spirals, and the word "down" written hundreds of times. The pen had torn the paper in some places. I lifted another page and found a crude map of Moon Basin, the mine roughed in underneath it. Different passages were circled or crossed out, arrows jabbing into corners and dead ends. It almost looked like a treasure map, like he was looking for something. Or like he was marking where he'd already *found* something.

"He's seeing things down there," I said. "That's why all the bells and cameras and shit. He's afraid they're going to come into the house. I think maybe it's talking to him. Like Mellie said it did to Sidney."

"Why?" Piper asked, looking at a heap of crumpled, bloody tissues. "Why him? Is it just because he went in?"

"I don't know, but that makes sense. Like going in is how it gets at you. And it has such a hold on him because he keeps going back. He spends so much time down there—"

I looked at Lisey as I spoke, warming to my theory.

"No one who lives here goes anywhere *near* the mine, and they still have enough freaky stories to fill a million ghost shows. We've only gone in once and it's had an effect on us. Proximity and exposure," I finished. "That's my best guess."

Piper turned to Nina, who had stayed quiet this whole time. "Go ahead," she said.

Nina looked at her. "I don't know. I know there's an explanation, but I can't see it yet. But this—" She swept a hand out, encompassing the room. "This is not normal. And if it started when you got here, then I admit there has to be at least *some* connection."

"There's one more thing," Piper said. "He only started doing it today."

She clicked the mouse on the desk a few times and motioned toward the monitor with the bloodstain. I almost screamed when the picture blinked up onto the screen. Carlisle was standing in front of the camera, eyes fixed on a point above it, and his lips were moving. Lisey breathed out, a long, shuddery exhale like someone had punched her.

"All morning," Piper said. "For hours."

She clicked again and the numbers at the bottom of the screen ran backward, and Carlisle never moved from his spot in front of the camera.

"He's talking to it," Lisey breathed, leaning over my shoulder.

"I feel like something bad is going to happen," Piper whispered. A tear shivered off her eyelashes and plinked down onto the space bar. "I don't know what to do."

She looked at us, eyes brimming with tears.

"Will you stay here with me tonight?"

Grave Encounters, Episode 12
Unused Footage

(Camera shakes. BATTY comes into frame, distorted through a smeary film over the lens. She is covered in ash and dirt. Her face is lit only by the glow of the camera display.)

BATTY, *whispering:* If anyone finds this, my . . . this is Batty—this is—my name is Rebecca Chambers. My mom's name is Pamela, she lives at—at—

(Camera swings away. Audible sobbing. Camera swings back to BATTY, but only half her face is in frame. She is looking somewhere behind and above the camera.)

BATTY: I can hear them. I can hear them in here with me. They tricked me and I followed them and now I'm down— down somewhere below all the others. I can't find my way out.

(BATTY sniffles and holds her hand up to the camera.)

BATTY: I used my chalk. I drew arrows, I did. You can see it on my fingers. I'm a *professional.*

(She wipes the hand down her face, leaving white streaks across the grime.)

BATTY: But I can't find them now. Even when I use the light. I'm trying not to use it, I don't know how much longer the batteries will last, but I can't see anything but fucking dirt and tunnels every time I turn it on.

BATTY, *whispering:* The camera should be dead. I don't know why it isn't.

(She brings the camera closer to her face, until her cracked and peeling lips are the only thing in frame.)

125

BATTY: Maybe it is. Maybe they just want me to think it's on. Maybe I'm just talking to myself. Fuck. *Fuck.*

(Camera turns off.)

(Camera turns on. BATTY's feet are visible, standing a few feet away from the camera, which seems to be on the ground. She is turning in circles.)

BATTY: Dawson! *Dawson!* Anyone! I'm down here, I'm down—

(Camera turns off.)

(Camera turns on. BATTY is lying curled on the ground, weeping softly. Camera turns off.)

(Camera turns on. BATTY is looking into the lens with feverish intensity.)

BATTY: I found the way out. I found it.

(As she speaks, it becomes apparent that she is walking with the camera.)

BATTY: I just had to go farther down, and I found the way. I can still hear them but it's getting quieter. I think—

(Camera turns around to reveal a dark, empty tunnel.)

BATTY: There's a light. There's a light.

(Camera swings and shakes as BATTY begins running.)

BATTY: Where are you—hey! Come back! *COME BACK!* Wait—

(Camera swings, falls lens-first into the ground with a crunch.)

THiRTEEN

We sat on the floor of Piper's room in tank tops and shorts, all of us covered in a sheen of sweat, pretending we weren't waiting for Carlisle to come home. We were listening to *Pet Sounds*, Lisey singing along to "God Only Knows" under her breath as she painted her nails. Her cards were caught between her first and second fingers, bent at the knuckles, and she put the polish brush in her mouth so she could pull one out.

"Hearts," she said.

I groaned.

She grinned. "I need your turn to last a while so I can finish this hand."

Lisey loved her nails, kept them long and perfectly shaped and always polished. She used vitamin-E base coats, top coats, strengthening, hardening. They made her long fingers look even longer, more ethereal, and she painted them pale wispy colors that made her look like she was disappearing from the fingertips up.

She squinted at her pinky, pulled a small wooden stick out from behind her ear, where the cloud of hair had hidden it, and ran it along the side of the nail. She tucked it back into her hair with a satisfied *hmm*. I pulled cards from the draw pile, cursing the entire suit of clubs, and finally a heart flipped up.

"Ha!"

"Baby gets one," Nina said.

I was opening my mouth to retort when the door slammed downstairs. Piper lifted the needle from the record. The silence only lasted for a moment and then there was a *thump-thump-thumpthumpthump*, far too fast, far too loud, for someone to be climbing the stairs on two legs. A vision of Carlisle skittering up the stairs on all fours shuddered across my mind. Piper rolled across the floor to her bedside table, was reaching for the lamp's cord, and then the door to the room banged open.

"Hi, girls," said Carlisle, looming huge in the door frame.

Piper froze, her hand outstretched, and settled back onto the floor slowly. "Hey, Dad." She tried to sound soothing. "It's late."

Carlisle was caked with dirt, shedding it onto the carpet with each breath. I got a whiff of something dark and ancient, musty stone and things choked with dying vines.

He smiled. "Piper, my girl. My little girl." He held out his arms to her.

"Dad, you have to go take a shower. You're dirty."

He laughed, and there was something *off* about it, something not quite right. "Right you are, my dear. Right you are. Where's your mother?"

The question surprised her. Her eyebrows lifted, her mouth dropped open into a tiny little O, but she gathered herself quickly and her tone stayed even. "She's not here, Dad. It's late," she repeated.

"She's sleeping in the guest room again, huh?" he said, that same off-kilter cadence in his voice. He almost seemed drugged, his eyes flickering around the room frenetically. Finally he landed on me. "My wife won't sleep in our bed anymore."

I recoiled and he saw me flinch.

"Oh, sorry. Secret. It's fine." He made a patting motion at the air, like he was stroking a horse. "I need to bring her down."

I could feel my voice crawling up my throat, willed it to stop, but the words forced their way through my teeth: "Down where, Mr. Wharton?"

"Down," he said, and smiled. I saw with a sick jolt that his teeth were stained with dirt, too. They looked like tombstones, lined up neatly, grimed with earth, and the grin pulled his lips back way too far. "Down inside the mine."

"Dad," Piper said. "You need to go to sleep."

He stepped farther into the room. "Are you upset, darling? I'll bring you, too. You don't have to be jealous."

"I'm not jealous, Dad! You're not thinking clearly. You have to go to sleep."

"I'll bring you all down, don't worry."

Lisey stepped up to him. "Mr. Wharton," she said gently. "What do you mean?"

His face cleared as he looked at her, and he almost sounded like himself when he said, "I'm so close to figuring it out."

Then his eyes glazed back over, his face sagged, and he shot out a hand and grabbed Lisey's wrist. Her hand closed into a fist and I could see her nail polish smudge from where I was standing.

"All the way down." He let go of Lisey's wrist, pivoted on his heel like a robot, and left the room as abruptly as he'd entered it.

There were approximately two seconds of silence as we all looked at each other, Piper crying silent tears. Then we heard Carlisle shout, "JANINE!" and slam his body against the guest room door.

"Fuck," Piper spat under her breath and darted down the

hall. "Dad!" she cried, and then there was a yelp and a thud. We ran out into the hall to see Piper slumped against the wall, clutching her head, and Carlisle hammering on the door he'd taken the lock out of less than a week ago. "Janine!" he yelled again. "Janine, you'll be fine, just let me in!"

A string of drool was hanging from his mouth, and it was brown with dirt. I could hear Piper crying, or maybe it was Lisey crying, or maybe it was Nina or me. The grave-smell coming off Carlisle was stronger in the closed-in space of the hall, and he left streaks of dirt on the door as he pounded on it.

"I have to do this!" he wailed. "Janine!"

Piper had gotten up and was yanking on his arm, trying to pull him away from the shuddering door.

"Dad." She was sobbing. "Dad, she's not in there, stop."

Carlisle swung around, a feral, mad light in his eyes, his hand raised. He froze like an animal in headlights, looking at the four of us, and his face went flat and dead. His hand fell to his side like a string had been cut. He shook his head slightly and winced. His hands twitched. The cords in his neck stood out as his jaw clenched. With what seemed like incredible effort, like his voice was coming from deep inside his body, he spoke.

"Cub," he said. "I'm sorry."

He turned away from us and walked down the hall to his office, and we could hear the bolt of the house's one remaining lock shooting home from where we stood.

We wedged ourselves onto the floor between Piper's bed and the wall like sardines, none of us wanting to be more than even an inch away from the others, but it wasn't enough. None of us could sleep. I kept waiting for the sound of the office door unlocking, opening slowly, stealthily, the sound of quiet footsteps in the hall, the tickling sound of dried earth as it fell to the floor. By the time the sun started to rise I'd been grinding my teeth for so long that I had a headache all the way into the backs of my eyes.

We stayed in Piper's bedroom until we heard the bells on the front door jangle, and then we waited another ten minutes, and then we bolted.

Encounters with the Other Side, Episode 130
Unused Footage

(A blurred face against a black backdrop. The voice, when it speaks, is distorted.)

SUBJECT: And this is—you won't tell anyone, right? Or, I mean—no one will know this is me. Yes?

LANCE DIMARCO, *from off-screen*: You'll be completely anonymous. We have state-of-the-art technology that will distort your face and change your voice. Your own mother wouldn't recognize you.

SUBJECT: Okay. All right.

DIMARCO: Whenever you're ready.

SUBJECT: I . . . I almost killed my baby. Right after he was born. I was—I was alone. I didn't have anyone. I was working all the time, and I wasn't sleeping, and he was so—he was so fussy all the time, he cried every time I tried to leave the room, and I just . . . oh God. I started—I don't know if I can do this.

DIMARCO: Take your time.

SUBJECT: I started—I don't know how to explain it. I started to hear things, but that's not quite right. It wasn't like I was really hearing them. I felt like something was whispering in my ear, but too quiet for me to hear. That's—I guess maybe that's how I have to explain it to myself, because otherwise I'm—you know. I started having these dreams, these waking dreams. I'd be in the bedroom and I'd hear him crying and I'd get up and go to the crib and put my hands on him, I'd put my hands on him and I'd—

(SUBJECT gives a muffled cry.)

SUBJECT: I'd put my hands over his face and push, just push down with all my weight, and I'd feel the little bones splintering, feel the skin give way and blood would bubble up through my fingers, and I couldn't stop until he stopped crying, until I was up to my wrists in blood. I'd be standing there panting, looking down at the—the *ruin* of his face, and then—I'd wake up. In my bed. And he'd be crying in the other room and I couldn't go to him. Because I was afraid I would—do it again. Do it for real.

DIMARCO: How long did that go on for?

SUBJECT: Until he was almost one.

DIMARCO: You spent a year unable to comfort your only child.

SUBJECT: Yes.

DIMARCO: And how often did you have that—that vision, so to speak?

SUBJECT: At least once a week.

DIMARCO: Why do you think it stopped?

SUBJECT: I tried—

(SUBJECT shakes head violently.)

SUBJECT: I was in a hospital for a while. To get better. When I came back it was gone.

DIMARCO: Why do you think it happened in the first place?

SUBJECT: I think . . . I think some people are just more susceptible to contact from the other side. I think something out there knew I was weak, and tired, and lonely, and it . . . it wanted to hurt something. And I was there.

DIMARCO: Can I ask why you didn't just leave Moon Basin?

(SUBJECT laughs ruefully.)

SUBJECT: Where would I go?

FOURTEEN

I went straight from Piper's house to the radio station, with a brief detour to the SuperStop for the biggest coffee I could physically carry and a clean T-shirt. My eyes felt like I'd poured sand into them; every blink grated painfully. I couldn't stop thinking about the way Carlisle had looked. I couldn't stop seeing that hungry, too-wide smile.

When I got into the studio the voice mail light was blinking. I jabbed the Play button, listening as Cecil's greeting gave way to the messages.

"It's me," Nina said. "Nadia called. The ghost lady, the one from the episode with Mellie. It's—"

Clunk. Pause.

"It's eight thirty a.m."

I looked at the clock. Eight fifty-seven.

"She woke my dad up at, like, eleven last night. Apparently did *not* sound thrilled about being contacted. Gave us a number, though."

I scrabbled in the drawer for a pen and clicked it, writing on the back of my hand as she recited it.

"I'm gonna crash," Nina said. "I know you have to be there for a while, so call Nadia and see what she remembers about the rest of Mellie's tapes. Maybe that can help us figure out what's going on in Carlisle's head. Try and get some sleep as soon as you can, and call me later. Like, way later."

I stood there staring at the numbers on my skin, and then I lifted the receiver. Nadia's voice was groggy when she answered.

"Shit, I'm sorry," I said. "I thought you were in my time zone, sorry, I can call back—"

"No, I am," she said. "Is this the girl from Moon Basin?"

"Clem, yes."

"It took me a while to decide to call," she said. "I probably shouldn't have."

"I'm really glad you did."

"Last night I stayed up late listening to those tapes. I'd almost forgotten . . ." As her voice cleared, the fear in it became much more obvious.

"So you still have them," I said. Relief and fear washed through me. She had the tapes. We would be able to watch them. We would have to watch them.

"Oh yes. I couldn't—I couldn't get rid of them. It's like they've climbed onto my back," she said. "I think about Mellie Harington all the time."

"Why?" I asked, dread metallic on my tongue.

Nadia sighed. "Because I don't think she was wrong."

I felt something squeezing my lungs, pressing me flat. "Why?" I asked again.

"I don't know. We never saw anything while we were there to indicate any kind of, I don't know, haunting, but . . . it felt off. Like there's an overlay of the town on the town, only the edges don't match up, so it makes you kind of queasy to look at it after a while. But it's so subtle you don't know what's causing it or how to fix it." She took a breath and chuckled. "I know, I'm not helping my case as an objective observer."

"No," I said, "I know what you mean. It's like something wearing a mask of a human face but you can see the bones beneath it and you know it's not human."

"Yes," she sighed. "Are you not from there?"

"No, I was born here," I said, confused.

She made a *hmm* sound. "I would have thought you came from out of town. It seemed to me like we were the only ones who felt it."

"Well, the out-of-town people are the ones who spend the most time near the mine, but I don't know," I said. "I think most of us feel *something*. But I don't know how strong it is, or how much anyone notices it anymore."

"Like living next to a waterfall," she said.

"Uh, sure."

She laughed. "Constant sound becomes a baseline, becomes no sound. Maybe people who live in the Basin don't realize how wrong it feels unless they leave."

I thought about the way it felt in the clearing, the perfect silence that fell in my head when I stepped inside it. I thought about the dark circles under Fish's worried eyes. "Yeah," I said after a moment. "Or until it gets worse."

My eyes fell on the clock and I yelped.

"Can I put you on hold?" I jumped up. "I'm so sorry, I work at the radio station; I need to queue up the—"

"Just call me back," she said, but nicely. "I need to make some coffee anyway."

I queued up a solid hour of music and commercials. I didn't know how long we'd be on the phone, but I didn't want to cut her off if she got into a groove. As I was sitting back down, Javi, one of the interns, popped his head into the booth.

"Coffee?"

I looked at the cup I already had, then at him, and said, "Absolutely." When he returned with an MBCR mug, I had the receiver pressed to my ear again. I mouthed *Thank you* at him and then flipped the on-air switch.

"Okay," I said when Nadia picked up. "You have my undivided attention."

"Well, thank you for that," she said dryly. She sounded almost like a teacher: Her tone reminded me she was doing me a favor, but somehow still conveyed that she wanted to help. "I went back and found my notes from when we were filming, but they're not very detailed. What are you looking for?"

"The one tape we saw, Mellie was talking about the mine telling Sidney to hurt her. And then she said it told her—"

"The same thing," she finished. "Yeah. The doctor asked if she meant it wanted her to hurt another person or herself, and she said, 'Both.'"

"Oh boy," I said quietly, thoughts flashing to Carlisle once more. "Did she ever say how long it took? Like, from the first time Sidney went into the mine to the time he started acting strange?"

"Not precisely, but the mine wasn't even running for a full year before the explosion, so I'd wager it happened kind of quick. She was also just dealing with life as a newly married housewife, so I think it might have slipped her notice a little longer than it should have."

"Why did she start wanting to go down there? Did she ever actually go in?" I asked.

"No. She just started thinking about it more and more, and then she started dreaming about it. During one of the later sessions she told the doctor it called to her. So he asks what she means by that, and she says she wants to go into the mine. It consumes her, how badly she wants to go in. She's never been in, of course, but she can see it when she closes her eyes. She says—"

A rustling of pages.

"She says it holds her 'in its mouth, like a lion with a mouse,' and it's still deciding whether or not to bite down.'"

I shuddered hard. I took a too-large gulp of coffee and burned my mouth, but it melted some of the chill I felt. "Did you go into the mine when you were here?"

"No," she said.

"So you came after *Grave Encounters*."

"I heard about that girl." The words were laced with bitterness. "That should have kept me the fuck away, but nooo. Nadia has to go where the ghosts are. Nadia has to win an Emmy. God, I was the worst." She sighed and circled back to my question, turning it on me. "Have you been down there?"

"Yeah."

"What does it look like? Just tunnels, right?"

"Yeah."

"So even if it was allowed, it wouldn't be worth much to go down there. Small space, hard to light, nothing visually interesting . . . We didn't complain. Not when there were so many abandoned buildings to traipse around in."

"But you said you could feel something—"

"Oh, of course I could. You don't have to be in the mine to feel it. It permeates the whole Basin, Clem. It's stronger in the old half, practically immobilizing near the mine, but it's everywhere."

"Okay," I said. "So Mellie—"

"There are ten sessions. An hour each. The first one is mostly crying and introductions, but the rest are solid. The one that you heard was the ninth, I think. Close to the end."

"And what about her dreams?"

"What about them?"

"How often did she have them? What were they like?"

Rustling again.

"Every night, eventually," she said. "Sometimes Sidney was there, sometimes just her."

"What happened in the dreams?"

"Look, I can't—do you want me to just send you these? I certainly don't need them. Honestly, it'll be good to get them out of my apartment."

"I guess," I said, taken aback. "I'll give you my address, that's probably best—"

"I'm sorry, I'm just—I have things to do, and I don't want to rehash this whole—"

"No, I understand—"

"I dreamed about the mine, too," she said abruptly.

I snapped my mouth shut, waiting.

"For almost six months after we shot the episode. That's why I quit the show." She took a deep breath and let it out, and I heard the clunk of a refrigerator door shutting. "I've been to a lot of places, you have to understand. A lot of very fucked-up places with very fucked-up energy. And none of them affected me like Moon Basin did."

I kept quiet, afraid to break the spell.

"The only place I've felt anything like it was this little house in the middle of Missouri. It was built on the edge of a river, this little tiny house. Red shutters on the windows. The woman who lived there, she, um."

She cleared her throat.

"She drowned her kids in the river, but she did it—she sort of hung them, I guess—hanged them, I mean—she put ropes around their necks and pushed them into the water and the current pulled the ropes tight. I don't even know if drowning is the right word."

A weak, watery laugh, and I could tell she was on the verge of tears.

"That house made me feel completely unhinged. It made me feel like I could understand a woman who would do that." She took a deep breath. "But Moon Basin made me feel like I could *be* a woman who would do that."

I was so cold with dread I was almost numb. I could almost see those kids, still and blue under the water as the shutters banged in the breeze. I wondered if their mother's face had gone slack and dead when she killed them. I wondered if she had smiled. I hadn't responded to Nadia for almost a full minute, but I couldn't seem to draw enough breath to form words. I hoped fervently that I'd never know what it was like to feel capable of something like that.

"I left my fiancé," Nadia said. "I quit the show. I started drinking, like, heavily. It was . . . it was a rough time. When I heard the tapes of Mellie saying she felt like it was whispering to her, I—it struck a horrible chord." Her voice was trembling, but she kept speaking. "It sounded so much like what I was experiencing. Everything she said. I never dreamed about her husband, but I—" She made a muffled choking sound. "I dreamed about her. About Mellie."

I was clutching the receiver so tightly my hand ached.

"Almost every night. And it felt so real. She was always dripping wet. She said Sidney was always on fire when he visited her, kind of smoldering . . . so I guess it makes sense that she would be wet. She would try to talk to me, but I could never understand her."

I let out the breath I'd been holding. "I am so sorry. I can't imagine."

"You won't have to," she said, so quietly I thought I'd misheard her.

"What?"

"I'll mail you these tapes, okay? I have to go."

"Okay, um, thank you—"

I was cut off by the dial tone. I replaced the receiver in the cradle, watching as the blood slowly crept back into my whitened knuckles. I flexed my hand a few times. I hadn't moved for the entirety of our conversation. My coffee was cold. I pushed it away from me; I didn't need my thoughts moving any faster than they were.

I was nearing the end of my set when the little red call light blinked on the studio phone.

"Moon Basin Community Radio," I said into the mouthpiece. My voice was tinny.

". . . there?"

"I'm sorry," I said, one eye still on the tables. "Could you repeat that?"

This time there wasn't even a hint of a word, just a crackling hiss.

"Hello? Nadia?"

The hiss narrowed and sharpened until it sounded almost like someone breathing.

"Look, we have star-six-nine," I said, trying to sound unflappable, channeling Nina. "What do you want?"

The breathing deepened, grew harsher, became panting.

"Okay, fuck this," I said, and slammed the phone down. A commercial was playing, and I busied myself queuing up the next song as I tried to ignore the fact that I was shaking. It hadn't sounded like perv breathing, as terrible as that would have been. It sounded more like animal breathing. Like something with teeth and claws hunting, tasting the air, looking for weakness. I shuddered and put the needle down, twisting the knob just as the last words of the commercial floated out over the air. Soft guitar spilled over into the world, obliterating some of my fear, and I closed my eyes for a moment and listened. When I opened them again, the red light was blinking.

I picked up the phone and put it to my ear, holding my breath. There was only the hiss of an open line on the other end. I pressed the receiver harder against my ear, trying to listen past the ocean of my own pulse, and I heard breathing. That same ragged, hungry breathing. I slapped the button in the phone's cradle, ending the call, and then I left the receiver off the hook.

At the end of the set, I wound the fader down to zero and then clicked the machine off. I took my mug to the kitchen and washed it, then poked my head into Javi's little closet-office. "I'm out of here, Javi," I said.

He yanked something out of the crate of records he was sorting through and waved at me. I almost told him not to answer the phone but stopped myself. It was his job, and I was being paranoid. I felt around in my pockets, making sure I had my keys, and then I lunged back into the studio and grabbed for the phone. I threw it onto the hook and leaped away like I'd been burned, pulling the door to the booth shut behind me as I trotted out of the studio. I looked back—I shouldn't have, but I did—and the little red light was blinking.

"Nope," I muttered, and slammed out of the station.

My thoughts kept spinning back to Nadia as I walked home, her words looping in my mind. *You won't have to.* Was it a warning? A promise? A chill crawled down my spine. *I don't think she was wrong*, she'd said of Mellie Harington. I was having the same thought about Nadia and it scared me badly.

My mother was home when I got there, rummaging through the fridge. It was one of the rare moments when we were both awake at the same time, and I was going to have to ruin it.

"Mom," I said carefully. "Did you know Mellie Harington?"

She backed out of the fridge holding a pie tin and a jar of artichoke hearts, turning to me and closing it with her hip.

"Not really," she said, sitting down. "I knew *of* her. Saw her around and such. Why?"

"No reason," I said. "Nina found some tapes of her at the motel and we just wondered who here even knew her."

"Maybe one of the other miners' wives," she mused. "None of them would really speak to her, but you never know. Maybe one of them softened."

"When you saw her, did she seem . . . sane?"

She fished an artichoke heart out of the jar and ate it. "She seemed harried. Like she was being followed, always looking over her shoulder, hearing something coming."

I didn't know I was going to say it until I did. It climbed up my throat and forced its way past my lips and fell flat onto the table, raw and glistening: "Why did you go into the mine after Dad died?"

She looked at me. "What? Why?"

I sat down across from her. "What was it like in your head? How did you feel?"

She opened her mouth and closed it again, at a loss. Her eyebrows furrowed as she looked at me.

"Mom," I said quietly. "Please."

She sighed and stabbed her fork into the pie tin, lifting a bite to her mouth before answering around it.

"Foggy," she said. "I felt foggy. I was doing a nephrectomy when they told me Thomas had been killed. Over the intercom, so I was still sterile, so I finished the procedure. But it was as if my mind had floated away from me. My body was down below me working, but my mind was getting further and further away. The light kept flashing off the instruments, and every time it did I heard something in my head. Not a word, but not—I don't know. Maybe I felt it more than heard it. It just kept repeating, like a heartbeat."

Her eyes misted.

"I went to the morgue to identify him, and he was barely recognizable, and I was so far above my body. I could see myself down there crying, and I could feel that I was crying, and the fog in my head got louder and louder until there was just a perfect, empty blank."

She paused, tears rolling down her cheeks.

"The next thing I knew, I was on a stretcher."

I put my hand on hers, the one that wasn't holding a fork. "What about after?" I asked, hating myself for putting her through this.

"What about it?"

"Was there ever anything . . . paranormal, I guess? Did you

see anything, or hear things again, or—?"

She looked like a statue for a moment, her gaze fixed on me, calm and sad. Then she tipped her head to the side. "Is that happening to you?"

A wave of despair and exhaustion swept over me. "Maybe," I said. "I don't know. We went into the mine last weekend."

She rocked back slightly in her chair, but her voice was even as she said, "Why would you do that?"

"Piper's dad," I said. He'd looked so hopeful. A tear spilled down my cheek. "He asked if we wanted to go."

"He's the one working for the town council," she realized. "Why would he bring you down there?"

"He wanted to spend time with Piper," I said as my chest hitched. "Bond with us."

She put both hands flat on the table and looked at me. I could tell she was chewing on the inside of her cheek. "I remember being your age. It's easy to talk yourself into things."

"I'm not *talking myself into* having nightmares every single night," I said. "And Mr. Wharton's a grown man, he isn't talking himself into—into whatever's going on with him. It's *coming* from somewhere."

"Clem—"

"It *happened* to you!" I cried. "You can't tell me it's a coincidence that you got hurt in the mine."

"Of course it was," she said. "I had a—a nervous episode, a grief-induced blackout. I could have ended up anywhere."

I thought about what Nina had said about everyone in town suddenly deciding to believe. My mom had done the opposite. Her resistance to the idea felt like a physical presence in the room, and I couldn't find a way around it.

I lifted my head and forced a smile. "You're probably right. Sorry to dredge up all that old stuff."

Her smile was just as forced, and she didn't say anything as I got up from the table.

I wandered into my room, rolling across my bed to the little shelf of tiny animals in the corner. I picked up a quartz rabbit, turning it in the dim light coming in from the hallway. I felt around on the windowsill, found a lighter, and flicked the flame over my favorite candle. The light danced over the animals, making them look a little bit like they were shifting in place. I pushed them around: turtle, kangaroo, Pomeranian. The ones from when I was small were ceramic, painted, with eyes and mouths and little delicate accents. The ones from more recently were stone, rougher-hewn. A frog made of dark-red jasper huddled next to a jade dragon and a small agate mouse. I hadn't gotten a new one in years. My mom used to bring them to me when she visited her mother. Every time she got back, I'd run to her as soon as the door opened and she'd kneel, unclasping her hands to reveal the newest pet she'd chosen for me.

The candle flickered and the rabbit's ears twitched. I had a sudden urge to hug my mom, hold her to me and tell her I loved her. I wanted to tell her I was sorry for what she'd been through, and that I was proud of her, and that I trusted her. I rolled off my bed and walked out into the hallway. The kitchen light was off. I pushed open her bedroom door just slightly, to see if I could hear the white-noise hum of her fan. She wasn't there. She'd left for work. I nodded to myself, kept nodding as I went back into my room, and when my cheek hit the pillow I felt that I was crying. I thought, *I forgot to call Nina*, and then I was asleep.

In the dark moonless middle of the night I woke to water dripping on me. The first drop hit my eyelid; I opened my eyes and shifted slightly, and the second one hit my forehead.

"Shit," I murmured, rolling toward my side table to turn on the lamp. The trailer didn't usually leak, but there was a first time for everything. I was reaching, my fingers fumbling under the shade, when a hand grabbed my wrist.

A scream died in my throat as I tried to make out who was holding me. I could smell the metallic, mineral tang of water. I knew who it was but I didn't want to, I wanted to be wrong, even though the fingers on my wrist were slimy and swollen with damp. I squinted into the black, hoping against hope, and then her face swam down out of the darkness toward me.

This time the scream came out, full-fledged, and I tried to yank my arm out of her grip but she was too strong. Her eyes were gone, clouded and fish nibbled. Her makeup ran down her cheeks. She opened her mouth and a tide of murky water spilled out, the cold of it shocking as it hit me. A whistling, reedy sound came from her throat, and as her mouth stretched wider, I saw something scrabbling there in the darkness at the end of her tongue. I pedaled my feet, shoving myself backward toward the head of the bed, bunching the wet bedclothes away from me. I couldn't make a sound, transfixed by her mangled eyes, and as she leaned closer I smelled the flat metal smell of the river, and I realized it was coming from her lungs, where it had pooled when she died. The scrabbling thing made a rustling, clicking sound, and I could see one bristly leg searching for purchase on her tongue and her mouth yawned, her jaw crunching as it dislocated. She was going to swallow me whole, put those horrible unhinged jaws around my head and bite, holding me there while the scrabbling thing climbed from her throat and forced its way between my lips, between my teeth, until it settled on my tongue and gorged itself on my blood and I suffocated in the yawning, fetid cavern of her mouth.

"Mellie," I said, still trying to pull myself away from her, "Mellie, please, please don't—"

The Mellie-thing made the whistling noise again, louder, ratcheting up like the buzz of a cicada, and her mouth kept opening. The skin at the corners of her lips split all the way back to her ears and still her mouth opened. I was sobbing, hyperventilating, wild, high shrieky breaths, and I couldn't get enough air, but my voice was stuttering *please-please-please* and suddenly my wrist slipped from her wet bloated grasp and I tumbled backward off the bed, cracking my head on the floor, and then, blessedly, there was darkness.

American Phenomena, Episode 30
Unused Footage

(WAYNE UNGER, county coroner, sits behind his desk eating a sandwich. There is a partially disassembled scale-model human skeleton in front of him. As he speaks, the camera loses focus; by the end of the clip he is nothing more than a mint-green blob.)

UNGER: My dad was a big hunter, back before the explosion. Pheasant, deer, you name it. He was just earflaps and a scope half the year, that's what my mama always said. But she couldn't complain too much, 'cause the freezer was always full. I wasn't born until '66, but I hardly ever saw him go hunting. I don't think I've ever even seen a deer, let alone something like a pheasant. I don't know why. I guess they just didn't make it over with the rest of us.

JOSS KYLE, *from off-screen*: Did he ever hunt the coyotes?

UNGER: Well, it's funny you ask that, really. He did try. Thought at least he'd keep his skills up, cut down on the scavenger population some. But it was the damnedest thing; it just . . . didn't work.

KYLE: How so?

UNGER: Well, like, okay, like, his gun would jam. He'd get one of their heads dead center in his crosshairs and pull the trigger and *click*. Nothing. Once the gun misfired and he blew off his two back fingers, right here. *(He holds up one hand and makes a chopping motion with the other, "severing" his pinky and ring finger.)* How does that even happen? I don't know.

(UNGER finishes the sandwich, balls up the wrapper, and

produces a Snickers bar from a drawer somewhere. He holds it out toward the camera.)

UNGER: No? All mine, then. (*While chewing.*) He got one once, though. That thing fuckin' scares me to this day. I'm afraid he's gonna leave it to me when he dies.

KYLE: You mean the trophy?

UNGER: Yeah, it's a rug, but there used to be a guy in town who did glass eyes, and he did all the preservative stuff himself, and it just looks so alive. Alive and *mean*. I felt like I could hear it following me through the house at night, if I went down to use the bathroom or something I could hear it sliding along the floor behind me. I never turned around. I had this weird waking nightmare about it.

KYLE: Describe it for us, please.

UNGER: Well, I'd turn around and it would be lying there on the floor staring at me, and then it would stand up, only it wouldn't stand like a coyote, it would keep going, up and up until it was on two legs like a man.

KYLE: And what happened to it?

UNGER: Nothing happened to it. It's still in their living room. Waiting for me.

(He laughs.)

UNGER: No, I'm joking. I am gonna put it in an incinerator when the old man goes, though. Just to be safe.

FIFTEEN

I'd had strange dreams since we'd gone into the mine, but Mellie hadn't been a nightmare. I'd been awake. I knew I had. I woke up on the floor with a still-swelling knot on my head, the bones of my wrist aching where her hand had gripped me.

I decided to visit her.

Mellie's grave was in the back of the cemetery, not far from where I'd met Nina. Her marker was a discreet little tablet set in a corner, overgrown and cracking. No one was maintaining it, that much was clear. Long-faded remnants of graffiti straggled across the engraving: MELODY HARINGTON 1939–1964. No dearly beloved, no mother-wife-whatever. Just her name and the short span of her life. There hadn't been anyone to buy her a gravestone. The city put a cheap one up because they felt guilty, just like they included Sidney Harington in the memorials for the dead miners. The one in the cemetery was a statue of a man, pickax slung bravely over one shoulder, looking off into the future. All seventeen of their names were engraved around the base. The one in the town square was just a little plaque in the gazebo, but he was on that one, too. Public opinion might have destroyed the Haringtons, but Moon Basin wasn't going to put the ostracism on record for everyone to see. Not when "tragic inexplicable explosion and subsequent haunting" was on the table.

I knelt next to the flat stone of Mellie's grave. There wasn't an aboveground tomb—they wouldn't spend that much on her—and I wondered what they'd done with her body. I saw her drowned, and she saw Sidney burning—was it the way they'd died, or the state of their bodies underground? I hoped they hadn't just buried her waterlogged corpse. Maybe they cremated her, let her leave here in death since she couldn't in life. Either way I doubted they'd had a real funeral. I put my hand flat on the browning grass.

"I'm sorry," I whispered, picturing it. Cheap coffin, Reverend Parker's dad reading the shortest Bible verse he could find. Maybe a friend. Did she have any friends? I dug my fingers into the earth. Something rustled behind me and I whirled around, a startled yelp escaping my lips, scaring Lisey into an answering yelp. There was a beat of silence and then we started laughing. Across the gravestones, I saw Piper and Nina winding their way toward us.

"Gee, are we edgy?" Piper asked, walking over to me.

"I think we are," Nina said. "But we found you."

We walked to the Half Moon and settled into a booth. I waited until we'd gotten through a plate and a half of cheese fries before I started talking. I told them about my conversations with Nadia and my mom, and my not-dream visitation from Mellie. By the time I finished, Piper had worried a thread out of the hem of her shorts, and Lisey was inspecting the ends of her hair. Nina kept her eyes down as she slid her water glass around in a puddle of condensation. Finally Piper broke the silence.

"So the mine really is doing something to my dad."

"I think so, yeah," I said.

"Well, can we—can we get the town council to shut him down? Fire him? If we tell them something's wrong—"

"They already know." Nina's face was somber as she looked at Piper. "They know what it's like down there, and they know what it does to people. That's why they let the sheriff close it off. Even if they didn't know for sure that something would happen to Carlisle, they knew it was a possibility and they sent him in anyway. They don't care."

Piper's lips tightened as she absorbed the words, trying to keep her chin from quivering. "So it's just us. What are we supposed to do?"

"We figure out a way to get him out of there for good," I said, "and in the meantime we keep an eye on him. We need to watch the rest of those tapes, figure out what kind of stuff it's made people do. If we can get a good enough idea of that, we'll be able to see the signs when he starts to do whatever it is it wants him to do. And then we can stop him."

I thought about the coroner stitching my mother's wrists, the fog in her mind clearing as suddenly as it came. I thought about the moment Mellie Harington's feet left the bridge, that whispering voice finally silent as the water closed over her head. I thought about Nadia, safe in her home somewhere far from here.

"Or save him," I said. "Or whatever."

Hauntings across America, Episode 58
Unused Footage

(Tracking shot through the Old Basin. The camera passes the grocery store, the hospital, the gazebo, lingering on the crumbling benches heaped with ash. It leaves the town commons and moves through the shrouded gray streets, panning slowly back and forth across the cracking asphalt. Ash spirals down past the lens. Over the course of the footage, it will accumulate into a smeary film across the glass, making the last several minutes look like a video taken underwater. The footage seems not to have audio, but during postproduction a sound engineer will notice and amplify a low, continuous droning like the hum of a thousand wasps, which seems to come from everywhere and nowhere. It is impossible to remove this sound from the footage, despite the engineer's best efforts. It isn't even really audible, in the strictest sense of the word. Even when the footage is viewed with a speaker at top volume, the overwhelming impression is that of a very loud silence. It becomes impossible to speak while viewing it, and to hear, and really to have any coherent thought whatsoever. In fact, it will so unsettle the crew of Hauntings across America *upon previewing the episode that they will pull not only the footage but the entire episode from broadcast, incurring a hefty fine from the network. The camera is in the graveyard now, drifting slowly past the rows and rows of lifted marble crypts. For a moment something like a candle flame is visible in the bottom right corner of the screen, but when the camera swings toward it nothing is there. The camera turns slowly in a full circle, the sky visibly darker now than it was in the town square. The angels poised above the crypts*

154

look hungry. Their eyes are obscured by the ash that settles into the hollows of their bones, drawing their features long and cruel in the fading light. Something ripples behind their faces. The ash seethes in the air and the picture moves and blurs, and before the camera shuts off there is, almost visible in the edge of a single frame, the barest twitch of a marble arm.)

SiXTEEN

We spent the weekend watching tapes, taking notes, trying to figure out what the mine wanted. There weren't a lot of common threads—everyone experienced different things, and only some of them ever expressed interest in actually going *into* the mine. Most just felt a low-grade fascination with it. I wished the girl from *Ghost Walk* would call us back; for some reason, I felt like Mellie and Sidney Harington were the key to understanding what was happening. Piper called her dad every few hours, checking to see that he was still at home, and he sounded normal each time they spoke. We made an unsuccessful attempt to convince him to take Monday off to drive us to the city, and we parted ways on Sunday night feeling more than a little defeated.

We spent Monday at the pool, trying to keep ourselves from worrying about him. Piper looked at her watch every ten minutes until Nina took it from her. Lisey snuck in a water bottle full of something with *breeze* in the name and we passed it back and forth until it was empty, giggling like kids. We had dinner at the Half Moon, burgers with all the trimmings, and half a pie between the four of us. When we finally walked her home, Piper seemed calmer than she had been all weekend. She looked almost happy. I toppled into bed feeling optimistic. We hadn't been able to keep Carlisle out of the mine that day, but we weren't giving up. We had more tapes to watch, more research to do. Even if he spent another few days down there, we had time. I was sure of it.

The ring of the phone jerked me awake. I flung myself across my bed and grabbed the receiver as fast as I could. I didn't know what time it was, or even if she was home, but my mom did *not* appreciate being woken up.

"What?" I whispered.

I almost didn't recognize Piper's voice. "My dad's still down there."

I sat up and rubbed my eyes, willing my brain to move faster. "What?"

"He never came home," she said.

"What?" I pinched my thigh. *Wake up, Clem.* "Is he on the cameras? Can you see him anywhere?"

"The cameras are off," she whispered. "He turned them off."

"I'm coming over," I said. "Call Lisey."

The sun was starting to rise as I knocked on Nina's window, hoping Paul was already at work. She pushed it open and leaned out. "What's up?" she mumbled around her toothbrush.

"Carlisle didn't come home. He turned the cameras off."

Her eyes widened and she ducked back inside without another word. Three minutes later we were half walking, half jogging toward town.

Piper was sitting on her front porch, looking small and defeated. She tried to smile when she saw us. We sat down on either side of her. The sun continued to rise. After a little while Lisey materialized at the end of the driveway, coalescing out of the already-forming heat waves like a bird lighting on a branch. She ran the last few feet to the porch and flung her arms around Piper, rocking her back and forth as she hugged her.

"It's gonna be okay," she murmured.

We went upstairs without speaking. The office was filthier than before; dirt had actually started to pile in the corners like snowdrifts. Piper looked nauseous as her hands flew over the keyboards, cycling the footage back until each screen showed the same thing: Carlisle with wide, unseeing eyes, reaching for the camera.

"Jesus fucking Christmas," Nina muttered, leaning forward.

Piper made a sound halfway between a laugh and a sob. "I know."

"We have to go get him," I said, uncertain. "Right?"

I wanted her to turn the monitors off. I wanted to be out of that room, out of that house.

"Right," Lisey said. The shake in her voice twisted a fishhook somewhere in my throat.

"We have to go get him *now*." Nina slapped the desk and straightened up. "How long ago did he turn off the cameras?"

Piper looked at the time stamps. "An hour, maybe two. They only refresh every fifteen minutes."

"And he was down there all night before that," Lisey said.

"Yeah, we have to move," Nina said, already halfway to the door. "We don't know if he's got any water, food, anything. Come on."

SEVENTEEN

The back of my shirt was soaked through with sweat by the time we reached the entrance of the mine. I was already nauseous and a little dizzy. I slung the bag I was carrying onto the ground and dug for a water bottle, twisting the cap off and drinking about half before offering it around.

"Okay," said Lisey after she'd taken a sip. She turned away from us, sat on the edge of the entrance, and kicked her feet down to the first rung. She pulled out the little camping lantern we'd brought, clamped the handle between her teeth, and then disappeared from view with a flash of white hair. The three of us stood there and looked at each other. Piper fidgeted with the end of one of her braids, and Nina rocked back and forth with her hands in her back pockets, eyes flickering around.

"Okay!" Lisey's voice floated up faintly. "Nina!"

Nina blew her bangs out of her face, resituated her backpack, and clambered into the mine. Piper and I watched her go. I reached out and squeezed her hand. It was clammy, even in the stifling heat.

"We're gonna find him, Pipes," I murmured, releasing her. As the words left my mouth, I wondered if I actually believed them.

She looked at me but didn't say anything, and as soon as Nina called up she was gone, vanishing over the ledge without a backward glance. I looked at the entrance to the mine, nausea still roiling inside me. I had the bizarre thought that the square frame was crooked somehow, like it had been set into the earth wrong. It made me feel off-balance. I tilted my head, trying to lessen the effect, but it seemed to move with me. I closed my eyes and opened them, and it seemed better. I blinked again and it was crooked. My stomach lurched. I closed my eyes again and kept them shut until I heard Piper's voice, and then I shuffled forward to the mine with my gaze fixed on the ground. I could feel the entrance tilting around me as I slid over the edge, and my hand slipped as I started down. I yelped, dirt and rock crumbling away under my fingers, and flattened myself to the wall.

"Clem? You okay?"

"Great," I called down, trying to slow my breathing. If I threw up now I'd fall and die. *And then your body would rot down here,* my brain whispered. *You'd be part of the mine.* I coughed sharply, like I could expel the thought from my body, then climbed down as fast as I could. I let go when my toes were still almost three feet from the mine floor, landing in a crouch and stumbling onto my hands and knees. My hands felt like they were crawling, like I'd shoved them into something rotting and slimy, and I couldn't touch the wall of that mine shaft for another second. I scrubbed my hands against my shorts, trying to rid them of the sensation.

"Jesus, Clem. Do you wanna break an ankle?"

"I lost my grip," I lied. "Sweaty hands."

Lisey's barely visible eyebrow arched, but she just turned around and started walking into the mine, holding the little lantern aloft. We followed her, falling into single file like kids on a field trip. I wished we had a big leash tying us all together.

Every time we passed a new tunnel, we stopped and yelled for Carlisle. Then we waited, holding our breath, for some sound to bounce back to us. It was always only our own voices.

The mine still gave me the feeling of being swallowed. It almost felt like being watched, eyes-moving-in-the-painting style, but more intimate. It felt like being *known*, like it was tasting us, deciding whether or not to swallow us whole. I shuddered hard, knocking into Nina, who was closer behind me than I'd expected.

"Chill out," she murmured, handing me another water bottle. I pressed it against my forehead.

"Do you feel sick?" I asked, keeping my voice down. "Like, nauseous?"

"I feel like I'm getting heatstroke," she said. "Does that count?"

I kept walking, rolling the bottle across my skin. It was barely cold anymore, but in comparison to the air it was almost arctic. There was a flat mineral smell in the air, tinged with rot and copper. I flicked my gaze upward, looking for anything that might look like it was dripping blood. Lisey's light was too far forward, though, and all I could see were flickering shadows.

We walked in silence for almost half an hour, our footfalls muffled by the earth. The soles of my shoes grew warm and sweat poured down my face in sheets. I kept blinking it out of my stinging eyes, licking it off my lips. My breathing grew shallow and slow, the heat scraping in and out of my lungs; I was being slowly roasted alive. I stumbled twice, and the second time I fell all the way to the ground, my knee landing hard on a rock. I heard a crack and bit off a scream.

"What was that?" Lisey asked, turning around to see me on

the ground. "Clem, what—"

She dropped down next to me and slapped my hands away, looking at my bleeding leg. She made a face and threw her pack down, digging in it until she found a length of fabric, which she wound around my knee and tied. Then she pulled the shoelace out of her shoe and tied it around my thigh, six inches above the knee. She placed her fingers on my kneecap, probing gently.

"I think everything is okay. I think it just sounded bad. Do you think you can keep going?"

"Yeah," I said, pushing myself carefully to my feet. "I might need to lean on one of you, though."

We kept moving, more slowly than before, stopping every so often so I could rest my throbbing leg. Lisey was right—I didn't think anything was seriously damaged—but I could feel each thump of my heartbeat in it like an animal trapped under the skin. I leaned on Nina, occasionally steadying myself on the wall of the mine, the feel of it sending cold waves of dread through me. After another fifteen minutes we'd made it to the little pocket of the mine where Carlisle had gone strange on the day we'd been there with him.

There were two tunnels branching off from the larger space. We went down each one about ten feet and yelled for Carlisle, then regrouped. I dug out another water bottle and passed it around. Lisey handed me a box of animal crackers. I shoved a few in my mouth and chewed, trying to quell the nausea that had been getting stronger as we moved deeper into the mine. She looked closer at me.

"Are you okay?"

"I feel sick," I managed through the crackers. "Like I'm on a boat."

"You've never been on a boat." Nina mopped her forehead.

"Well, it feels like the ground is moving."

Piper finished the water and tucked the bottle back into my bag.

"Now what?"

"We need to split up," Lisey said, at the exact same time that Nina said, "We're not splitting up."

Nina sputtered. "Lisey, we're not the fucking Scooby-Doo gang."

"No, listen," Lisey said. "Not, like, two of us in each tunnel. Two of us go down one tunnel until there's a dead end or something, and the other two stay here to guide them back. Then we do the same with the other one."

Nina folded her arms. "And what if there's no dead end? What if we're in the one tunnel that goes all the way to the center of the Earth? Should we just turn around when we hit lava?"

"Nina," I said quietly.

She sighed. "Sorry. It's just so goddamn hot."

"Piper, you come with me. Clem has to stay here so she can rest that leg. Keep this—" Lisey handed me the little camping lantern. "When you hear us calling you, just come down the tunnel a little ways and yell back until we reach you."

"We should have brought a ball of yarn," I muttered, lowering myself to the ground as carefully as I could.

"We *should* have," Lisey said. "Shit. That would have been way easier."

"Or chalk," Nina said. "Jesus, we're amateurs. At least we brought water."

Piper was just shifting from foot to foot, eyes a little too wide. She looked almost manic.

"Okay," Lisey said. She took Piper's wrist and pressed a few buttons on her watch as she spoke. "If we don't find any more tunnels, or anything that seems like it's Carlisle-related, then we'll turn around in half . . . an . . . hour. There. I set the timer."

She let go of Piper's arm and it just stayed in the air for a second, like Piper had forgotten she was in charge of it. After another moment, Piper shook her head and pulled her flashlight back out of her belt loop.

I closed my eyes and tried to ignore the pain in my knee, which was for some reason worse now that I was off the leg. The nausea was slightly better when I couldn't see anything, even though the darkness made the swaying feeling intensify.

I heard Nina sit down next to me, and then she knocked her shoulder gently into mine.

"Do you think he's down here?" she whispered.

"I don't know," I whispered back. "Most people who come in here don't come back out."

"I know. But you know that's just a coincidence, right?"

"What do you mean?"

"Well, clearly there was some kind of collapse that buried the original miners, they fell into some kind of pocket in the earth, and that's why no one's found them. That one ghost-hunter girl came out pretty fucked up, yeah, but she came out. And we can't *prove* anyone in town who's missing went down here. Causation and correlation and all."

"Those are some fancy PSAT words," I said.

"Still not ready for jokes," she said, her spine stiffening.

"Noted." I leaned back against the wall. We needed to be listening for Lisey and Piper anyway.

I gripped my legs tightly, tried to stop my body from moving, thinking of boulders, thinking of tree roots. Our breathing became smoother, more synchronized, until it was just one sound, getting larger and louder until it filled the little chamber. It pressed against my ears, into the hollows of my eyes, weighing on my shoulders, and with a shudder I realized it was the mine breathing, the hot, stale air rushing past us, carrying our scent deeper into it. It was inhaling us, tasting us, making us a part of it. We were *inside* it, pulling it into us, exhaling ourselves out into it, becoming less and less and less until we were just the mine. I felt myself starting to hyperventilate even as I fought to control it, trying to take slow, even breaths. I wheezed as my lungs stuttered, struggling for air but at the same time afraid to breathe at all, afraid to lose any more of myself. I could feel the mine pressing itself into my mouth, my nose, curling down into my lungs, the strange poisonous warmth of it spreading like ink inside me. I gagged, choked, gagged again, and I opened my eyes to see only darkness.

"Nina? Nina!" I shrieked, putting my hands out. I couldn't find the lantern, couldn't feel anything except the rotting-skin earth beneath me. "Piper! Lisey!"

I shuffled forward on my hands and knees, waving one hand in front of me as I moved.

"Where are you? Where—"

My throat snapped shut like a mousetrap, like something had put its foot on my neck and stomped. My mouth opened and closed uselessly as I clutched at my neck, my fingers scrabbling against sweat-slicked skin. There was nothing there, nothing wrapped around my throat. The darkness was inside me, swelling and barbed and lodged there like a blood clot, killing me. I pitched forward, my face smashing into the dirt, and the feel of the earth on my lips made me retch. I rolled to my side, still trying desperately to breathe, my hands grasping at nothing, and suddenly a flashlight beam pierced the darkness. I could see it in the distance, like a lighthouse. I staggered to my feet, stumbling toward it. My lungs heaved and a sip of air scraped past the darkness in my throat. Light sparked behind my eyes and a small wheeze escaped me, scratching up into a high, thin keening sound as I fell to the ground again. The beam of the flashlight swung toward me, then away, and then it flickered out completely. My lips and tongue were heavy with ash and dirt. Hot tears streamed down my face. I reached out one last time into the darkness, but it swallowed me whole.

I woke up drenched in sweat, panting and gasping, my breath sobbing out of me in great heaves. I was lying on the ground exactly where I'd been before, the little camping lantern glowing softly against the wall. Nina was lying on the ground next to me, hair thrown over her face, arms flung out.

I sat up, wiping my face with the damp hem of my T-shirt. My mouth tasted like a grave. My leg was pulsing with pain, crawling like a thousand fire ants.

"Nina?" My voice scraped out of me like broken glass, barely audible. I put a hand on Nina's arm and shook her gently. "Neen. Nina."

She drew her hand over her mouth and turned her head, rumbling a little in her chest.

"Nina," I said more urgently. I patted her cheek, moving her hair away from her face. Her eyes opened slowly, and when they focused on me there was no recognition in them.

"What?"

I moved closer to her, looking down into her face. Her eyes tracked me, eyelashes flickering, and gradually some awareness came back into her face.

"Clem?" She sat bolt upright, her head swaying. "What the fuck just happened?"

"I have no idea," I rasped. I touched my throat and the pain made me jerk my hand away. "I think something choked me."

She rubbed a hand over her mouth. "Maybe we have heatstroke. Maybe we're breathing some fucking hallucinogen down here. Fuck!" She balled up her fist and thumped it into the ground. "We didn't think this through at *all*."

My heart was tripping over itself and I was still having trouble taking a full breath. I pressed my hands against my sternum, trying to ground myself.

"Shit!" Nina scrambled to her feet like something had bitten her. "Clem, we have to—we have to get Lisey and Piper; they're farther in than we are, they're probably closer to it—"

I shook my head.

"Honey, I'm sorry, I'm so sorry, I'm not leaving you—"

She put her hands under my arms and yanked me to my feet. I grabbed onto her to keep from falling. My knee felt like it was full of needles and boiling water, and I couldn't put any weight on it. She put one arm around my waist and I held on to her shoulder, and we staggered into the tunnel.

"Lisey!" I yelled. The lantern seemed to be dimming as Nina swung it back and forth in front of us, trying to find them.

"Piper! Lisey!"

As we moved deeper into the mine, my nausea, which had been drowned out by the pain in my knee, returned with a vengeance. I was horribly dizzy. The tunnel seemed to be splitting away from us like we were inside a kaleidoscope, but we kept going in a straight line.

"Hang on," Nina said. I leaned against the wall while she turned the lantern off. "Do you see that?"

I looked ahead of us. "No . . . Wait."

My stomach heaved violently and I put a hand to my mouth. There was a point of light up ahead, like the beam of a flashlight, like the one that had led me—

She was propping me back up, moving forward, and I couldn't use my legs to brace and stop her.

"Nina," I said. "Nina, Nina, wait, I saw this—I saw this already; it's not—"

"Clem, that's a flashlight," she said. "That has to be them. Just keep holding on to me."

I bit back a moan of terror as the light flashed in front of us. The darkness around us was too close, too heavy, and I started to suffocate as I fumbled for my flashlight and clicked it on.

"We won't be able to see if you—"

We stopped moving at the same time. At the end of the flashlight beam, in front of a wall of earth, was Lisey. She stood with her back to us, hands dangling limp at the ends of her arms.

"Lisey, what the hell, didn't you hear us yelling for you?" Nina called.

Lisey turned and ran down another tunnel.

"Lisey!" Nina made a strangled sound of rage and hoisted me against her, jerking us into a swaying half run, like we were in a three-legged race. "Lisey, come back here!"

We turned the corner, I swung the flashlight, and the tips of her hair flickered as she vanished around another corner. We hobbled after her, still yelling. It was getting hotter at an alarming rate. My lungs felt like they were full of steam.

We turned again, and again, and each time we caught just a glimpse of her. I'd lost count of the corners when we finally turned and slammed right into her. Nina was drawing breath to start yelling when Lisey spoke.

"I found her." Her tone sent a chill through me. I looked behind her to see Piper standing there, eyes unfocused.

"Piper?" I walked toward her, watching her eyes. I waved my hand in front of her face and she didn't respond. Her body swayed slightly as she stood there. "Piper!" My tone was sharper this time. I snapped my fingers next to her ear. She blinked.

Lisey took her hand, squeezing tightly. "Pipes," she whispered. "Are you in there?"

Piper's eyes rolled slowly toward her and all three of us gasped. I resisted the urge to shake her, to do something dramatic that would snap her out of this horrible stillness. She blinked again, slow, like she was trapped in molasses, and then a few more times. She seemed to focus on Lisey—not fully, but enough that it looked like there was something behind her eyes. She opened her mouth. Her lips moved. She mouthed, *Lisey*. But no sound accompanied it. Her eyes sharpened a little more, the first hint of panic entering them, and she tried again to speak.

Something *you guys*, something *I can't. What the hell.* She grabbed at her throat, fingernails scraping at the hollow under her necklace. A faint whistling came from her as we watched, a wheezy teakettle sound that never escalated into actual noise.

"Pipes, you can breathe, right?" Nina asked. "Is this a breathing issue or a talking issue?"

She was calming down now that she had a problem to solve, someone else to focus on. Piper mouthed *I can breathe* and we all relaxed a fraction. Her eyes flicked from face to face and tears started to run down her cheeks.

"What happened, Piper?" I asked as gently as I could.

She gestured back behind her and raised her hands helplessly. Then she pointed upward.

"Yeah, we should leave," Nina said. "Right? I mean, Clem can barely walk, and we have to get all the way back to the entrance—"

Piper was crying harder now, but she nodded.

"We'll come back," I said. "We'll come back and find him."

I couldn't meet her eyes when I said it.

As we wound our way toward the entrance, I tried not to vomit, not to think about what had happened, and to generally keep my shit together. I kept my eyes forward, and gradually I was distracted from my fear by a new and worsening concern.

"Shouldn't we be seeing some light?" I asked, keeping my tone even. "From the entrance? We're close, aren't we?"

"Yeah." Lisey tromped forward. "I think—"

She rounded a corner and there was the ladder, carved steps casting strange misshapen shadows in the flashlight's beam. There was no light whatsoever coming down from above.

"What time is it?" Nina's voice was quiet and thready. Piper lifted her wrist and Nina seized her hand, pulling her watch toward her face, and swore under her breath. "It stopped. Of course it did." She looked at me. "Can you climb? If I go right behind you and sort of, I don't know, you can put your shin on my shoulder?"

I pulled myself up a few steps, high enough that she could stand underneath me, and she climbed up enough to let me rest my injured leg on her. We climbed in tandem, counting out loud. Making contact with the soft warm earth turned my stomach. Each movement sent shocks of pain through my injured leg, radiating up and down from the knee. I closed my eyes and tried to breathe through it, letting the pain temper the fear, letting the fear keep me moving. I had no idea how close to the surface I was. I had no idea how long I had been climbing, how long I'd been in the mine shaft, how long since I'd taken a real breath.

My searching hand slapped onto a flat surface above my head, too deep to be another step. A slight breeze stirred the hairs on the back of my hand. A cry of relief escaped my lips as I scrambled upward, hauling myself over the edge of the entrance, and as I tumbled onto the ground, I realized it was pitch-dark outside.

I pulled all my limbs in save the injured one, folding myself into as small a package as I could. I couldn't see anything. I couldn't see the mine shaft I'd just climbed out of, and knowing it was somewhere close by in the darkness gave me a sick, crawling feeling.

"Nina?" My voice barely made a dent in the blackness. I cleared my aching throat and tried again. "Nina?"

No response. I could hear a slight ticking sound, like earth shifting, and something that might have been breathing. I shook my head hard, digging my fingers into the earth, and started dragging myself across the ground. *She was right behind me.* Maybe she was caught—if I could just find the entrance again—

I thought about long arms reaching up out of the mine, fingers scrabbling across the dead forest floor until a terrible thin hand reached me, scuttled up to my face, settled itself across my mouth and nose and suffocated me.

Something brushed across my cheek and I screamed, flattening myself to the ground and covering my head. I lay there, heart hammering in my chest, and cried for Nina. My face was still pressed into the earth when I heard her voice.

"Clem?"

It sounded so far away. I lifted my head cautiously. "Nina?"

"Where are you?"

"I'm out, but I don't know where. A few feet from the entrance, I guess."

"It's so dark." Her voice wasn't getting any closer, but I couldn't make myself move. "Can you see anything?"

I cast my eyes back and forth, willing them to adjust. "No," I said, trying and failing to keep the panic out of my voice. "Can you?"

"No."

Something moved to my left. I yelped and covered my face. "Was that you?"

"Maybe?" she said. "Why aren't the others up here?"

"You took forever," I said.

"What? I came out right after you. I thought I was gonna crawl up your butt."

I laughed. My throat objected. "Maybe it just felt really long. After all that. My time is all fucked up."

I saw a faint lightness, the smallest fraction of color in the dark, and as I watched it grew brighter, delineating the shaft entrance. I shuddered to see how far away I'd gotten and scrambled closer almost involuntarily, colliding with Nina, who was doing the same thing. The light was interrupted by Piper's head and shoulders as she climbed out. Lisey was right behind her, and my sigh of relief was audible as the light emerged with her.

"It's *night?*" Piper asked, looking at the sky. "Oh God."

All of us turned toward her.

"Your voice is back!" Lisey cried.

"Yeah," she said. "It felt like something loosened in my throat right as I climbed out."

"Well, that's telling," I muttered, shouldering my backpack. I could feel blood rolling down my shin.

"What are—"

"I think—"

"We should—"

All of us started and stopped almost at the same time. Lisey huffed a little laugh.

"Piper, you go," Nina said. "It's your dad."

"I just didn't realize it would be so bad," she whispered. "We weren't ready at all."

"We will be, though," I said. "Next time."

I felt Nina look at me and I avoided her gaze. Lisey looked a little sick, but she nodded.

"We should go home right now," she said. "We should get some sleep, and then in the morning we'll all meet up at Clem's—is that okay? And we'll talk about what happened down there today, and then we'll make a plan of attack for when we go back in."

I nodded when she glanced at me. I didn't know if my mom would be home, but maybe hearing from all of us at once would convince her I wasn't jumping at shadows.

"*Attack,*" Piper said. "That feels like the right word."

"Yeah," said Lisey. She smacked her fist into her other hand. "And we're gonna win."

EIGHTEEN

The walk back was agony, even with the three of them taking turns supporting me. By the time we got to Piper's house I was covered in sweat, my teeth were chattering, and my head hurt almost as badly as my knee.

"I'm sorry it was so bad," Piper said as we stood at the end of her driveway.

"Just get some sleep," Lisey said. "We'll see you in the morning."

She nodded but didn't speak again. Her chin trembled as she turned away. We watched her walk down the driveway, listening to the crunch of her footsteps fading into the night. We waited until she was safely inside and then started walking toward Lisey's house.

"You guys can stay here tonight, if you want," she offered as we crossed the street toward her driveway.

"We're okay," I said, "but thanks, Lise."

Lisey's parents were "wellness consultants," whatever that meant, and they were out of town for work more often than they were home. They'd changed their lifestyle very little when they had a kid, and the consequence was that the house felt more like Lisey's than their own. She was self-sufficient almost from birth, and it made her seem both older and younger at the same time. She liked being alone, drifting through the big empty house with only herself for company. I knew she was just offering in case I thought I couldn't walk all the way home, and I loved her for it. I gave her an impulsive hug, feeling the strange lightness of her, the fragility of the bones just beneath the surface of her skin.

"See you tomorrow." She slipped away across the lawn, hair trailing behind her like the streak of a comet.

Nina and I hobbled along in silence until we hit the cornfield, turning onto the white crushed-shell road that ran through the stalks.

"Where do they get crushed shells, anyway?" she asked. "We're nowhere near an ocean."

I could hear a hint of a smile in her voice. We had done this bit a lot as kids.

"Well, this whole country was underwater once," I said, taking my cue, doing a fifties-style newscaster voice.

"The whole world was underwater once."

"Surprising there aren't more crushed-shell roads, when you think about it."

"It's the most economical thing, really. Poor planning on the government's part."

The conversation trailed off as my steps got slower, the corn rustling around us. There was a strange heaviness in the air, and in my body. There wasn't enough oxygen in the darkness. My whole body was freezing, except for my knee, which was molten steel. I wondered if I had an infection.

"Do you feel weird?" My voice wavered a little as I spoke. I took a tiny breath, sipping at the air like a hummingbird.

"How?" she asked, turning to me.

She was silhouetted by the lights of the trailer park in the distance. We were near the end of the path, about to come out of the cornfield onto High Grange Road. Half her face was in shadow as she moved closer to me.

"Like, shivery," I said. "Fever-y."

She put her hand on the back of my neck and pulled me toward her. My heart did something convulsive and swoopy in my chest and I sucked in a breath. She smelled like black tea and clove cigarettes. Her pulse beat steadily in her neck just a few inches from my face. She pressed her lips to my forehead and then released me, stepping away.

"You feel warm," she said. "C'mon. We have to clean your knee, and then I'll make you some tea."

We started moving again. My heart was pounding like I'd just run a mile. What had I thought was going to happen? What had I *wanted* to happen? Her lips were cool and soft when they touched me, and for the split second it took me to inhale, I had thought maybe she would put them somewhere else.

I'd thought about it before, after she told me she thought she was bisexual, but never seriously. It was never more than the flicker of an idea, a casual what-if. She was my best friend. We'd had a long, strange day, and the electricity in my body, in the air between us, was an aftereffect.

She deposited me on the sofa and went into the bathroom. I could hear things rattling, drawers opening and closing, a muffled "Damn it" as she dropped something. She came back into the living room with her arms full, spread everything on the coffee table, and went into the kitchen. She started opening cupboards immediately, looking for tea.

"Fruit bowl," I said as I started picking through the pile. "Last time I saw it, anyway."

My mom was usually on autopilot when she got home from

an overnight shift; household items tended to turn up in weird places afterward.

"What about the kettle?" Nina asked as she filled the little bell-shaped diffuser and plunked it into my favorite mug, one I'd made in third-grade art class. It sat crooked, but it held liquid and it said I LOVE MOM. It made me feel better.

"Hey." She pointed at the bandage I'd just unrolled. "Stop that. Go wash it in the bathroom first."

"The kettle's in there somewhere," I said, levering myself up off the couch.

I carefully unwrapped the fabric Lisey had put around my knee, but it was stiff with blood and when it pulled away from the skin the wound started bleeding anew. I sat on the edge of the bathtub and inched closer to the faucet until I could get my knee under the water.

I gasped as the water touched me. The pain had settled into a deep ache, but it flared bright and hot like I'd jammed a live wire into it. I gritted my teeth and leaned forward. My knee was swollen and purple, and the gash below my kneecap looked like a ragged, bloody smile.

"Holy shit," I muttered. It hadn't looked like that after I fell. Maybe I'd slammed it into something when I blacked out. I took a deep breath, pumped some soap into my hand, and set just my fingertips on my knee. Black spots danced in front of my vision for a moment, but I shook my head and they cleared. I tried to be gentle, to touch it as lightly as possible, but it was still agony.

"Fine." I exhaled through gritted teeth. *"Fine."*

I pressed down into my skin, started rubbing dirt and ash out of the wound as hard as I could. I could hear that I was crying, making a long, drawn-out keening sound that I couldn't have kept inside if I wanted to. I felt like all the blood was leaving my limbs, rushing toward my heart, and I wondered if it would explode. My head dipped as my vision went blurry, but I dug my fingers in deeper and the darkness receded. When the water was clear—still deep red, but no longer muddy—I shut off the tap and leaned my head against the wall. I was still sobbing quietly. I got to my feet as carefully as I could and pressed a wad of tissues against my knee, then limped back into the living room. I put my foot on the coffee table and watched myself bleed, swabbing away the drops that rolled down before they could fall on the carpet.

"One second," Nina called. "I found cookies."

I reached for the remote and turned on the TV, keeping the volume low. Someone was trying to sell me a tiny blender, dropping all sorts of things into the cup and watching them disintegrate. Orange still in the peel—it shreds. Handful of unshelled walnuts—it shreds. Thin paperback book—it shreds. I changed the channel when he picked up a chunk of raw meat with a bone in it.

"Well, I can't find the kettle," Nina said, coming around the bar counter. She set a plate of cookies on the table and dropped heavily onto the couch next to me. "I just used a saucepan. Remind me to check on it so it doesn't boil over."

"'Kay," I said.

"Jesus." She looked at my knee. "What *happened* to it?"

"I don't know. It wasn't that bad at first, right?"

"It looks like someone hit you with a bat." She soaked a cotton pad with hydrogen peroxide. "Hold my hand," she said, and used the other to press the wet cotton firmly into my bloody knee. I squeezed her hand until I thought her bones would crack.

"Fuck you," I said through clenched teeth.

"Love you, too." She set the blood-soaked cotton aside and picked up a can of something. She sprayed what looked like insulation foam into the wound, let it dissolve, and then put a new cotton square over it. She stuck that in place with medical tape, then wrapped the entire thing in a two-foot-long bandage.

"You won't be able to bend it a lot," she said, "and we should definitely ask your mom to look at it, but you should be okay for tonight."

"Thank you," I said, leaning sideways until my head was resting on the arm of the couch. The adrenaline was finally ebbing away, and the only thing in its place was exhaustion and defeat.

She pulled both my feet carefully up onto the couch and set them in her lap, then reached over and grabbed the remote.

"There's nothing on this late," she said, clicking away. I watched the channels flip by, my vision blurring as I slid toward sleep.

"Hey," she said after a minute, putting her hand on my ankle and squeezing lightly. My heart jumped. I cracked an eye open and looked at her as she continued. "Did you say someone choked you?"

"Some*thing*," I said, sitting up. "I couldn't see."

She leaned closer to me and put her fingers under my chin, tilting my head up. "You have bruises," she said softly.

I could feel my blood beating in my temples. Her fingers slipped lower, to my collarbone. There was a crackling hiss from the kitchen as the water boiled out of the pan onto the stove.

"Shit—"

She yanked her hand away and maneuvered herself off the couch, trying not to jostle me. I closed my eyes and tried to calm down, listening as she moved through the kitchen. She came back into the living room with a steaming mug, which she set in front of me on the coffee table. I sat up and took it by the handle, bringing it to my lips. It burned, but I needed the distraction.

"Lemon, honey, whiskey, tea," she said. "Never fails."

I nodded and watched her over the rim of the cup as she turned her attention back to the TV. She settled on a crime show, something with a lot of hand-waving and bad reenactments, and wriggled down comfortably into the couch. We watched in silence as I drank my tea. The whiskey made me drowsy almost immediately, and by the time the cup was empty I could barely keep my eyes open.

"C'mon." She patted my leg. "Time for bed."

We'd always shared a bed, I reminded myself as I went into the bathroom. Since we were little. I ran my head under cool water, watching streaks of ash swirl down the drain as I took deep breaths, but my cheeks were still flushed when I looked in the mirror. *Fever. Alcohol.* I brushed my teeth without looking at myself again, then opened the door and darted into bed. I rolled as far toward the edge of the mattress as I could get and tucked my stuffed giraffe next to me, where it would be between us. I pulled the covers up all the way over my head and listened to the familiar sounds of her going through her nighttime routine. The water was still running when I fell asleep.

NiNETEEN

I dreamed of the mine, of course. I followed Lisey down into the dark and lost her, and then I ran screaming through the tunnels. There was a piece of red string caught on one of Carlisle's probes and I took it, followed it, let it pull me forward until I realized I was at the edge of some kind of slope. I walked deeper, winding always to the left, down and down until I came to the end of the string. It lay on the ground tied to nothing, which was strange, because I had felt resistance when I tugged on it. I stooped to pick it up and heard Lisey's voice from behind me.

"You don't build a labyrinth to keep something out," she said. "You build it so you can lie in wait."

Then her hands reached out from behind me, picked up the string, and pulled it tight around my throat.

I woke up gasping and choking, my hands wrapped around my neck trying to untangle a string that wasn't there. As I sat there the pressure lessened, and then only the ache remained.

"Nina," I rasped. "Nina?"

She lifted her face out of her pillow approximately two inches and made a noise that sounded like *whuh*.

"I'm getting up. I can't—I'm gonna go watch TV or something."

She pressed her hands to her face, raked her hair back. "'M coming. Gimme a second."

I swung my injured leg carefully out of bed while she tried to mobilize. It seemed like the swelling had gone down. I probed at it gently, like it was a bubble that would pop, and was grateful to find it was no longer a ten on the rate-your-pain-from-one-to-vivisection scale. I stood up, keeping all my weight on my other leg, and then managed to do an inelegant little hop-step that brought me toward the dresser.

"This works," I said, trying to convince myself. "This is probably fine."

"We're obviously getting you a crutch. Or a brace at the very least. Something."

"Well, I'll look forward to that," I said, making my way out of the room.

"Do you have any cereal that doesn't have marshmallows in it?" she asked from behind me.

"I think you know the answer to that."

She groaned.

"My mom has, like, granola," I said. "If you really wanna bum me out."

She rolled her eyes and started to say something, but then the door banged open. Lisey was wide-eyed, out of breath, and Piper was behind her.

"Did you dream about it, too?" she demanded.

A shard of ice formed in my heart. It was in our heads. It had a hold on us. How long had Mellie dreamed about the mine before she ended up in the river? How much time did we have? I closed my eyes, tried to push the panic aside.

"Yeah." I kept my voice from shaking. "You were there."

"We did, too." Lisey gestured at Piper. "I woke up in the *kitchen.*" She lifted her eyebrows, but we just looked at her. She sighed. "It's the west side of my house. Toward Old Town."

"Oh, shit," I murmured.

Lisey nodded.

Piper looked as if she was barely holding it together. Her eyes were shiny and vacant, like she was looking at something beyond us, and her hands twisted into each other ceaselessly. The corner of her mouth wouldn't stop twitching as she tried to get control of herself.

"What about you?" I asked her.

She shook her head. "I was, uh . . ." She paused. Her eyes glittered with tears. "My dad was in there. With me. I was dead. My dad was—" Her throat worked. "He was burying me. I couldn't move, couldn't speak, and the dirt was in my eyes and my mouth—" She broke off, put her hand over her face. "It took me so long to wake up."

"Well, fuck," Nina said. "I almost feel left out."

"You didn't dream about it?" I asked in shock. "Not at all?"

She shrugged. "I don't remember. I don't usually remember my dreams."

I shook my head in disbelief. I'd always had to tell her what she said whenever she talked in her sleep—she really didn't remember most of the time—but I thought for sure that the mine would *make* her remember somehow. It would lodge itself in her mind. Wasn't the whole point for us to think about it, to know it was inside us? I couldn't believe it wouldn't have come to her, too, but I didn't want to think she was lying.

"I guess I felt kind of bad when I woke up, though," she said after a moment. "Like, almost hangover-y. Like after we drank all those wine coolers at the pool and fell asleep in the sun."

Piper cleared her throat. "Can we—sorry. Can we talk about yesterday?"

"Of course." I had to get out of my own head. "Do you guys want anything to eat?"

Lisey shook her head. "I haven't been hungry for days, actually."

"I'm not either," Piper said. "I just want to know what the fuck happened down there."

"Let's just go one by one." Nina looked around at all of us. "Okay?"

"Can I go first?" Piper asked.

"Sure, Pipes," Lisey said, patting her knee. "Go ahead."

She took a second to compose herself, rubbed her eyes and smoothed her shirt where she'd been worrying at the hem. She kept her eyes on the floor as she spoke.

"So we're walking down the tunnel," Piper said. "And I get out in front of Lisey, just a little bit, and suddenly I notice her light is out. There's, like, a glow coming from somewhere, kind of like undersea phosphorescence, you know? Like the *walls* were glowing. It felt unfriendly, kind of . . . You know when the moon is full, the way the light feels like it's watching you? It made me shiver when I saw it on me. And the air was freezing, like, so cold that I could see my breath. And I turned around to ask Lisey why she turned off the light and—"

She blotted her eyes with her shirt.

"She was gone. She wasn't there. It was just me, alone, in that fucking glow. So I yelled for her and then I listened, and I heard scuffling sounds coming from somewhere. Like footsteps. I started walking toward it before I really realized what I was doing. And as I moved forward, I could hear something breathing. *Panting.* Like a dog. And it was weird, but I felt like . . . I knew where I was going. Like the mine was leading me."

I glanced at Nina. She was leaning forward, listening intently.
"It kept getting colder the longer I walked. The panting
sound never got closer, but I could smell an animal."

"An animal?" Lisey asked. Piper turned to her.

"Something with wet fur. Wet fur and musk and something
metallic, maybe blood."

Lisey wrinkled her nose but didn't say anything else.

"I realized I was . . . whispering, I guess?" Piper continued.
"I know how that sounds. I kept zoning out and then coming
back to myself and realizing my mouth was moving, and I had
no idea what I was saying. Then I heard something behind me.
I turned and it was just that horrible empty tunnel, stretching
back into the dark, and that awful sickly light."

She shuddered, looking down at her hands. She had picked
off most of her nail polish.

"I said, 'Hello? Is someone there?' And I took a few steps
back into the tunnel, and then the breathing got so much
louder. *So* much louder. It started to sound like there was more
than one of them. Whatever they were. All I could hear was that
panting bouncing off the walls, echoing, and it started to sound
like voices, and then I thought I heard it say my name—"

Her breathing was shallow but steady.

"I turned and I ran, just ran into the dark, and my brain just
kept going *Help me, help me, help me.* I don't know how long I
was running. And then I felt—this strange urge, something in
me that said turn *now*, and I threw myself sideways into this
tiny side tunnel, and I was still running, and it was so cold—like
something wrapped around my chest—I couldn't breathe, but
I kept running and turning and running and turning, deeper
into the dark, and then I turned again and—"

She put her hands over her face and muffled a vicious, wracking sob.

"My dad was standing there," she said. "With his back to me."

I shivered. My mouth filled with bitter, metallic saliva. It made me think of the way Lisey had stood at the end of the tunnel, turned away from us in the beam of the flashlight— shoulders slumped, hands hanging lifeless. She'd looked hollow, like something inside her was missing. I could barely handle seeing Lisey like that; I couldn't imagine how I'd feel if it was my mother.

"He had his head down. I said—I said 'Dad, it's me, are you okay?,' and he didn't move. I could see his back moving, like he was breathing, and I could still hear that sound. And it got louder and louder, and then he turned around, my dad turned around, only he—"

She shook her head, tears flying.

"His face was—he was—he was a coyote," she wept. "Standing there in my dad's clothes. He had his head down, and those fucking yellow eyes were staring right at me, *glowing*. He took a step toward me and I stepped back. I was kind of babbling, I just kept saying 'No, no,' and every time I stepped back he stepped forward. And I knew—I knew even if I turned and ran, if I was even still capable of running, he would catch me. So I just stopped. I stood still and I waited for him to get me, but he didn't. He stopped short. And his mouth was open, he was panting, with that horrible tongue just lolling out between his fucking *fangs*. And it was still so cold I could see my breath, but I couldn't see his. So I looked at him and I said, 'Are you real?' I said, 'Are you alive?'"

A chill ran through me from the base of my spine to the backs of my eyes. I could see it: saliva-slicked teeth, patchy fur drawn too tight over bone. Those lambent yellow eyes.

"He blinked, and—"

She took another breath and looked at us one by one.

"Then he had my dad's eyes. My dad's eyes in that fucking face, just for a second, but he recognized me. I know he did. And then he blinked again and they were gone, and then—"

She covered her face again.

"He smiled," she said, her voice muffled. "His lips, it was like something was pulling them with strings, the way they just wrinkled back into this hideous, awful grin. And then he opened his mouth so wide, so much wider than I thought a coyote could, and he *shrieked* the way they do, and it was so *loud*—I backed away, and I tripped and almost fell but I got myself turned around and started running. And behind me I could hear the shriek turn into laughter, this insane, jagged laughter. It chased me. Not my dad, just that laugh, the sound . . . it chased me back into the darkness. I don't know how long it was from then until Lisey found me."

"She was just standing there," Lisey said quietly, looking at her hands. "Just staring into the dark. She wasn't blinking."

I turned to Lisey. "Where were you before that? What happened to you?"

She sighed, twisting a lock of her hair. "Did you know crows have funerals?"

"What?" Nina asked.

I put a hand on Nina's knee. Lisey did better if you didn't interrupt her.

"They do," she said. "They gather around their dead friend

and they shriek in the trees and it sounds like people crying."

We waited. Piper looked ready to scream. She'd moved on from her nail polish to the arm of the chair, picking at it like her sanity depended on it.

"I was walking behind Piper," Lisey said. "We turned a corner and then she was gone. I doubled back because I thought somehow I missed her, or she got lost, and then I panicked and started running, and then I tripped over something. I fell and hit my head and I guess I blacked out."

"Jesus, Lisey," Nina murmured. "We have to take you to a hospital."

"Shh," she said, squeezing Nina's hand. She smiled for a second, like it was silly that Nina would worry about her when all of this was going on. Then her face settled back into an almost serene blankness. "I woke up and the lantern was next to me and all of my crows were there. At first I was happy to see them, but then I realized I couldn't move. My arms were so heavy, my legs . . ."

She closed her eyes briefly, as though the effort of remembering was costing her.

"It felt like I was falling asleep, but under such heavy weight. Like sand was filling my whole body. I was almost sinking into the ground."

She started checking her hair for split ends. It was meditative for her, one of the many ways she self-soothed.

"The crows were all looking at me, but not like normal, like they knew me. They were looking at me the way they look at food. They kept hopping toward me and then back, toward me and back, and my eyes were so, so heavy. I kept trying to reach my hand out, to let them know it was me, but I couldn't. One of them jumped onto my arm and I thought *Good, now they'll realize*, and then it—"

She dropped the lock of hair she'd been holding and shook her head.

"It *bit* me." Sorrow and outrage mingled in her voice. "It jabbed its beak down into my arm and bit me. I screamed and it fluttered away and landed back on the floor, and they all looked at me, and then I just—I was so *tired*, my eyes finally closed, and then—" Her mouth trembled.

"They started shrieking like I was dead," she whispered. "It sounded like you guys. Like you were all crying. I felt them jump onto me, felt their wings brushing all over my skin, and they kept crying and crying and I couldn't move, and then I opened my eyes and there you were."

She looked at Piper.

"It felt like after your arm falls asleep, only all over my whole body. Like all my blood was rushing back at once." The ghost of a smile crossed her face before she focused on me again. "I could tell she wasn't there. You know? I put my hand on her shoulder and she just kept staring straight ahead. So I took her hand and I just started walking. I didn't know if we'd gotten turned around, and I couldn't see any light besides ours. I yelled for you a few times before you found us."

"We didn't even hear you," Nina said, a faint note of fear in her voice.

"Nina, what happened to you?" I turned toward her. "You still haven't told me."

She sighed. "There's really not a lot to tell."

"Nina." I tried to put some threat into it. "*Tell* us."

"Fine." Her jaw clenched. I knew she didn't want to admit

that she'd experienced something down there, but she wouldn't lie to me. "The light went out. I felt around for it or for you, Clem, and I couldn't find either, but then my hand landed on something really hard and it dug into the heel part, the part that takes your weight when you crawl, and I sort of crumpled over. Like, I smashed my shoulder into the ground. So I got back onto my hands and felt around again, and I found the tiny thing. I picked it up and kept crawling until I found another one, and I followed the trail until something grabbed me by the hair and lifted me off the ground. Then there was enough light that I could see, and I saw all the little things I'd been picking up were teeth, and then I realized they were *my* teeth, and my mouth was just this empty, slick . . . it was just gums and blood. There was blood pouring down my chin and I kept swallowing it, too, choking on it, and I was trying not to scream. I turned around a few times, but whatever had picked me up was gone, and I was alone. And then it hit me that I picked up all my teeth so there wasn't a trail back, and then I *did* scream, and then—"

The corner of her mouth pulled up into a tiny smirk.

"Then, because there's no logic to hallucinations, I decided that if I threw my teeth back into the tunnel I'd have the trail back, and I'd be able to find you. So I threw them out in front of me one at a time as I walked in the dark, and I did that until I ran out of teeth, and then . . ."

She shrugged. "Then you woke me up. I don't know."

"I kind of had a dream like that," I murmured. "Only it was a trail of string."

"Like we talked about bringing next time," Lisey said.

A chill ran through me as I remembered her hands at my throat. "Yeah," I said. "Just like that."

"So what happened to you?" Piper asked me.

I pulled my hair up off my neck so she could see the bruises. "Something grabbed me. The light went out and I started choking, and then I saw your flashlight in the dark and I tried to go toward it, but I blacked out."

"Holy fuck," Piper said, inspecting my neck. "That—those are *real*. Something *touched* you."

"I guess," I said. "And I must have whacked my knee on something while I was asleep or unconscious or whatever because it was so much more fucked up after that. It's still pretty bad."

"So your thing was real," Piper said. "It had to have been. So does that mean—"

"No," Nina said. "I hear where you're going, and no."

Piper shoved the heels of her hands into her eyes, grinding them into the sockets for a moment, and then dropped them back onto the arms of the chair. "Why not?"

Nina barked a laugh, a sound that stopped just short of being mean. "Because ghosts aren't fucking *real*, Piper."

"Then how do you explain this?"

"Well, I said it already but it seems like no one was listening, so let me resubmit my vote for heatstroke."

Piper sighed.

"Fine, not heatstroke, then. Collective madness à la *The Crucible*? Toxic fumes making us hallucinate? Piper, there is no *end* to the number of possibilities—"

"Nina!" Piper yelled. "My father is *fucking missing* down there. I don't care what you come up with to explain it, okay? Something is wrong in that mine, and he's lost in there, and I need to help him." She dashed away an errant tear. "I don't need you guys," she said, her mouth twisting. "I'll go back in alone."

"Piper." My voice was too loud, too harsh. Her 'I don't need you' had stung badly, and I wanted her not to mean it. "Don't."

"Maybe you should," Nina snapped. She saw I was about to speak and cut me off. "No, Clem, don't. We haven't even known her two *months* and we're risking our lives for her. Risking our *souls* if you believe this haunting shit."

All of us were quiet for a moment. I was stunned, trying to understand where Nina's anger was coming from. Piper was our friend; her problem was ours.

"She doesn't mean that." Lisey patted Piper's knee.

"Don't speak for me, Lisey," Nina said.

"Nina," I said sharply. "Enough."

She turned to me, and I was shocked to see her eyes were filled with tears. "You do everything she wants. You're still trying to impress her. You'll go down into the fucking mine for her, but you won't even think about going to college with me?" She looked at the ceiling and blinked fast, trying to keep the tears from falling. "I've been with you on this. I've been right beside you doing research, I've gone down into the dark, I've devoted all my time to dealing with this, and you've never asked if I'm okay with it. You've never even *acknowledged* it."

I was opening and closing my mouth like a fish, trying to process what she'd said. Nina was jealous of Piper. I'd dragged her into a situation that she didn't want to be in. She coped for as long as she could, and now she was drawing a line.

"I—" I sputtered. "I didn't realize it was so—"

"You believe the mine is haunted, right?" Nina's voice was low and dangerous.

"Yes," I said.

"And you let your best friends go inside it? *Encouraged* them to do it? All for a girl we barely know?"

"That's not fair," I whispered.

"I think it's completely fair." Piper pushed herself to her feet. "Don't worry. You won't need to help me anymore."

"Piper, wait—"

The door slammed on my words. Lisey looked at me like a wounded puppy, eyes accusing. I felt caught, like I'd done something wrong, and I had no idea what to do. Nina was right—I hadn't asked them—but it hadn't been only my idea. We had all wanted to help Piper. I didn't know what had changed. A lump formed in my throat.

"What do you want me to say?" I asked Lisey. I needed to know I wasn't wrong, that we were on the same team.

She just shook her head and then went after Piper. Nina got up from the couch, the space next to me suddenly cold with her absence.

"Nina," I said, pleading. "I—"

She held up a hand, not looking at me. "I'll call you," she said, then slammed the door behind her.

I leaned my head back and stared at the ceiling. How had that gone so wrong? We had all been united; we had a plan. We wanted to save Carlisle. I knew Nina well enough to tell when she didn't want to do something, and I hadn't gotten that from her at all. She didn't believe the mine was haunted, but she knew it was affecting him, and she cared. I knew she did. What had changed?

I sat there watching the sun move across the room until my mother came in, a box clutched against her side. She dropped it onto the couch next to me. "That was outside."

I turned it over and saw that the sender was *Ghost Walk*. My heart lurched and I ripped it open, using my nails and teeth, to reveal ten neatly stacked VHS tapes. They were labeled "MELLIE 1" through "MELLIE 10."

"Nadia!" I said to myself, pumping my fist.

"What is it?" my mom asked.

I debated how much to tell her, then decided maybe honesty was the best policy. "It's tapes of Mellie Harington at her psych appointments. Between Sidney's death and hers."

"Good God, Clémence." She knelt and ripped open the Velcro on her shoes with a little more force than necessary.

"I know, but—it's research."

"For *what*?" She had the same look she'd given me when I'd tried to bleach my hair at fourteen: confused exasperation, with a little disappointment. What did you do, why did you do it, how am I supposed to fix it?

That look made me feel fourteen again, and all I wanted in that moment was for my mom to sigh and smile and say *Well, how can I fix it?* It made me feel like crying. I dropped my gaze to the box in my lap. "Piper's dad is somewhere in the mine and we can't find him. I'm just making sure we don't ignore something that might be a lead."

"Well, doesn't he work down there? How long has he been gone?"

I thought back. "Today will be the third day if he doesn't come home."

She nodded and then pulled the phone off the wall and started dialing.

"What are you doing?" I asked.

"Calling the sheriff," she said. "Where's Piper's mother?"

"Boston."

"Well, we might need to—yes, hello," she said, her back straightening. "What's the process for filing a missing-persons report?" She listened, nodding slightly, tapping her foot. "What if it involves the mine?" She looked at me. "Now I'm on hold."

I watched her nervously. I didn't know what I'd wanted her to do, but this wasn't it. I had a pretty good idea of how this conversation was going to go. I could practically hear Sheriff Nelson saying, *Well, he shouldn't have gone down there if he didn't want to get lost.* He'd closed the mine for a reason, and even with the town council's approval, he probably saw Carlisle as defying him.

"Hi, Marshall," she said after another minute. "It's June Marchand. I—" Her eyes rolled heavenward like she was praying for strength. "I'm actually *not* calling about your son, Sheriff, which I'm sure is a pleasant change of pace. I'm calling about Carlisle Wharton—the man who was hired to check out the mine, yes—he's been down there for about three days now without coming out." In response to some question, she said, "His daughter. No other family members in town."

She started winding the cord around her fist, pulling it like she was going to use it as a garrote.

"Marshall." Her voice was pleading. "It'll be on you, then," she said after a long silence. "You're lucky you always run unopposed."

She slammed the phone into the cradle so hard that it bounced back out and dangled, spinning, from the cord. Then she ran a hand through her hair and blew out a breath.

"That man is such an *asshole*," she said with venom.

"What did he say?"

"Her mom has to file the report. And even when she does, they don't send search parties into the mine, per town policy. Apparently when Carlisle got the job he signed some kind of waiver, so he knew that."

Despair swept through me. The sheriff had a legal excuse not to help us. "So there's just nothing we can do? Piper's dad is just *gone?*"

"He may still come out, Clem." She sat down next to me and put an arm around my shoulders. "All we can do is give it time."

"We can *look* for him," I said, shaking her off and standing. "We can try and *help.*"

"You are absolutely forbidden from going into that mine again." She looked up at me.

"I'll go when you're not home," I said. "Who's going to stop me? All I have to do is get down the ladder and even the sheriff won't come after me."

"Ah, Christ," she muttered. Her skin seemed to draw tighter over her face and I had a sudden, vivid image of what she would look like as an old woman. She dropped her head into her hands.

"Look, I need to watch these tapes," I said, picking up the box. "There might be something here that can help."

"I need coffee," she said through her fingers. "And a new, more obedient child."

"I can help with the first one," I said.

Dr. Lawrence Palmer, M.D.
M. Harington, Session 2
Transcript

MELLIE HARINGTON: I can't explain it. I can't explain it so that you'll understand it. I see him all the time. When I'm sleeping, when I'm awake, when I'm at the market. He's—he's always on fire.

LAWRENCE PALMER: When you say he's on fire, you mean—

HARINGTON: He's burning. He looks at me and I see fire behind his eyes, he opens his mouth to speak to me and all that comes out is smoke. His skin—*(unintelligible)*

PALMER: I'm sorry?

HARINGTON: His skin comes off of him like ash. It drifts to the ground as he moves. No one else can see it.

PALMER: What do you think he's trying to say to you?

HARINGTON: He says it wasn't enough. He says he was trying to *(unintelligible)*.

PALMER: Do you believe him?

HARINGTON: Yes. Yes. He would never. He loved those men. He would never steal from them. He would never hurt them.

PALMER: What do you think happened down there?

HARINGTON: It made them suspect him. It made them all turn against each other. Vinnie Freeman was Sidney's best friend and two days before he died he almost put him in the hospital. Some kind of fight about a missing helmet. Does that sound like best friends to you? Terry Kilgrave stabbed Gil

Orton with a pickax. Missed his heart by *that* much. Terry was married to Gil's *sister*.

PALMER: So it's your view that the mine was responsible for what Sidney did, but also for the way the town reacted to it?

HARINGTON: There's something wrong with that mine.

PALMER: In what way?

HARINGTON: It's not right. It . . . it's not right. It's alive.

PALMER: Alive. Is there any part of you that thinks perhaps the miners are still alive? The empty tunnels, the missing bodies . . . is there a part of you that thinks you'll see Sidney again someday?

HARINGTON: You're not listening. It did this. It killed them.

PALMER: Wren, can you get Mrs. Harington a cup of tea? She's upset.

HARINGTON: They're all dead.

PALMER: *(unintelligible)*

HARINGTON: But they're not gone.

TWENTY

Three hours later, we'd made it through two and a half tapes. Well, I had. My mom had fallen asleep on the couch sometime during the second tape. I had two pages of scribbled notes, the paper damp where I'd pressed my hands into it. I went into the kitchen, put my mouth under the tap, and drank cold metal-tasting water until I felt like I would burst. Then I straightened up and reached for the phone, but before I could take it off the wall it rang. I snatched it up and pressed it to my ear.

"Nina?"

"No," Lisey said. "Listen, you need to come over. Piper can't be alone, she's—she's freaking out. And I think it would be better if we were all here, but I don't know if Nina . . ." She sniffled.

"I think I might know what's going on with her, Lise," I said. "The Mellie tapes came today. One of them, she talked about how all the miners got more and more pissy with each other over time. Like, guys who were totally cool suddenly beating the shit out of each other. Sound familiar?"

"Yeah," Lisey said. Her voice was hesitant.

"Don't you think?"

"I don't know, Clem," she said. "Nina seemed like she had a lot of stuff bottled up."

I leaned my forehead against the wall.

"But," she said, a new note of interest in her voice, "we can't prove it's not the mine, either. Maybe it's enough to get her to apologize."

I sighed. "I really don't know, but we have to try. Are you at your place?"

"Yep," she said. "My parents are leading a mindfulness retreat in Nevada all week."

"Okay," I said. "I'm gonna talk to Nina and then we'll be over. Both of us, I swear. I'll do my best."

"Good luck," she said. "Bring batteries if you have any."

She hung up. I looked at the phone in confusion for a moment and then put it back on the wall. I found a sticky note and a pen and wrote a note: *Going to Nina's and then to Lisey's. Not going into mine yet.* I left Lisey's number at the bottom and stuck the note carefully to the afghan, which my mom had pulled onto her lap. I showered and dressed. I rummaged through the junk drawer and came up with a handful of batteries, which I shoved into my pockets. Then I let myself out silently and knocked on Nina's door.

"The mine is making us fight," I said as soon as she opened it, trying to cut right to the chase before she slammed the door on me.

"Bullshit—"

"I got Mellie's tapes," I said. "She said the miners were turning on each other left and right."

She folded her arms and stared at me.

"You love Piper," I said. "She completes us. We literally made a blood bond with her, which, by the way, was your idea."

She glanced away and down, and I knew it was working.

"She'd do this for you, Nina," I said. "In a heartbeat. You

know she would."

She worked her jaw like she was chewing gum and sighed. "Fine," she said, and came down the steps.

We walked in silence for a bit. I kept trying and failing to form a sentence, and finally I just said, "I'm sorry."

Nina stopped and looked at me. "For what?"

"For everything," I said. "For the college thing, and for not asking if you wanted to do this. I haven't been the greatest friend this summer."

She rolled her eyes. "Clem. You're the best friend, always, which is why it sucks that you don't wanna go to school with me. I hate that I have to lose you if I want to do something different with my life. I'm not mad about Piper, and I do want to help her, and I'm sorry I blew up at both of you. I'm just . . . I guess I'm a little jealous that you'll follow her into the spooky haunted mine."

"I'd follow you into the mine," I said. "I'd follow you anywhere. Just because I'm not going to college doesn't mean I'm never leaving the Basin, okay?"

She bit the inside of her cheek as I continued.

"I don't know for sure what my future looks like, but I know you're in it. Even if I end up living in the weird drawer underneath your tiny, weird dorm-room bed."

She snorted.

"Even if we're apart for a bit while I figure my shit out," I said. "We'll never not be friends, and I'll never not love you more than anyone else."

"You know, you make it really, really hard to be mad at you," she said, offering me her arm. "Ugh. I love you, too."

I looped my arm through hers and we started walking.

TWENTY-ONE

"What if we don't find him this time, either?" Nina asked as we neared the center of town. My stomach rumbled as we walked through the cloud of cherry pie smell that always hovered outside the Half Moon. I cast a brief, longing glance at the doors. We hadn't eaten since that morning, but there wasn't time to stop for dinner.

"We can't keep going down there," I said. "It's not good for us."

"It's really bullshit that the sheriff won't help look for him." Nina jammed her hands into her back pockets. "Like, how is that allowed? Isn't there, like, a duty to serve or whatever? Maybe we should call the FBI or something." She stopped in her tracks. "Wait. Hang on. I've got a better idea."

She broke into a run, through the commons toward the other side of town, and I followed in a swaying half jog. By the time we reached the motel we were both panting, drenched in sweat, and my knee was throbbing so hard I could feel it in my fingertips. We burst in through the front doors and Nina rushed up to the counter.

"Are those ghost hunters still here?" she asked.

Sherlene put her pen down (*she does the crossword in pen*, my brain had time to note) and looked up at her. "Why?"

"We need them," Nina said. Her voice was urgent, just shy

of hysterical. "It's important."

Sherlene made a huffing sound as she picked up the phone and pressed three numbers. "Mr. Carey," she said. "Are you still here?" She listened. "Lovely. Well, I've got some girls here, and they'd like to tell you a story." She nodded and made *mmhmm* sounds for a moment and then hung up and looked at us. "Room one seventeen. He's expecting you."

Glen was waiting in the doorway, drinking a minibar Scotch. He looked like he'd been asleep; he was wearing sweats and a T-shirt with a picture of Ozzy Osbourne biting the head off a bat. Behind him I could see video equipment strewn around the room, a laptop open on the bed. *Probably conked out trying to edit their boring-ass footage*, Nina's voice said in my head. I smothered a laugh.

"That was a shitty trick you pulled, setting me after that Nelson kid," he said. "He was useless."

"I can't be responsible for what you believe," Nina said. "But," she added as he started to open his mouth, "I have a way to make it up to you."

"I'm so sure."

He was older than I'd thought he was when we first saw him. The beret had been hiding a sizable bald spot.

"No, I'm serious." Nina nudged me. I stared at her. I didn't know what her plan here was. "We can take you into the mine."

I bit my cheek to keep from speaking.

"No one's allowed in," he said, squinting at her. "The sheriff was very clear."

"We've been inside twice this summer already," she said in a hushed, conspiratorial tone. "And we have to go back in because there's a missing person in there, and get this—the sheriff knows about it, and he won't do anything."

"Wait, what?"

She nodded. "It's policy. But think of the episode." She framed her hands in a square around his face. "*GhostWatch* becomes the first crew in years to enter the fabled Moon Basin mine, and not only that, they save someone's life in there."

He stroked his goatee as he thought about it. "And what do you get from us?"

"You help us search," Nina said. "We need light—a lot of light—and more eyes. More *tech*. Radar. Night vision, infrared, all that shit you guys have, we need it all."

He folded his arms. "I want to interview the missing person when we find them. In depth."

"Done," Nina said. She saw me start to protest and grabbed me by the wrist, her meaning clear: *Don't.* She had no intention of keeping that promise.

"Let me talk to my crew," he said. "Where can I reach you?"

Nina turned to me. "Do you have any paper? Like, a wrapper or something?"

I started feeling around in my pockets while Glen ducked back into the room. He emerged with a pen and a pad, saying something, but I couldn't hear him over the ringing in my ears. I was staring at the thing in my hand, the thing I'd just pulled out of my pocket. Nina said something to me, her voice muffled like she was underwater, and I turned to her and held my hand out.

She took it out of my palm and held it up, and the three of us stared at it together.

It was a tooth. A human tooth.

"Is that—" Glen started to ask.

"Yes," Nina said. "It is." She grabbed me by the hand as she shoved the tooth into the front pocket of her overalls. "And there's probably more where that came from, which is the mine, obviously, so call us when you decide."

She yanked me away from the door and down the hall, leaving him staring after us.

I stumbled in the parking lot and almost fell. Nina caught me by the elbow and pulled me upright, and then she took me by the shoulders and held me at arm's length. The sun was going down, and the neon sign bathed us in red light.

"Breathe," she said.

"Nina, that's a fucking tooth," I managed to say.

"I know it is," she said. "It's mine."

I jerked away, out of her hands, and then I did fall. I just sat there on the ground, tailbone aching, and stared at her.

"I mean, it's not actually, obviously," she said. "But the mine wants us to think it is." She helped me up.

I squinted at her, absorbing the words. "Did you just say the mine *wants* something?" It was the first time she'd willingly attributed some kind of sentience to it.

"Yes," she said. "I still don't believe it, and I'm working on a rational explanation, but until I find it all I have are the facts: I had some kind of hallucination where I threw all of my teeth into the mine. On the same occasion, in the same place, you also blacked out, hallucinated, and then apparently found and accidentally stole a tooth."

I closed my eyes tightly, trying to process.

"What if it belonged to one of the miners?" I asked.

"It probably did," Nina said. "But that's still a pretty big coincidence."

I felt sick, and my knee ached. I felt like I was sliding over the edge of something, scratching at the ground trying to stop myself, and at any moment I would slip all the way over and fall.

"Let's go," Nina said, tugging at my arm. "Lisey and Piper are waiting."

East Coast: Ghost to Ghost, Episode 17
Unused Footage

(A young woman leans against a low stone wall. The trees above her shift in the wind, dappling her face with sunlight, and MARNIE WILLIAMS keeps having to move her so that her eyes aren't shadowy pits.)

WILLIAMS: So this is it.

AYELET NADIR: *(nervous laughter)* Yep. In the flesh.

WILLIAMS, to camera: The Moon Basin River Bridge. The very same bridge that Mellie Harington jumped from when she tragically ended her life.

(Pained embarrassment flashes across NADIR's face.)

WILLIAMS, flourishing mic: And what is your connection with this bridge, Ayelet?

NADIR: I used to sleepwalk. A lot. Almost every night until I was probably twelve.

(WILLIAMS widens her eyes at the camera, rolling her head toward NADIR. The shot zooms in slightly.)

WILLIAMS: How old were you when that started?

NADIR: Nine. I remember because the first time it happened I had a broken arm and I got the cast hung up on the door frame. *(She laughs.)* My older sister dared me to roll down the hill into the Sugar Bowl, it's like this dried-up riverbed in Old Town that's filled with ash—anyway, I hit a tree root on the way down, busted my elbow, blacked out for a second. I had to just lie there in the bottom of the wash for, like, half an hour while she ran to get help. So that night, even though I'm all drugged up, I somehow get up and try to leave the house. The next night I didn't get stuck and I made it all the way into the woods. Every night I got a little farther west. My parents had to put a lock on the door. *(She grins.)* My sister had to share a room with me so I'd still be able to get out if there was a fire or something. Serves her right, huh? She hated it. She'd find me just standing in front of the locked door every morning.

WILLIAMS: When was the first time you made it all the way to the bridge?

NADIR: High school, I think. It stopped for a while, kind of when I hit puberty, and we all got less careful with the lock.

WILLIAMS, *nodding sagely*: I see. And what happened that night?

NADIR: I woke up and I was standing right here. *(She pats the top of the stone wall.)*

NADIR: Just in my sweats, bare feet. Standing on the edge of the bridge.

WILLIAMS: And were you frightened?

NADIR: Yeah, I mean . . . yeah.

WILLIAMS: What did you feel in that moment?

NADIR: I don't know. Nothing, I guess. I've been doing it my whole life. This is just the farthest I've ever gotten.

WILLIAMS, *disappointed, pausing to adjust NADIR's position*: I see. You didn't feel any, mmm, any sort of presence? Anything to suggest that maybe you were led here?

NADIR: Not really.

(WILLIAMS wipes a hand down her face and then pinches the bridge of her nose the way people do when they're trying to convey annoyance without speaking.)

WILLIAMS: Didn't it frighten you to see that you were

standing on the bridge where Mellie Harington took her own life?

NADIR, *nonplussed:* Well, yeah. It's—I mean, the river's really deep.

WILLIAMS: Do you feel you might have been drawn here by her spirit? Perhaps your troubled soul reached out and found hers?

NADIR: Not . . . really.

(She tugs at the edge of her shirt, looking out over the water. WILLIAMS makes a heroic last-ditch attempt.)

WILLIAMS: Do you think you would have taken your own life that night if you hadn't woken up?

NADIR: I think I would have died. But I don't think it counts as suicide if you just sleepwalk off a bridge. I mean, Mellie was awake, right? Everybody says she jumped. I would have just kind of tipped over.

(WILLIAMS sighs for a very long time before the tape cuts off.)

TWENTY-TWO

Lisey answered the door with her cordless pink princess phone in hand.

"Why is there some dude named Glen calling for you?"

Nina waved her hand. "Tell him to stay in the motel room and we'll call him back. Wait—ask him if he's in or out."

Lisey put the phone back to her ear. "She wants to know if you're in or out." She nodded. "Okay. I guess we'll call you back?" She put the phone on a side table and motioned for us to follow her.

"New painting?" Nina asked as we walked down the hallway.

"Please don't ask," Lisey said.

"Well, now you have to tell us." I looked at the painting, which was an abstract mash of blue and red, fading to purple in places.

"My parents went to some couples art therapy thing, and they had everyone cover themselves in paint, and then they gave each couple a canvas . . ." Lisey shuddered. "You get it."

"Your parents are truly wild," Nina said. "Whatever happened to painting a garden gnome while you drink wine?"

Lisey laughed. "At least they haven't started doing, like, erotic sculptures."

"Not yet, anyway." I looked around the living room, which was lit entirely by salt lamps and candles. It felt soft, friendly, like a night-light. The stained-glass appliqués in the windows seemed to glow, and for a moment I wanted nothing more than to curl up in the deep, tufted couch and pull a blanket over my head until morning.

The basement was blessedly cool and dark, the smell of palo santo curling toward us from the incense burner in the corner. Piper was asleep in a beanbag chair. Even unconscious, she looked miserable.

"So what's the Glen thing about?" Lisey asked in a low murmur.

"Ghost hunters," Nina said. "They're going to help us."

"I found a tooth," I volunteered. As they looked at me, I realized it wasn't the time to say that. I was having a hard time staying focused on the conversation.

"Help us do what?" Lisey demanded.

"Find Carlisle," Nina said.

"We're going to take them *with* us?" Lisey's voice was loud enough that time that Piper lifted her head.

"What's happening?"

"I had an idea," Nina said. "And we need more people to test it. But I wondered if we could, like, dilute the mine's . . . thing. Its influence. Like, if there's only one person down there—like Carlisle—they're getting hit with the full force of whatever it is. But if there's more of us, then it has to spread itself thinner, and maybe that keeps us safe. Safer, at least."

"That . . . kind of makes sense," Piper said, rubbing her eyes.

"But we're risking everyone that we take down there," Lisey said. "Including us."

Nina glared at her. "Were you not the one arguing with me *last night* about—"

"No, I know," she said. "I just don't like making that decision for people who don't know what might be at stake."

"So we tell them," Nina said. "They'll be thrilled. This is, like, their white whale."

"Yeah, they *want* stuff to happen to them," I finally managed to say. "For the show."

Lisey frowned, but I could see the wheels turning in her head. "It might work."

"They have so much equipment that we can use," Nina said. "They have, like, sonar and heat sensors and shit. It's absolutely our best chance to find him."

"What if we still can't find him?" I asked, trying not to look at Piper.

"We get her mom to file a missing persons report," Nina said, "and then we get our new friend Glen to put this episode out and tell the whole country that Sheriff Nelson didn't even bother to search for him. Then every ghost hunter and true crime weirdo for miles will come down on the Basin like a tidal wave, and then we finally get a real, official search party in there. Dogs and scanners and whatever the fuck else they need, and then we find him."

Piper was nodding slowly, looking more and more awake by the second. "This could work, Nina. This could really work."

"I know." Nina sat down on the floor next to Piper's beanbag and took her hand. "I'm sorry about last night."

"I'm sorry I got you guys into this," Piper said.

"Well, we're in it, for better or worse, so we're gonna be in it all the way."

Piper's smile was small, but it was real, and it warmed me from the inside out.

"Hang on," Lisey said. "Did you say you found a *tooth*?"

Nina pulled it out of her pocket and held it up like a jeweler inspecting a diamond.

"Whoa." Lisey took it and brought it so close to her face that it made her slightly cross-eyed.

"Probably one of the miners'," Nina said. "But our first thought was my weird vision of me losing all my teeth, which I think is what the mine wanted."

Lisey looked at her, eyes narrowing slightly. "Who are you, and what did you do with Nina? Is this *Invasion of the Body Snatchers*?"

Nina sighed. "Listen, if everyone keeps giving me shit for it, I'm gonna lose the tiny, tiny amount of belief that I *might* have. So just be cool, okay?"

Lisey giggled. The sound loosened something in my chest. "I think we're owed at least a little more teasing. You were on *such* a high horse."

Nina rolled her eyes, picked the tooth off Lisey's palm, and tucked it back into her pocket.

"Can we go to my house before we call Glen back?" Piper asked, extricating herself from the beanbag. "I want to look through my dad's stuff again and see if there's anything else that could help us."

"Yeah, sure," Lisey said. "Let's go before it gets any later."

We climbed the stairs out of the basement and as we emerged into the warm night air, I felt the first small flicker of hope.

American Ghosts, Episode 35
Unused Footage

(A group of school-age children stand in front of the motel, waving and cheering. In front of them is a banner that says WELCOME GHOST HUNTERS.*)*

(The camera sweeps down the hill into the valley. From a distance, Moon Basin appears to glow faintly. As the shot moves through the outskirts of town, the light grows brighter and colder, until the camera comes to rest on the shuttered windows of a local residence. The picture shudders faintly and the camera turns, panning across the glowing street. A pack of coyotes stands motionless in the middle of the road, heads lowered, tongues lolling. The lead coyote raises its head and its eyes flash strangely in the alien blue light.)

(A woman opens the door to her backyard, revealing a tiny garden. The camera follows her out into the little grove, where she kneels and pushes aside a flowering shrub to reveal a small stone marker. Engraved on it is the name BLUE. The woman's eyes fill with tears as she looks back at the camera.)

(The old hospital. Ash drifts against the walls, in the corners. The hallways are dark and shadowy. Something flickers in the corner of the screen, but when the camera tries to center it, it is only a pillar of smoke, twisting away.)

(A thin, pale girl standing still enough to be a statue, arms outstretched, crows fluttering down to land on her delicate wrists.)

TWENTY-THREE

We moved all the research material out of Carlisle's office, where the lamps had burned out, into the hallway and upstairs bedrooms. Nina tore page after page out of his notebooks and laid them out side by side, searching for some kind of larger picture. Piper dug through boxes while Lisey looked through a folder of maps—they all seemed to show the mine, but none of them matched. There were scribbled notations, tiny symbols scattered across them that I didn't understand.

Lisey peered over my shoulder. "What is that?"

"Where?" I asked.

She pointed at some writing in the corner of the page I held that had been double boxed with deep lines.

"It looks like ingredients," I said. "Kind of. Like if you look at the back of a Twinkie or whatever. Just all chemicals."

She nodded and tapped her chin, reaching for a lock of hair.

"Guys," Piper said. We all turned to see her holding up the little recorder that Anson Perry had given her to give to her dad.

"He only had it for a few days before—" She clicked a button and then another, and then Carlisle's voice, tinny and small, started speaking to us.

"I don't know if it can be done, but I think it has to," he murmured. "Can't think about it when I'm down there, though. Gets cloudy. Gets . . . crowded."

215

A rustle, a metallic scrape. What might have been the flick of a lighter.

"Was he *smoking*?" Piper whispered, horrified. "He *never*."

On the recording, Carlisle laughed a weird, wobbly laugh. "My heart wants it filled in. There's no concrete evidence that it needs to be, but something about it . . . No one's supposed to go inside it, but it feels like—it feels like they aren't really trying to keep people out." A staticky sound shrouded his next words, but the ones after that were clear. "It's incredible that it's still completely accessible. It's almost—"

He laughed, sounding embarrassed.

"It's almost like it wants people to go down there."

His voice started to change.

"Like an open mouth, like a Venus flytrap . . . it's waiting."

The tone deepened, warped; he sounded like a slow smile with too many teeth. "They must be allowed to go down. They must be *encouraged* to go down. Down below the cold, dead ash and dirt, into the warm embrace of the living earth—"

The sound of a door opening scared Piper into dropping the recorder. Carlisle's voice was muffled as she scooped it up and turned the speaker back toward us.

"Cub!" he yelled, distant like he'd pulled the recorder away from his face. "That you?"

There was another burst of static and then he spoke once more, his voice low and urgent, but unmistakably *him*.

"It has to be fast," he said. "Take it by surprise. I'll have to—"

The recorder beeped a few times and then died.

"How could he sound so normal and then so *off*?" Piper murmured. "What was happening to him?"

"There's this fungus that bugs get," Lisey said. We all turned as one to stare at her. "No, listen. It takes over their brains and it makes them, like, climb up the tallest plant they can find and then they die there. And then the fungus spores, like, blow away and disperse all over the place, and that's what the fungus wants."

"Okay," Piper said.

"It makes the bug think it *wants* to climb the plant," Lisey said.

"So my dad is the bug?" Piper asked with more than a little skepticism. "And the mine is the fungus?"

"It's not a perfect metaphor," she said with a touch of irritation. "But think about it like an infection. You don't go from being totally fine to being, like, dead of Spanish flu or whatever. There's stages. Your dad's sick, Pipes. He's been getting sicker, but—"

"Good days and bad days," Nina said.

"But the end goal is for him to bring other people down there," I said. "And what happens then?"

Lisey shrugged. "The zombie bug fungus doesn't really have a plan. It just wants to keep sending more of itself into the world. Maybe the mine is like that. It just takes the world into itself instead."

"How do you get rid of the fungus?" Piper asked.

"I don't know," Lisey said.

Nina reached out and tapped a fingernail on one of the maps, where a single word was written and circled: *EXPLOSION*.

"You kill it," she said.

TWENTY-FOUR

"You think my dad wants to blow up the mine."
Piper stared at Nina.

"I was trying to figure out what all these maps were." Nina looked down at the papers strewn all over the floor. "They're all, like, *almost* the same, but they have these little marks—see—and they're all in different places. But this one"—she pointed at the one I'd been holding—"this one looks different. Decisive. This one looks like a plan."

The marks were firm red Xs, slashed into various points of the map like wounds. There were numbers next to each of them, small decimal-pointed kilogram measurements. She slid her finger over to the boxed list of chemicals that Lisey and I had been looking at.

"And this looks like a bomb," she said.

Piper's chin was trembling as she took the sheet of paper from my hand and inspected it. She picked up the recorder and pressed it to her chest.

"He knew it was happening," she said. "That's why he said he had to do it fast, take it by surprise. He couldn't—" She made a tiny sound in her throat. "He couldn't stay himself for long, and I bet every time he went under it saw what he wanted to do." A tear dripped from her face onto the paper. One of the red slashes began to bleed. "He's not coming back out."

I looked at the first map, the one that had *EXPLOSION* printed on it in block letters. "I bet this is where Sidney's bomb was. It didn't work. Carlisle must have been down there all this time trying to figure out how to do it right, where to put the explosives and how much to use."

"They'd have to be connected," Piper said, blotting her eyes. "So they would all go off at once. Otherwise it wouldn't be strong enough."

"Do you think—do you think—how far do you think he got?" Lisey asked, clearly formulating a thought as she spoke. "Do you think he built the bombs? Do you think he put any of them down there yet? Would we have seen them?"

"How hot does it have to be for something to detonate accidentally?" Nina asked. "He probably couldn't leave them in there, like, long term. So they might not be in there, but they might be in the house somewhere."

"Hang on," I said. My chest was getting tight. "Are we talking about blowing up the mine right now?"

"Aren't we?" Lisey asked.

"You want *us* to do it?" My voice cracked.

"Who else?" Nina's tone had just a trace of anger in it.

"What if he hasn't made the bombs yet?" I asked, trying to stall while I slowed down my breathing.

"Maybe he got the supplies, though," Piper suggested.

My lungs burned. "We cannot *make a bomb*," I whispered.

"Everyone hush," Lisey said. "We have to make a plan. Attack, remember?" She rearranged herself so she was kneeling, then sat back onto her heels. "We're going in one more time, with those hunters. We're gonna be prepared this time, and we're gonna do it right." She put the sheet with the Xs in the center of our little group, and we all looked at it. "While we're in there, we're going to be pirates."

"X marks the spot," Piper murmured.

"We put a mark everywhere he did," Lisey said with some satisfaction. "All its weak points." She looked at Piper as she continued, "We come back out with or without him." She chewed on her lip for a second.

Piper nodded. "Yeah."

"Then we make the next plan." She looked smaller than usual in that moment, subdued in a way that didn't sit well with me. She seemed not paler, exactly, but less substantial somehow.

"Lise," I said. "Are you okay?"

She looked at me and smiled, a quick puppety jerk of the lips that didn't reassure me. "I should eat something before we go back down there," she said, looking faintly ill at the thought.

"We all have to eat and pack and get some rest," Nina said. "I'll call Glen and let him know when it's going down tomorrow. Here, let's—" She started sweeping all the papers back into a loose pile, which she then picked up and clasped to her body. "Let's go to my house, eat a fuck-ton of Tater Tots, and make sure there's nothing in here that we missed."

Honey Martine: Medium, M.D., Episode 22
Unused Footage

(HONEY MARTINE stands in the backyard of a suburban residence. Holes of varying depths and sizes have been dug in the grass in no apparent pattern. The homeowner, RORY CORLISS, paces back and forth as he talks.)

CORLISS: See? Look. I don't know how it keeps moving, but it's down there somewhere. Little bastard. It's got a den somewhere in this yard and I'm going to find it, I'm gonna drag it out of there and put its tiny head on a stick. It's scaring my wife.

MARTINE: And what is it, exactly, Mr. Corliss?

CORLISS: Not sure. Some kind of rodent, I guess, whatever burrows.

MARTINE: And you've never seen it?

CORLISS: No. But I had to uninstall the damn motion lights back here because they come on every half hour, every single night, for the past eight months. It's like it waits until they go out to pop up again. Like it's doing it on purpose.

MARTINE: And you're sure it's an animal that's doing this?

CORLISS: What do you mean?

MARTINE: Well, most of the stories about Moon Basin indicate that there aren't a lot of, mmm, prey animals in the area.

CORLISS, *somewhat confused*: Well, sure. Because of the coyotes. But what—

MARTINE: It seems to me you might be overlooking a more likely scenario.

CORLISS: What?

MARTINE: Mr. Corliss, have you ever considered that you are being haunted?

CORLISS: Good Lord, no. What?

MARTINE: Mr. Corliss—Rory—may I call you Rory? I have to tell you I'm getting a very strong supernatural vibration from this house. A *malevolent* one.

(CORLISS seems at a loss for words.)

MARTINE: Rory, I'm prepared to offer you a service that I don't extend to most of the people I see in my line of work. I'm prepared to perform an exorcism for you right now, today, for less than the cost of the work it will take to repair your yard.

CORLISS, *after intense consideration*: I thought you couldn't do exorcisms on a ghost.

MARTINE: Well, ah, hmm. Yes. You can't, usually, but because I am able to communicate with the dead, I am able to . . . convince them to move on, as it were.

CORLISS: So not really an exorcism. Just kind of askin' it to leave.

MARTINE: It's still a highly dangerous endeavor, Mr. Corliss. Especially given that this spirit feels *so* angry.

CORLISS: Does it, now. Who does it say it is?

(MARTINE pauses. She puts a hand to her temple, as if receiving a transmission.)

MARTINE: She says—

(CORLISS makes a noise like a game show buzzer.)

CORLISS: Look, lady. I appreciate the hustle, and I respect it, but the only ghost in this house is my gramps, and he's about as far from angry as you can possibly get.

MARTINE: I—well, I—it's possible that there are multiple—

CORLISS: Look, I'll do you a favor. Go talk to Cassiopeia

Bossert. Anyone in this town needs an exorcism, it's her.

MARTINE, *scribbling rapidly in a notebook she has produced from somewhere in her tentlike dress*: Cassiopeia . . . Bossert . . .

CORLISS: Mm. Daughter's all kinds of kooky. Cass had to pen her up when she was a kid so she'd stay away from the damn mine. Now if you don't mind, I've got a gopher to hunt. *(He turns back to her.)* Oh, and Doctor? I'd leave the big-ass crucifix in the car. She's more of a new age gal.

TWENTY-FIVE

We met at the mine the next morning. Glen had offered us a ride in the *GhostWatch* van, but we told him we'd walk from Nina's place. It helped us work out at least a little of the jitters we were all feeling, and by the time we got there, we were feeling almost optimistic.

"This is my dad." Piper pulled a framed picture out of her bag and handed it to Glen. I caught a glimpse as he gave it back. It was the two of them in front of a Disneyland castle, identical delighted grins, mouse ears and all. She stared at it for a moment before putting it away.

"He's been in there for almost a week now," she said. "I don't know if he has any food or water, but he's got a ton of equipment with him. Maybe your shit will pick it up? A lot of it is magnetic. I don't know." She ran a knuckle under one eye. "His name is Carlisle."

It took Glen and his camera guy a good fifteen minutes to assemble everything once we'd all climbed down into the mine. He looked nervous, but he struck a pose next to the ladder and made a rolling motion with one hand. The cameraman gave him a thumbs-up.

"I'm Glen Carey," he said, his voice half an octave deeper than usual. "I'm standing now in the entry tunnel of the Moon Basin mine. No ghost hunter has set foot down here since the crew of *Grave Encounters* was rescued. The town sheriff doesn't know we're here. What he *does* know . . ."

He paused, clearly counting in his head. One . . . two . . . *drama.*

". . . is that there's a man lost down here. That's right, *Ghost-Watchers.* A town resident is missing, and it's been five days since he was last seen. We know he's down here, and so does the sheriff, but he's refused to search for him. He's too *afraid.* But *we're* not."

Nina made a quiet gagging sound. I elbowed her. If he had to do more than one take, we'd never get started.

"We're about to begin the search for Carlisle Wharton, who moved to Moon Basin just two months ago," Glen said. "We've got all our state-of-the-art equipment with us. We'll be using all our tools to communicate with the spirits in the mine, asking them to help us find him. The only question now is, Are you ready?"

He turned and took three big steps down the tunnel, just far enough for him to vanish into the dark. The cameraman yelled, "Perfect, come on back," and Glen jogged toward us.

"Okay," he said. "We'll go me first, with the Handycam, then Mitch, then you girls, so you're not in view of the camera. Unless—have you changed your minds about appearing in the episode?"

"Absolutely not," Nina said. We'd already told him we had one goal, finding Carlisle; we didn't need Glen constantly maneuvering us around and asking questions.

"All righty, then. Let's get a move on."

We filed into the tunnel. It was weird to see it so lit up. It almost looked fake, like a movie set, all the rough edges and clods of dirt thrown into sharp relief.

"Carlisle!" Glen yelled. He had good projection, I'd give him that. "Carlisle Wharton! My name is Glen Carey! I'm with the television program *GhostWatch*! I'm here to rescue you!"

"Now you can gag," I whispered to Nina.

It was hard to see around Glen and the camera guy with his rig, which might have been why it felt less scary in there. It was sort of like being stuck in line at the supermarket, but underground. I didn't have to look down those blank, empty tunnels.

"Dad!" Piper yelled. "Can you hear me?"

"We can't have you yelling in the shot unless you agree to be in the episode," Camera Guy said, almost in a singsong.

"Edit me out, asshole," she snapped. "DAD!"

"Fucking teenagers," he muttered, fiddling with the camera. I squeezed Piper's hand and we all yelled for Carlisle as we moved deeper into the mine.

I hadn't worn a watch this time. I didn't know how long it had been when Glen stopped walking.

"What is that?" he asked, his voice hollow. "Who—what is that?"

"What do you see?" Lisey called. "We can't see."

"It's an animal," he said. He was starting to sound fuzzy, almost sleepy. Like he was drugged. "It's an animal . . . with yellow eyes."

My heart gave a hard thump in my chest. Could a coyote have gotten down here somehow? Was it alone, or was there a pack somewhere deeper in the tunnels? What would they *eat* down here? The walls drew toward me as I started to panic.

"Glen." Lisey kept her tone even, but something in her voice spiked my fear even higher. She sounded like she knew what he was seeing. "Don't look at it."

"It's smiling at me," he said.

Lisey reached out and grabbed the back of the cameraman's shirt, pulling him toward us. "Stop him."

Camera Guy shook her hand away and made a shushing motion. She ducked under his arm and darted forward, yanking at Glen's arm. He spun around, eyes vacant and murderous, and raised the Handycam like he was going to club her with it. She cringed back and Camera Guy shoved her aside, into the wall.

"Glen," he said. "Dude, what—"

"You can only see it through the camera," Glen said, putting his eye to the viewfinder and turning back to the tunnel. "A real paranormal phenomenon."

"Okay, well, I'm not seeing it on the big camera, so I'm not sure—"

"Wait," Glen said, voice suddenly full of anguish. "Wait, don't go."

He started walking forward. Then he started jogging. Camera Guy ran after him for a few yards, then slowed to a stop as Glen disappeared out of the beam of his light.

"Glen," he called. There was no response from the tunnel. I could hear a low chuckling sound like slow-moving liquid.

"Lisey, what was that?" I heard the fear in my voice and tried to dial it back. "Are there coyotes down here?"

"It wasn't a coyote." She tucked her hair behind one ear and looked at me seriously. "I promise. But I think—"

"Guys," Nina whispered, glancing in the direction Glen had gone. "Now's our chance." She pulled Carlisle's map out of her pocket. "Quick, c'mon. The first spot is this way—" She turned and ducked down a side tunnel, and we followed. She trotted along, checking against the map, until she found the arched support she was looking for. She pulled a stick of chalk from her fanny pack and scrawled an X high up on the beam. "Let's keep moving."

We had plotted the route from point to point, avoiding doubling back as much as possible. We made our way deeper into the mine, leaving our marks as we went. The heat got worse, closer somehow. It felt like a towel soaked in boiling water wrapped tightly around my body. The air in my lungs was too hot. I kept listening for footsteps, for animal breathing, but all I could hear was my own blood rushing in my ears.

A man yelled in the distance. The voice was so distorted I couldn't tell for sure who it was. "Should we go back?" I asked. "Maybe they need help."

"Carlisle needs help," Lisey murmured, shining the light around.

"Maybe they found him," I said. "What if that was him yelling?"

Nina wordlessly held up a walkie-talkie, and I nodded. They could reach us if they needed to. We soldiered forward, all of us drenched in sweat. Ash coated our skin.

We were maybe halfway done with the marks when the walkie clicked.

"Girls?" It was Glen's voice, sounding surprisingly calm. "I need you back now, please."

"On our way," Nina lied, consulting the map and turning into a new branch of the mine.

"Now, please," he repeated, an edge to the words this time. "I need you back now." There was a series of clicks. "I can see you."

"What?" Nina looked at the walkie. "How?"

"I know where you are." His voice was getting slower, deeper, like his throat was clogged somehow. "I'll come get you myself."

Piper grabbed the walkie out of Nina's hand. "Have you found my dad? Do you see my dad?"

A burst of static, and the little device went silent. Piper pressed the buttons frantically, twisting the frequency knob, but Glen was done speaking, at least for now. She made a movement like she was going to throw the walkie, but at the last second dropped her arm to let it hang at her side. "Fuck."

"Let's just keep moving." Lisey tugged at her arm gently. "We're getting close to the end of the marks."

Piper pulled her arm away, but she started walking again. We followed Nina through the tunnels, marking through the Xs on the map as we left them on the walls. The back of my neck prickled like something was watching me, but I never turned around.

"Piper?"

The word blared out of the walkie-talkie so suddenly, so loudly that we all jumped. Nina dropped the chalk and swore, scooping it back into her hand as Piper fumbled with the walkie.

"Dad?" Her voice was shaking. "Dad, is that you?"

Nina turned the map so I could see it. Only one *X* left. She tilted her head like she wanted to walk away, but I held up my hand. *Not yet.* I was watching Piper. She pressed the walkie to her ear, eyes wide and desperate.

"Dad?" she asked again. "Can you hear me?"

"I know where you are," the walkie spat. "I can see you."

Lisey pulled at Piper's hand. "Turn it off," she whispered. "Please."

Piper just held it tighter. "Dad, say something. Tell us where you are and we'll find you. Just tell us—"

"You have to come down," he said. "All the way down to the bottom."

"The bottom of the mine?"

"All the way down," he repeated. His voice was thick and clotted, almost bubbling out of the speaker. "Then we can be together."

"It's not your dad, Pipes." Lisey spoke as gently as she could. "You know it's not."

Piper shook her head, a low moan building in her throat.

Nina suddenly turned and sprinted away. She was going to make the last mark, and I didn't want to leave Piper, but I couldn't let her do it alone. I ran after her.

"I thought you'd stay with them," she said as I caught up. It hurt, but I deserved it.

"Let's leave this X and get the hell out of here," I said.

She nodded and slashed the mark onto the wooden beam. "After you."

We ran back to the others. Piper was sitting on the ground, her body curled around the walkie-talkie like she was protecting it. Lisey stood over her, hands moving through her hair in a blur.

"It's not her dad." Lisey looked at us. "It—"

"It was my dad."

We all turned to look at Piper. She lifted her head. "It was my dad. Whatever that thing on the radio is now, it used to be him. I can feel it."

"You always were too smart for your own good." The radio crackled and it sounded like laughter. "He tried to fight, but he lost." The voice was joined by another, many others, and when all of them spoke in unison it was like the buzzing of a gigantic mechanical wasp. "The way all of you will lose."

Fear churned inside me, and somewhere in my throat it turned to anger. "Fuck you!" I spat. "You have no idea what's coming for you, you—"

Nina grabbed my wrist so tight I could feel her nails puncture my skin. "Stop talking to it," she whispered. "It wants you to engage. It wants you to make it real."

"*Stop talking to it,*" the voices whined at her. "You're just as afraid as she is."

She shook her head, visibly fighting the urge to reply. She held out her hand to Piper and yanked her up off the ground.

"We need to go," Lisey whispered. "We need to go right now."

Piper dropped the radio, intending to leave it, but I picked it back up. "In case we get lost."

We started moving, holding on to each other, following the beam of Lisey's flashlight.

"It's inside you now," the radio hissed. "You'll never leave. You belong down here with the rest of them."

I turned the little wheel, searching for a different channel, but the voices kept talking even as it cycled. "If you were strong you'd stay down here. You'd fight. Pitiful. Sad little girls running away, back to the light, can't save Daddy, can't save themselves—"

Piper snatched the radio out of my hand and raised it above her head. "Keep talking," she snarled. "Keep fucking talking."

The voices *screamed*, the sound vibrating in my jawbone, making my teeth ache. The insectile whir of it crawled into my ears, into my brain, and I could feel my mind shivering apart. "Do it, Piper," I managed to say over the din. The screaming got louder; the ground started to tilt under my feet. Piper bared her teeth and lifted the radio higher and then—

There was a small, tinny pop before everything went silent. Glen's voice crackled out of the radio.

"Can anyone hear me?"

"Glen?" Piper's voice was hoarse. "Glen, is that you?"

"Yes, it's fucking me, where the hell are you girls? I've been yelling my head off into this frickin' radio for the last half an hour. Is Mitch with you?"

"No." I leaned toward the radio. "Where are you?"

"Fuck if I know," he said. "I don't have a goddamn heat signature on anything for almost a full mile. It's like being down here is fucking up the equipment."

"Can you make it back to the entrance?" Nina asked.

"I—tunnel—farther down." The transmission was garbled.

Piper shook the radio. "Glen, you're not coming in clear. Go toward the entrance, okay? Don't go any deeper into the mine. Okay? Glen?"

Nothing answered.

"Fuck." Nina started walking again, picking up speed rapidly. "Come on. We have to get back aboveground."

The radio clicked again.

"Goddamn it, Piper, just throw it already," Nina said. "I'm tired of that fucking thing."

"It's back," Glen's voice said. "I recognize the yellow eyes."

"Glen, just go toward the entrance, don't follow it—" Piper broke into a jog, trying to keep the signal from fading.

"I have to film it," he said dreamily. "It's proof."

Then, from behind us, so close I could have touched him, he said, "It's waiting."

Then he screamed.

Lisey swung the light around, trying to find him, but there was nothing there. His voice wasn't coming from the radio. It was too clear, too loud, too present.

Run, something in my head said. The screaming started to wobble like a top about to fall, and that low liquid chuckling slid by my ear so close I could feel hot stale breath on my skin. I grabbed for Nina and the others, yanked them toward me, and whispered, "Run!"

We ran. We ran through the warm, seething darkness, crashing into the sides of tunnels and each other. I fell and got up and kept running, and after a thousand years we found the ladder and the sound of Glen screaming was still right behind us. I scrambled up the steps and I felt my knee leaving a kiss-print of blood every time it touched the earth. Then finally I was out, crawling across solid ground, pulling myself away from the mine as fast as I could. The four of us stumbled to our feet and ran, and the screaming became a high, jagged giggling. It chased us, snapping at our heels, until we reached the road and the empty *GhostWatch* van.

Piper sat down hard beside the van and we crowded around her, trying to calm ourselves down. After a while she took a deep, shuddering breath and looked at us.

"My dad's never getting out of there," she whispered. A tear cut a track down her ash-caked cheek. "He's gone."

I reached for her hand. I didn't know what to say. She was right.

"That laugh," she said. "The eyes. I think . . . I think Glen saw my dad. The coyote-thing version of him."

"We have to go back," I whispered, almost to myself. "We can't leave them down there."

Piper sniffled. "I don't think I can go down there again." She stood up slowly. "When my dad was talking to me, I . . . I wanted to go to him. I could feel him looking for me, and I wanted to find him. I'm afraid—" She wiped her eyes. "I'm afraid if we go back in I won't make it out."

"We don't have to go back." Lisey saw me look at her in confusion. "Think about it. It never keeps out-of-towners. It'll spit them out eventually."

It was surprisingly callous coming from her, but she wasn't wrong.

"We still have to go back to place the explosives," Nina said.

Piper looked at her sharply. "We don't even know if we *have* any explosives. I just really don't think any of us should be going down there anymore."

"Pipes, if we don't kill it, I don't think just staying out of it will be enough." Nina's brow creased. "It *wants* us."

"It's like Sauron," Lisey said. "We put the Ring on too many times and now it can see us."

I thought about that flaming, searching eye opening wide, looking up at us from the bottom of the mine. I shivered. "So what do we do?"

"We need to get far enough away from the mine that it loses its grip on us." Nina folded up the map, shoved it into her pocket, and started walking. We fell into step beside her. "Right? Proximity and exposure, like Clem said. We've been exposed. Way too much. The only thing we have any control over now is how close we are to it."

"So we just leave?" I asked. "Just go away from it?"

"And then what?" Lisey's hand made its way into the nest of her hair.

"I don't know," Nina said.

"How will we know?" Piper asked. "That we're far enough away?"

I thought about what Nadia had said about living next to a waterfall. "We'll feel it. Or, I guess, we won't feel it. Like in the clearing."

"And then what?" Lisey twisted a single strand of hair around her fingertip tighter and tighter, watching as the skin turned purple. "We just never come back?"

"Not *never*." I looked at Nina. "Probably not. Right?"

"I don't know," she said. "We might not be able to."

"But we can try. We just have to get out first." I was trying not to think about Mellie, who drove away from Moon Basin once a week to see her psychiatrist. I was trying not to think about the fact that she'd died here anyway.

"If my dad's really gone, then there's nothing keeping me here," Piper said, her shoulders slumping. She looked utterly defeated. "Except you guys, so I'm in."

"We can't think about it like we're leaving forever." My mom's face flashed across my mind. "Because then we won't be able to make ourselves do it."

"Just a trip," Nina said. "Just a road trip. We take it one day at a time, one hour at a time, one minute at a time. We figure it out as we go."

"Like that movie we saw on Valentine's." I was ping-ponging from thought to thought, unable to focus on anything for too long. "Britney Spears and her girls drive to LA, or whatever."

"Exactly," Nina said.

"I didn't see that," Piper said. The normalcy of the response was so absurd under the circumstances that a tiny, wild laugh burbled out of me. I put a hand over my mouth.

"They don't have a plan, they just go," Nina said. "It's actually kind of perfect. They're just, like, about the journey. We can do that."

"When?" Piper's voice was hardly more than a whisper.

"As soon as we possibly can," Lisey answered.

We were almost all the way to Lisey's when the *GhostWatch* van roared by us, clipped a mailbox, and slewed onto the road leading out of the valley.

GhostWatch, Episode 18
Unused Footage

(Black screen, staticky audio, as if the camera has been thrown into a bag without even being turned off, by someone in a hurry.)

GLEN CAREY: Holy fuck. Holy fuckin' shit. What the fuck was that? What—*(muffled cry).*

UNIDENTIFIED: We have to go back for the equipment.

CAREY: Fuck the fucking equipment, dude, I am not stopping this van until it fucking stops itself.

UNIDENTIFIED: *(unintelligible)*

CAREY: You didn't see its fuckin' eyes, man. You were messing with the Geiger counter, no, with that stupid spirit box—

UNIDENTIFIED: It works.

CAREY: We didn't need a fucking spirit box to hear that thing. It talked.

UNIDENTIFIED: What did it say?

CAREY: *(unintelligible)* sounded like it was chewing on glass.

UNIDENTIFIED: I think those girls have my goggles.

CAREY: They can fucking keep them.

(Long, loud blast of a car horn.)

CAREY: Get out of the FUCKING WAY, ASSHOLE!

UNIDENTIFIED: *(car horn)* Most of a paycheck, you know?

CAREY: Oh, now, what's this jackass doing? *(louder)* Get off me, dude.

(An engine roars. There is a remarkably loud crunching sound.)

UNIDENTIFIED: He rear-ended us. On purpose. What the—

(Crunch, screech of tires across pavement.)

CAREY: What—

(Squeal of brakes.)

CAREY: Oh, sweet Jesus, no, oh, no—

UNIDENTIFIED: Stop jerking the wheel around, Glen, what the fuck—

CAREY, *sobbing*: Don't you see it?

UNIDENTIFIED: *(unintelligible)*

CAREY: Its eyes, its fucking eyes, it's behind us, it found us—

UNIDENTIFIED: What do you—oh my God. What the fuck. Is that what you saw? That's not—that can't—no. No, no—Glen, what—wait, wait—

(Metal on metal, shrieking, grinding, as perhaps one might hear as a van slides along a guardrail before finally toppling over it.)

(Twin screams, underlaid by the crumpling of metal. Audio deteriorates as the sounds slow and then stop. Brief silence.)

CAREY: *(garbled)* down the hill, is it, can you see it—*(burst of extremely loud static.)*

(Scraping metal again, like a car door being pried out of a frame, followed by a distant thud, as if thrown. Screaming, loud and strong, trailing down into bubbling whimpers. Sounds of licking, chewing, something very distorted which could almost be a laugh.)

TWENTY-SIX

"So California." Nina opened the road map with a flourish. "It's almost three thousand miles. Forty hours, give or take. If we keep switching out drivers, we won't have to stop except for gas."

We'd spent a sleepless night in Lisey's gigantic bed, and now we were walking down the side of Motton Road, contemplating our route out of town. Nina and Piper each held one side of the map and Lisey drifted over their shoulders, looking warily excited. None of us was paying attention to the actual road, so when the whistle blew, we all jumped.

A herd of deer had been killed on the road just ahead of us. The deputy with the whistle stood in front of the carcasses, waving us away. There were cones lined up, a path around the carnage, and we followed them as we stared at the entrails scrawled across the cracking pavement.

We picked our way through the underbrush on the side of the road, trying to breathe through our mouths, trying to ignore the shriek and chatter of the crows descending to eat. A sound I couldn't place made me turn toward the road, and my gaze fell on a dead doe. Her legs were twisted underneath her, and there was blood still leaking from her nostrils. I slowed down, staring. Her head was turned almost all the way around; I could only see one glittering black eye above the splintered ruin of her neck. As I watched, the eye blinked.

I stopped moving. The doe blinked again and her head turned, scraping toward me on broken vertebrae. I could hear them grinding. A scream was building somewhere inside me, terror rising in my throat and threatening to choke me, but the rational side of me was talking sweetly, soothingly, saying *No, this is not happening, this cannot be happening, this is impossible,* and then the doe staggered to her feet with a sickening crunch of bone. I felt my stomach heave and I clapped a hand to my mouth, looking wildly around for Nina.

It was then that I noticed how silent it was. No crows, no Nina. I was alone and around me there was nothing but ash. A thin white fog was curling around my ankles, shrouding the trees, pulling their trunks into tall thin skeletons, waiting, watching. I heard a creak and looked back at the doe. Her head hung down by her chest, the twisted ribbons of her neck barely still intact. As she turned to face me I realized with a lurching, gasping shudder that she had only one eye. The right side of her face was caked in blood, the hollow of the empty eye socket glaring raw and weeping in the middle of her sticky fur. The doe's intact eye fixed on me, and I heard a low moaning, a wretched crawling, begging sound, and I realized it was me. I tried to run but I was held captive by that awful bright eye.

The doe lurched toward me, head swaying like a gory pendulum. The keening sound (*me*, I reminded myself, *that is me*) was all around me, in my ears, roaring like water and thunder, and then all at once, it was gone.

I stood in a vacuum, the silence pulling at my eardrums, and the deer was still moving closer. She stopped a few feet away and slowly, laboriously tried to raise her head. Tears streamed down my face as I watched her struggle and finally I moved forward and put my hand under her mangled chin.

I lifted her head slowly, feeling the shattered bones of her spine grate against each other, and fought back the urge to vomit. It didn't seem to hurt her. Her fur was cold and tacky on my fingers, and the smell of animal musk and shit and blood was all around us. I knelt in front of her, holding her head level with my own, and I looked into that dark eye. She looked at me, blood still oozing from the empty socket like tears. I was sobbing again, but I still couldn't hear anything, and the deer looked at me, and inside my head there was a strange tickling feeling. We stared at each other and the tickling became a scratching and then a burning, a scraping, fiery pain. It carved words into the ruined walls of my mind.

Where would you go?

All the sound in the world came rushing back as the deer collapsed onto the ground in front of me, her ravaged head thudding to the pavement with a spray of blood. I opened my mouth and I screamed.

"Clem! Clem! Clémence!"

There was a sound like a whipcrack and a strange flat pain.

I opened my eyes and Nina's face was inches from mine, her curtain of hennaed hair falling around the two of us, maple syrup on her breath.

"Oh, thank God," she said, and gasped, touching the side of my face. "I'm so sorry, I didn't know what to do, I slapped you, it was so fucking—God! Are you okay?"

She put two fingers on my neck, brushing my hair back from my face with the other hand.

"Clem. Please. Say something."

I looked up at her, her perfect eyeliner, the freckle beside her mouth, and all of a sudden her eye was gone, a gaping, bleeding socket in its place. I screamed and rolled away from her and vomited onto the pavement. I shut my eyes and pressed my forehead into the road, red pulsing behind my eyelids, and sank my teeth into my tongue. *That did not happen.* Tears welled in my eyes and I could taste my blood. I lifted my head and spat onto the road. Nina was crouching, the fingertips of one hand bracing her on the ground, the other held out to me.

"Come here."

I got up, my knee singing with pain, into a sort of half crouch and stumbled the few steps to her. I sat down and she shifted from her haunches to the ground in front of me. She took my hands and pulled me into her, cradling my head, and I pressed my face into her neck and wrapped my arms around her, fingers digging into her back, and cried.

Gradually I realized we were on the side of the road, just a few feet away from the deer. The deputy was standing clear of us, carefully watching-without-watching. I bolted to my feet and felt all the blood rush out of my head.

When I opened my eyes again it was to three anxious faces under the ceiling fan in Lisey's living room, the gigantic dreamcatcher hanging from the cord twirling lazily above me. I tried to move my arm and realized I was rolled up in one of her mom's braided blankets.

"What the—did you swaddle me?" I asked, feeling a bizarre urge to laugh.

"Fuck yes, we did," Piper said. "You kept thrashing."

She started freeing my right side, Nina on my left. I sat up, touching the bandage on my knee. It was wet.

"How did we get here?"

Lisey sat down in front of me. "That deputy drove us."

Nina cleared her throat. Her eyes were shiny, and her jaw was flexing like she was gritting her teeth. "What the hell happened?"

The deer's ruined face flashed across my mind and I shivered. "Another weird hallucination. Sort of like Piper's coyote, but it was one of the deer. It stood up off the ground."

Nina's face wrinkled in disgust.

"Did yours say anything to you?" Piper asked, her voice filled with dread.

It came out of my mouth before I could even think about it. "No. Just looked at me."

Lying felt like the right thing to do. We were all on edge. If I told them about the deer's warning, they might take it to heart. There couldn't be any bad omens, anything making us doubt the plan. I was keeping all of us safe.

"Well, we have a bunch of weird electrolyte drinks," Lisey said, handing me a bottle filled with purple. Nina was looking at me, and I averted my eyes as I drank.

"Thanks for getting me out of there, guys," I said. "What a nightmare."

"It'll be over soon," Lisey said. Then she sighed. "I still wish there was a way I could bring my crows."

"There'll be crows in California," Piper said. "Don't worry."

"So where were we before I, you know, derailed us?" I capped the bottle and set it beside me. "When do we leave?"

"We're telling our parents it's a road trip, right?" Nina spread her hands. "The weekend seems like the most believable option. No one leaves for a road trip on a Thursday."

"Makes sense," Lisey said. "My parents get back from their retreat tomorrow, and then they've got some weird thing in a yurt that starts really early on Saturday, so we can take their car."

"So we have the rest of today and tomorrow to get our shit together." Piper clapped her hands together and stood up. "Everyone better make at least one mix CD, okay? I am not driving through corn country with nothing but the radio."

Sometime during the night something—maybe the deputy, maybe not—dragged the deer off the road one by one, depositing them in a sad heap a little ways into the brush. On our way into town the next morning, we saw three coyotes crouched low over the mangled remains. They didn't move as we passed them; two of them didn't even raise their heads. The largest one lifted its bloodstained muzzle toward us, wrinkling its lips back from its teeth. Then it threw its head back and shrieked, loud enough to hurt my ears, and plunged its face once more into the heap of carrion.

TWENTY-SEVEN

Lisey fainted at exactly 11:47. The four of us were sitting on the curved benches next to the fountain in the town commons, eating ice cream, and suddenly she gasped and dropped her cone. She sat bolt upright, legs unfolded, hands resting upturned on her thighs. Her eyes were huge, the pupils dilated almost to the edge of her irises. I looked at her and behind her head I could see the clock out front of the bank, the red-glowing numbers on it, and as the six melted into a seven, Lisey slumped forward off the stone bench.

I dropped my own ice cream, moved to catch her, and she fell against me hard, teeth clacking together as her chin hit my shoulder. I put my arms under hers, around her back, feeling her chest heaving against me. She weighed almost nothing. I lowered her onto the ground, cupping the back of her head. Her eyelids fluttered. Her lips moved, her breath coming in tiny shallow puffs and sips, and in the soft, sibilant rush I could almost hear words. She trailed off into a sinuous whistle through her teeth, chattering and hissing, and then her eyes flew open and fixed on me and she screamed, "Oh, don't, I'm sorry, please—"

Her arm came up, jagged fingernails catching me below the eye all the way to the corner of my mouth. I gasped and jerked away from her, blood gushing down my face. She was screaming

245

in earnest now, thrashing and kicking, fighting some invisible demon. I backed away in a crouch, all the way into Nina's legs, and she yanked me to my feet beside her.

"What do we do?" I shrilled, looking around wildly. How was there no one coming to help us? "She's gonna choke, she's—what are we supposed to do—"

I started toward Lisey, ready to do something, anything, and before I could take another step she slumped back to the ground, motionless. I knelt at her side and put my hands on her cheeks, patting her gently, trying to bring her out of it.

"Lisey," Piper said urgently, shaking her shoulder. "Lise."

Her eyes opened, and after a split second of haziness, they focused. "Whoa." She blinked a few times. "What happened?"

A watery laugh burst from Nina's lips. "You tell us."

I could feel the adrenaline coursing through me. Lisey had been fighting something, begging it to stop, and I couldn't help but think it was the mine. Like it knew we were about to leave. The deer's words lurked in my head, circling like an animal at the edge of a campfire.

Lisey shook her head. "I don't know. It was dark. It was dark and I could hear something coming."

"What was coming?" I asked.

"I don't know," she said again, a nervous edge in her voice. "It was just something, coming toward me. Like a heavy, shuffling, dragging sound, something dragging itself toward me in the dark, and I could hear it getting closer." She shuddered hard and pushed herself to a sitting position, looking at us with wide eyes. "Whatever it was, it told me—it told me we can't leave."

"What?" Piper looked as if Lisey had slapped her.

"It had hold of me by my hair, and I kept hearing something

muttering, 'Can't leave, can't leave' over and over again. I kept asking, 'Why, why?,' but it wouldn't come out of my mouth."

"Oh my God," Piper whispered, stricken. "It knows we're trying to leave. It won't let us leave."

Nina put her hand out as if to stop her, gentling her like a horse. "Piper, no, it's not—it doesn't *know* things, it's not—"

"It knows," she said again, eyes filling with tears.

Nina looked at me, raising her eyebrows, asking for my help, and my heart gave a vicious lurch.

"She's right," I said, the words scraping out of me.

All of them froze. They turned to me slowly.

"What?" Nina's voice was so, so quiet.

I closed my eyes and heard a crow shriek somewhere high above us. "Please don't be mad," I said.

Nina shot out a hand and grabbed my wrist. "Clem—"

"I lied," I yelped, the words splattering out as I pulled away from her. "I lied, I'm sorry—"

"What?" Piper's voice was thin with terror. I turned away from them and felt a tear slip down my face. I was shaking. I could feel hurt and confusion coming off all of them in waves and it made me queasy. They were looking at me, waiting. I breathed in as deeply as I could.

"I lied," I said again, lifting my eyes from the cracked stone of the bench to face them. "About the deer. It did say something to me."

Piper's face did something shivery.

"It was dying. It should have been dead. Maybe it was." The thought made me ill. "It came up to me and it didn't really speak, exactly—not like your coyote, Pipes—it sort of . . . *thought* at me. I don't know if that's right. It just felt like nothing was there and then suddenly these words were in my mind and they *hurt*, like something was physically shoving them into my head."

"What words?" Nina was modulating her tone very carefully.

"Where would you go?" I recited. "That was all."

"Taunting us," Lisey murmured. *"You can't leave, where would you go?* It's trying to make us afraid."

"That's why I didn't say anything," I said. "I don't know what I was thinking. Well, I do, I just—I thought it would be better if I was the only one who knew. Like, I could carry it so you all wouldn't have to. I didn't want you guys to be scared. I didn't want you to change your minds." I looked at Piper as I continued. "I know that's not fair. You can all make decisions. I just . . . in the moment it made sense. I'm sorry."

Lisey smiled wanly. "I guess I get it. If I was more collected, I might have done the same. I mean, I wouldn't have, but I do get it."

"It was using you a different way," Nina said. "Not trying to keep us from leaving by threatening us, but by making us fight. Making us not trust each other."

My lungs hitched as I realized she was right. I had forgotten all about what Mellie said. The impulse not to tell had been so strong and clear, I'd assumed it had come from some reptilian part of my brain, the survival part. But it hadn't come from me at all. I leaned forward, clutching my head with both hands.

"Fuck," I whispered. "How am I supposed to trust myself? How am I supposed to know what's real?"

"Here's how you know," Nina answered. "If you have any impulses that are telling you to stay, or to lie to us, or to do some weird third thing that results in us staying or fighting or both, that's not you. That's not real. Anything else, you can trust. Anything that helps us leave, that gets us away from the mine and from the Basin, is you."

"We just have to get through today," Piper said, putting her arm around me. I rested my head on her shoulder. "One more night and then we're out of here. Then we're safe."

TWENTY-EiGHT

My mother wouldn't be there for me to say goodbye to,
I realized as I stepped into the quiet trailer that night. We'd
missed each other like always. By the time she got home tomorrow I'd be somewhere on a highway. That thought, more
than anything else, brought the reality of what we were doing
home, and all at once I was overcome with grief. I went into
my mother's room and sat on her bed. I was feeling too much
to cry, somehow; all I could summon was a kind of gulping,
hiccupping sound. My heart thudded against my ribs and my
head swam as I tried to breathe normally. I tipped sideways,
laying my head on her pillow. As soon as the familiar scent of
her shampoo hit my nose, my lungs heaved, drawing her in. As
I breathed out I heard myself whisper, "Mom," and then the
floodgates burst. I curled into a ball, hugging her pillow against
me, and cried myself to sleep.

The next thing I knew Nina was sitting beside me, shaking
my shoulder gently. I rolled over to look at her.

"What time is it?" I asked, rubbing my eyes.

"Almost one," she said. "I couldn't sleep."

I sat up and looked at her. She had the remnants of cried-off
eye makeup smudged into her lower lashes.

"Did you see your dad?" I asked.

She nodded. "I made us dinner. It was just a normal night,

but it was—" She ran her thumbnail under her right eye. "It was so hard to just sit there and lie. I could tell he was a little nervous—because of my mom, you know—but he was still so excited for us, he kept telling me all these places we should stop—" She looked at me and her mouth twisted. "Oh, Clem, I'm so sorry. You didn't even get to see your mom, did you? I'm being such an asshole."

I took her hand and squeezed it. "You're not. It's awful either way."

She laced her fingers into mine and shook her head, looking down at her lap.

"Still," she said, blotting her nose on her shoulder. "Tactless."

"It's okay, Nina," I said softly.

She nodded, a quick bob of the head that swung her hair forward around her face. I looked down at our clasped hands, the still-healing cuts on our palms pressed together. When I raised my face again I almost smacked my head into hers. She'd leaned in, and she was close enough that I could see the dark spot in the amber iris of her left eye.

"I'm scared," she said, barely above a whisper. "Everything is going to be different."

I could feel her breath on my skin. She raised her free hand, touching my shoulder so briefly I could have blinked and missed it. Her fingers hovered just above my collarbone, wavering between my neck and my face, never making contact.

"I don't know what's gonna happen," she said. "So I just—"

She touched my cheek, her fingertips grazing lightly over the side of my face before drawing away again. I realized I was holding my breath.

"I wanted to do this," she said, looking at me steadily. "Before it's too late. And I wanted you to know that I wanted to."

I sat frozen, watching as she leaned toward me. She closed the distance between us slowly, carefully, her eyes on mine, gauging my response, waiting for me to react. She curled her hand loosely around the back of my neck, her skin warm and soft, and then she stopped moving. I could feel her eyelashes brush my skin as she blinked. She was too close for me to even see her clearly. My heart was beating in my throat, in my ears; electricity crackled at my fingertips where my hand met hers. Fear and joy and something I couldn't name coursed through me as I made a decision.

I tilted my head just slightly, just enough to press my lips to hers for a second, and pulled away. Her hand tightened on the back of my neck and slid up into my hair and this time she kissed me, just as quick, just as nervous. I put my hand on her side, above her hip, and then on the wing of her shoulder, and then on her face. I felt her smile as I kissed her again, and when her lips opened under mine a shock ran through my entire body. She pulled me against her, I held her tighter, and for a little while we set our fear aside.

"I didn't want things to change," she said later. We had moved to my room, to the bed we'd shared for the first time when we were seven years old. I sat with my back against the wall, her head on my lap as she looked out into the room. I was stroking her hair, running my fingers through it from root to tip and watching the red glint in the lamplight.

"I know," I said. I'd felt the same fear when I first realized my feelings.

"But everything's changing anyway," she said.

"I know," I said again.

"Are you mad?"

I laughed, tucking a strand behind her ear with one fingertip. "I think you know I'm not."

"One likes to be sure, though," she said mock haughtily, turning so she was on her back looking up at me. Then, sincerely, almost shyly: "Are you sure?"

I looked down at her. "Ehh. Like, ninety percent."

She smiled so wide it seemed like her face would crack and then put her arms around me as best she could from that position.

"I suppose that'll do." She rolled off my lap and arranged herself on her side of the bed. I slid down the wall until I was lying next to her. I moved closer, tucked myself against her, felt her sigh with contentment. When I opened my eyes again it was morning.

TWENTY-NINE

We hadn't packed much. We had money, we had Lisey's parents' car, and we had each other. We were as ready as we were ever going to be.

I don't know whose idea it was. It seemed to come from all of us at once. We pulled out of Lisey's driveway and she turned the wheel sharply the wrong way and something flickered uneasily in the back of my mind, but none of us said anything.

We had to go back to Old Town one last time.

We left the car at the edge of the woods, walking to try and rid ourselves of some of the weird, nervous energy that hounded us.

"It's really happening," Lisey said. Her voice was filled with wonder.

"Yeah." Piper stopped walking. She yelled into the gray forest. "You hear that? We're *leaving*." She spat on the ground. "*Fuck* you, Moon Basin."

Nina laughed a high, wild laugh. "Yeah, fuck you!"

Lisey and I looked at each other.

"Fuck you!"

Our voices bounced off the trees, coming back to us muffled and hollow. Lisey spun in a circle, middle fingers extended, her hair a white cloud in the gloom. Piper smiled, really smiled, for the first time in weeks. Lisey giggled and darted away, leaping like a gazelle.

"I love you guys," she called, turning to face us. "Come on!"

She started running and we followed, streaking through the woods like wild creatures. Our blood thrummed in my veins, urging me on. Shadowy tree trunks stretched endlessly into the eternal graying twilight of the ashfall, flashing by us and fading away. Once I thought I saw the doe, pacing us, but she was gone as soon as I blinked. We ran in silence through the trees, tall and straight and black, and little by little a small black pinpoint appeared and began to open in front of my eyes in the gray. I slowed to a trot, then to a walk. It was the entrance to the mine.

"How—" I started to ask. I hadn't realized we were moving toward it. My thoughts scattered like frightened rabbits, my mind fuzzing and fraying. The hole in the ground drew all my focus. It looked hungry. With a jolt of panic, I realized the mine was sucking at me, pulling, the edges of me raveling outward and forward as the black mouth yawned wider and wider. *Wake up,* I thought, *wake up, wake up,* but in my bones I knew I wasn't dreaming. I was close now, too close, my heart thumping, blood roaring in my ears, and I suddenly became aware that Lisey had slipped ahead of us. She was almost to the mine. *Wake up,* I thought again, even as I screamed.

"Lisey!"

My feet stopped moving and I was rooted, frozen, my terror a small panicked animal climbing the walls of my mind and clawing me bloody. Nina's hands were clenched into fists, blood dripping from her palms where her nails had cut her. Piper's eyes were wide, her face anguished. All three of us were breathing like we were sprinting; none of us moved.

"Lisey!" I screamed again. I mustered all my strength, pushed through the paralysis, and took a tiny step forward. Something inside me *twisted* and suddenly I was on hands and knees gasping, fingers plunged knuckle-deep in dirt and ash scratching clutching scraping *get it out of me get it out out out.* There was something inside me that burned like fire, I was on fire—out of the corner of my eye I saw Nina sprawled next to me, I heard Piper gasping in tiny bubbling breaths, and then everything stopped. Everything was quiet. A flake of ash hung in the air in front of me. I lifted my head and Lisey was standing, just barely on tiptoes, on the edge of the entrance to the mine.

"Lisey," I said, and she glanced at me over her shoulder. She looked like an angel, or a stained-glass depiction of a martyr, the flat gray light filtering through her hair and giving her a strange, somber glow. *Like a ghost,* my brain whispered, and the thought sucked all the air from my lungs. She rocked forward, backward, and then she turned to face me full-on, but it was too sudden, too quick, and the soles of her shoes made no sound as her feet slid off the edge. I had one disoriented flash of her small white hand against the earth, and then the hole was empty, black, impassive once more.

I screamed and scrambled to my feet, half a second behind Piper as she lunged over the edge of the entrance. She was panting, clutching her side.

"Lisey!" she yelled. "Lisey, can you hear me?"

Her voice bounced back out of the mouth of the mine distorted, flattened, but there was no other answer. She leaned farther in, craning her neck. Her body went rigid, the tendons in her hands standing out as she gripped the wooden frame. I could hear Nina behind me murmuring the Hail Mary as I took another step toward the mine.

"No," Piper said, her voice hollow. Something in my heart crumpled. She turned around. "She's not there."

"What?" My lungs spasmed as I tried to breathe, sending a fresh spike of pain through my chest. I jostled her aside to peer down into the mine shaft. I couldn't see anything at the bottom.

"We need a light," I said, my voice rising. "We need a light!"

"The only one is down there." Nina stepped around me. "That little one that Carlisle always left at the bottom of the ladder. We have to go down and get it."

"How could she have gotten up?" Piper asked. "She couldn't have just walked away!"

"It's too dark," I said, panic taking hold. "She's down there and we just can't see her. We need the light, Nina, we need to get it so we can see her—"

She took me by the shoulders. "Clem. Take a breath. We're going to get the light. I need you to focus."

I took an uneven breath. I heard Piper next to me doing the same thing.

"We're gonna climb down now, okay? Nice and slow. Nice and easy." Nina released me carefully, watching my face. "I'll go first. Just stay calm."

Every step down the carved-out ladder was a horror like nothing I'd ever known. *Her corpse is down here*, my brain whispered. *You're climbing down toward her. The flashlight is gone, and she's lying somewhere below you and any moment now those long thin fingers will wrap around your ankle—*

My foot hit the bottom of the mine shaft with a thud, and I barely kept my knee from buckling. I could see absolutely nothing. There was a faint jingle and scrape and then Nina said, "Oh no."

"What?" My voice was weak.

"The keys," she said. The despair in those two words sank like knives into my heart. "The car keys are here with the flashlight."

I heard the centipede-leg sound of the flashlight crank tick-tick-ticking slow and steady, and gradually a faint glow began to emanate from a few feet away. Nina started moving, pacing in smaller and smaller circles as the light grew brighter and brighter, until she was in the center of the mine shaft and it was clear we were alone.

"Fuck!" she said, the sound sharp and agonized as it bounced around us.

"What do we do?" Piper asked. "We have to find her. What if she has a concussion and she's walking around down here—"

She made a rattling, choking sound in her throat and retched, putting a hand on the wall to support herself.

"Oh God," she whispered. "Oh God."

"We have to go farther in," I said, the words heavy in my mouth.

Piper sobbed once and covered her face with her hands. Then she straightened up and screamed.

"Lisey!"

It echoed back to us, doubled and trebled itself, and when it faded there was silence.

Nina looked at us and held out her free hand. "Come on."

I took her hand and held mine out to Piper, and we made our way into the dark.

THIRTY

Even as the heat increased, I felt a chill creeping up my spine, up the back of my neck, pulsing in the base of my skull. It throbbed and needled as we moved deeper into the mine, holding on to each other as if our lives depended on it. Piper cried a slow, steady river of tears that made almost no sound at all; Nina muttered prayer after prayer. Every twenty steps we screamed Lisey's name and waited for even the slightest sound to come back to us.

I don't know how long we'd been walking when we saw it, but we all stopped at the same time. There was a light up ahead of us, a distant pinprick that shone toward us as if out of a very long, very narrow tunnel. As soon as I saw it, I knew it could see me, too. It was the single eye of something gigantic and shapeless crouching in the darkness, forced into the depths of the mine, waiting for us. It peered at us from the bottom of its hole, its den. I felt a sudden and unshakable certainty that in the black void underneath that bright watchful eye there was a ragged, smiling mouth.

As we watched, it began to move toward us. The pinprick grew, became a dime, became a single headlight, until the light was no more than ten feet from us. I squinted at it, willing my eyes to adjust, and as I did, a strange numbness washed over me. My muscles relaxed; my hands dropped to my sides. Our own light slipped from Nina's hand and fell into the dirt without a sound. The light was still moving toward us, somehow, but it never grew bigger. I was going into the light, and that thought made me laugh. *Going into the light.* I tried to say it out loud, to include Nina and Piper in the joke, but my mouth was filled with gluey saliva and I couldn't. There was a strange weightlessness to all of my limbs, as if I were floating in water. I wondered if I could swim toward the light. Maybe Lisey was in there, inside the light. It was cold; it would be warm inside the light. It would be—

A hand closed on my arm and yanked me sharply backward, tearing my eyes away from the light as I fell hard onto my tailbone. Pain lanced through me and I cried out, spraying flecks of blood from my bitten tongue. I whipped my head around, trying to see my assailant, but the afterimage of the light was the only thing in my field of vision.

Don't look at it, said something in my head. *Get the others.*

The fuzzy glow in front of my eyes seemed to lunge sideways, flashing past Nina and Piper, and as it arced away, I saw they were both standing still, staring fixedly ahead of them. The little flashlight lay on the ground next to Nina, still shining. Keeping my eyes away from the light in the back of the mine, I grabbed each of their hands and pulled as hard as I could, sending all three of us flying.

"Don't look at it," I said, dimly aware that my chin was covered in spit and blood. I wondered if my knee was bleeding again, too.

"Get the light. Don't look at it!" I snapped again as I saw Nina start to turn around. "Use your hands."

She felt blindly around her, fumbling the flashlight into

her hand. I struggled to my feet, still holding on to them, and pulled them up off the ground.

"Come on," I said, panting. "Come on, you guys."

They were still in the grip of it, their limbs heavy and clumsy, but they let me lead them back down the tunnel. My teeth chattered; I couldn't stop sweating. The light at the back of the mine floated behind my eyes and I wanted so badly to turn around, to go back to it, to give myself over to that numbness once more. I stumbled and almost fell, narrowly avoiding losing my grip on Nina. We had been walking for so long. My face was wet with tears and sweat and blood-tinged drool, and I wanted nothing more than to lie down. I slowed down, my feet dragging.

Get the fuck out of here, Clem.

Something shoved me in the small of my back, snapping me out of my stupor. I tripped forward, yanking Piper and Nina with me. I could feel them waking up, coming back to themselves.

Not that much farther.

I pulled them with me, kept walking, and after an eternity I saw the thin gray light of Old Town filtering down from above. A sob exploded out of my chest.

"Thank you," I whispered. I turned to Nina and her eyes were clear and sane, and I pushed her toward the ladder and she started climbing without a word. Piper followed her and then it was just me, the handle of the flashlight clamped between my teeth, the dead light flickering inside my head. I pulled myself out of the mine and collapsed next to the other two, cradling the flashlight to my chest. All three of us were crying.

"What do we do now?" Piper asked. She pulled her knees to her chest and rocked herself like a child.

"I don't know," Nina said. A sob tore out of her and she covered her face with her hands. I scooted closer and wrapped my arms around her.

"It won't let us leave," Piper said.

I looked at her over Nina's head.

"It won't let us leave," she repeated. "It killed Lisey. It won't let us—"

"That's why we have to go now," Nina said, lifting her head off my shoulder. "It's trying to keep us here. It's trying to stop us from leaving. We have to go now or we'll never be able to."

Piper made a low, miserable sound in her throat. "We can't just leave her."

"We have to," said Nina, tears still dripping off her down-turned face.

"She wanted us to leave," I said. I hurt all over; grief etched itself into my bones as if with acid. "She'd tell us to get the fuck out while we still could."

"She'd be so pissed," Piper whispered, "if it killing her managed to keep us here."

We looked at each other and the world wobbled around me as I tried to reconcile the threeness of us. It seemed impossible. We were leaving a point of our compass behind, and I didn't know who we were going to be without her.

Nina stood up. "Lisey, I love you," she said through tears, staring at the mine.

"I love you," Piper echoed.

For a moment I couldn't speak, and I thought the words as hard as I could, projecting them for whatever lingered. *You were so brave. You made us all better. I'm so sorry we're leaving you. I'm so sorry.*

"I love you," I said at last.

Nina slipped her hand into my right, and I took Piper's in my left, and we stood there looking down into the mine as the ash fell around us. Then we went back to the car.

THiRTY-ONE

The Honda rattled and wheezed as we climbed up the hill out of the valley. I looked out across the dying grass, the empty fields, the motel sign blinking against the strange distant nothingness of Old Town. There was a small flayed animal corpse in the crook of a tree, and as we rounded the curve onto the freeway, I saw a crow flutter down onto the branch next to it. I moaned low in my throat and put my head back against the seat, closing my eyes. Piper reached her hand up from the back seat and I took it. Her fingers were cold. After a while Nina turned on the radio and the car filled with Carole King and a soft, white wash of static. I was still holding Piper's hand when I fell asleep.

I was standing in the town commons. The moon was full, the light so bright that everything around me looked like daylight filmed through a blue filter. I stood in the center of the commons, the town radiating out around me, and there was no one there. No sound, no movement. Not even wind. I wanted to walk away, go home or to Lisey's house, but my legs wouldn't cooperate. I could only turn, looking around me, trying to understand why I was there, and then I heard it.

It was a slow, dragging sound, a liquid shushing noise punctuated by the sharp echoing rap of something against the road. *Rap, thud, shush. Rap, thud, shush.* The rhythm of it settled into my bones, took my heartbeat along with it. *Rap, thud, shush.* It was getting louder, closer, and still I turned in circles and saw nothing. The sound came again and I realized that it was hooves. Hooves on stone. The dead doe had returned for me and she was digging her hooves into the ground and pulling herself toward me, her head hanging low and thumping against her bloody chest as she moved.

"Hello?" I called out, desperate, eyes roving back and forth almost uncontrollably. "Are you here?"

Rap, thud, shush. A low, bubbling moaning sound, the breathing of something whose lungs were filled with blood, whose throat was crushed flat.

"Hello!" I yelled, the sharp edge of panic in my voice making me cringe. "What do you want!"

The sound was louder, faster, and my blood beat in my temples harder and harder as it drew closer to me. *Rap-thud-shush-rap-thud-shush.* I turned and turned and I couldn't see it, the sound was everywhere around me, and I knew it should have been right there and it wasn't. The moaning became a gurgling wail and the hooves were louder and louder as it rushed toward me and I *could not see it*, and then the hooves clattered to a stop in front of me and there was silence.

I opened my eyes slowly, slowly, slowly, and the town commons was empty. I started walking, moving through town into the woods, toward the mine. After a moment, behind me, I heard the sound of hooves. It followed me all through the night, pacing me, keeping time.

Nina woke me up somewhere in Indiana. It was dark. We were parked under an expanse of sodium lights, semitrucks nosed up to the pumps on either side of us. I looked at my watch, then at Piper. She was still out, folded sideways onto the seat, her arm curled up and over her face. Nina said, "Let her sleep," and got out, jerking her head at the convenience store. I trotted in while she reached for the nozzle.

I filled two coffee cups and left them on the counter, wandering through the aisles in a daze. I scooped up candy, sunflower seeds, granola bars. I couldn't stop hearing that sound.

"Awfully late, isn't it?"

"What?"

I looked up to see the clerk staring at me.

"Sorry," I said. "Yeah. It's late."

He started sliding the bags across the little scanner. A rustle, a thump, a hoofbeat behind me. I closed my hand around a clear plastic lighter.

"Where you headed?"

"California."

Thump. Shush. Lighter into my pocket. Fingers inching toward the lip balm.

"You travelin' with someone bigger'n you, I hope."

Rattling inhale. Lip balm pressed into palm.

"Yeah," I said again. I put the lip balm in my pocket. Pulled my wallet out. I could feel it behind me, watching me, shifting its weight back and forth, head dangling.

"Have a good night," he said in a bemused voice.

I pushed out into the parking lot. There was a crow perched on one of the streetlights. I looked up at it; it screeched and flew away into the dark. When I got back to the car, Nina was in the passenger seat. I groaned.

"Just follow the road," she said. "There's at least a few hundred more miles before you even need to switch lanes."

I sighed and climbed in, cranking the seat forward while Nina watched, sipping her coffee. As I pulled out, I glanced into the rearview mirror and slammed on the brakes, whipping my head around. Piper shifted and murmured but didn't wake. My heart was pounding in my ears. Nina looked at me quizzically. I turned back around and pulled onto the interstate. I didn't tell her that for just a moment I'd seen something standing behind the car on long, spindly, broken legs.

Once we were back on the highway, she held out her hand. "You have that look."

I sighed and dug in my pocket for the lip balm and the lighter, slapping them both into her palm.

"Come on, Clem." She sounded tired, and when I glanced at her she just looked sad. "It's not the SuperStop anymore. I know it's a coping thing, but you gotta try."

I nodded, shame spiking through me as I imagined our entire plan derailed by my arrest for shoplifting. "I know. I'm sorry."

I wrestled the car into the fast lane and stepped on the gas, then looked at her again. She was trying to drink her coffee in one gulp while still sifting through the candy.

"You're not sleeping?"

"No," she said. "Not yet. Piper drives next, so I figured I'd keep you company until it's daylight out."

"Thanks," I said sincerely. "I probably need that."

The Honda liked the fast lane, ran smooth and steady once it got past sixty. I took a sip of coffee and held up the cup.

"Free hand. Thank God it's not a stick."

She laughed. "I still say you would have gotten it eventually if you hadn't given up."

"Yeah, or I would have dropped the engine out the bottom

of Fish's car."

She waved a hand. "He'd have been fine. You would have gotten it."

"Listen, count your blessings that I'm driving competently in this thing." I put the cup in the holder and bopped the steering wheel. "The last time I drove a car was when you had your appendix out."

I saw her grimace out of the corner of my eye and laughed. "See? Bird in the hand."

She sighed and settled farther into her seat. "Someday you'll learn. Flexibility is key in the event of an apocalypse."

"Yeah, yeah," I murmured. "Until all the gas runs out and we have to walk anyway."

She snorted and reached for the radio, clicking through the channels.

"Stop," I said suddenly, and she froze, her hand hovering in front of the knob. "It's Stevie." I pushed her hand gently toward her lap. She laced her fingers with mine and rested our hands on her leg.

"You and your Fleetwood Mac." Her thumb brushed across my knuckles and a little thrill coursed through me. I didn't know if she felt me shiver, but she didn't let go. The headlights sliced down the road and we followed them through the night. Even when she fell asleep, Nina didn't let go of my hand.

The sun rose as we were driving through a field of sunflowers, the light cutting low and flat across the land to light them up like tiny halos. Piper rolled down her window and stuck her head out, then made me stop the car. She stood at the edge of the field, lit up around the edges just like the sunflowers, and then she walked carefully out into them. We followed her into the waist-high ocean of gold, everything glowing, and we stayed there among the flowers until the sun slipped higher and the gilt edges of everything melted away. Piper walked back to the car and got in the driver's seat. I climbed into the back seat. We drove on. I lay on my back with the seat belt unbuckled and watched the clouds go by. A crow soared above us, riding the freeway thermals. I slept again, badly, but I didn't dream.

We stayed for an hour at the next rest stop, which boasted a forty-flavor soda fountain and Illinois's best fried tenderloin sandwiches. We sat in a red-vinyl booth licking grease from our fingers as the engine cooled. Nina put every single flavor into a cup and it tasted almost like nothing, the way white contains all the colors but just looks white. We got back in the car. Somewhere in the night an animal ran across the road. Piper didn't flinch and kept the car steady. The animal made it to the other side and kept running, stayed alongside us, eyes glowing. A star blazed across the sky and Piper said, "Lisey would say that's an omen," but I couldn't tell from her inflection if it was a good or bad one.

The thought repeated over and over in my mind: *Lisey should be here.* It was so strange, so fresh. Her absence was everywhere but it was so incomprehensible. It was like someone had cut off my hand and I kept reaching for things. Every time I thought of her was like losing her all over again, but it was also somehow a fact in my mind. She was gone. She shouldn't have been. I cried silently in the back seat. My dreams were filled with the sound of ragged, hungry breathing.

On the fourth day we passed through the shadow of the mountains and kept moving into the flat red desert. A crow paced us as we moved south and west, winding across miles of red, dry ocean. We kept the windows down, the warm dry air buffeting our skin. We stopped at a motel surrounded by towering pink stones and paid cash for a room.

"Well, it's no Moon Basin Motel," Nina said, flopping onto the bed. "I bet there's not a single ghost here."

None of us laughed.

Haunted after Dark, Episode 47
Unused Footage

(A young woman sits on a bed in a small hotel room. She is attaching a long silver wand to the cord of a flat black box. She sets these two objects on the bed and looks at the camera.)

TONYA PRICE: I'm here in the Moon Basin Motel, getting ready to spend the night in one of the nation's most notorious ghost towns. Anson Perry, the owner of the motel, has just locked us into the room, where we will be trapped until eight a.m., no matter what we encounter.

(She clamps a pair of headphones over her ears and lifts the long silver microphone.)

PRICE: I'm calling out to any presence that lingers here in the motel. Is there a spirit here with us now?

(She points the microphone out, into the room, and stays silent for five seconds.)

PRICE: What is your name?

(She points the microphone out again. A low hum begins to emanate from somewhere in the room, although PRICE shows no sign of noticing it. The picture fuzzes as the sound's frequency climbs higher.)

PRICE: *(unintelligible)*

(The camera is no longer picking up her voice. It is no longer picking up anything besides the sound, which has become a cicada-like whine. The cameraman does not appear to notice this, and the tape continues.)

PRICE: *(unintelligible)*

(PRICE appears to ask three more questions, leaving space for answers, before her eyes focus somewhere behind the camera. Her lips continue to move as the whining sound intensifies, becomes almost a shriek, and then she stands up and the video cuts off.)

THIRTY-TWO

I was driving when we crossed the border into California. Nina rolled down her window, pulled herself up and out to sit on the edge, and screamed, a wild, wordless sound, victorious. I grabbed her ankle like I could keep her in the car if she fell, and Piper was laughing behind me. We shot down the road with the sun at our backs and I dared—I dared for one moment to believe that it was going to be okay.

That night we parked on a side street and ran screaming into the ocean. The sun was setting and the horizon was a sheet of gold. We stood there in the surf, in the strange sucking feeling of the ground shifting beneath us, and watched the sun sink down.

"My mom used to say sometimes when it hits the water you see a green flash," a voice said from behind us. I wheeled around to see a woman standing on the beach next to our shoes, smoking a cigarette.

"Where you from?" she asked, her words slow and languorous. She held the cigarette between her thumb and forefinger.

"Why?" Nina's voice was slightly combative. She began to wade back toward the shore.

"Never seen someone from here scream at the ocean," the woman said. "And, no offense, but you all look kind of homeless. Did you run away?"

"We escaped," Piper said.

"We're on a road trip," Nina said, giving her a pointed look.

The woman watched us for a moment, sucking her cigarette down to the filter, and I knew she knew Nina was lying.

"You can crash at my place," she said, jerking her head back toward the road. I looked at her hard.

"Why?" I asked. "You don't know us."

"My wife was a runaway once," she said. "I have a soft spot."

We stood there in the water looking at her, silently reading each other, and the woman shrugged and started to turn away.

Nina blurted, "Wait."

The woman smiled. "All right, then. But so help me God, if you try to pull squatters' rights on me I will literally—*literally*—kill you. Come on."

She turned and walked up the beach and we followed her.

Her name was Naomi. Her house was a small square box on stilts. Her wife's name was Marikh, and she was dead. We learned all these things as she laid out blankets for us, got us water and towels, microwaved plates of lasagna. She was on bereavement leave from work, she said. Aneurysm. Just like that, snap of the fingers. We showered in rotation as she smoked her way silently through the consumption of dinner and a jar of clear liquid that smelled like gasoline. Finally she said, "You're tired," shoved her chair back, and disappeared into her bedroom. We bundled ourselves down onto the floor.

"I'm so happy to be *clean*," I said.

"Me too," Piper murmured.

Nina was silent and I thought she was asleep, but then she whispered, "Do you feel different?"

I rolled toward her. "I can't tell for sure. I think so? I haven't had a nightmare since the pink motel."

Her throat clicked as she swallowed. "This seems too easy."

"I know," I admitted. "But maybe the Basin made things seem too difficult."

"Maybe it worked. Maybe we're finally out of reach," Piper said.

I made a sound of assent, but that night I dreamed of a huge dead hand looming up out of the mine, searching, seeking, casting its long, long shadow across the country.

THiRTY-THREE

Naomi woke us up early, her face creased with sleep.

"Sorry," she said. "Not enough space in here that y'all can be on the floor once I'm awake." She opened the fridge and took out a carton of eggs. "So. No more than a week here. Nonnegotiable."

Butter, pan, hiss of flame. Eggshells into garbage disposal.

"I have a friend who works at a hostel. You can go there if you don't find anything else. It's about two hours inland."

"Thank you," I said. "Really. We probably won't need it, but—"

Nina put her hand on mine. I shut my mouth. Naomi looked at me a moment longer and then sliced into a grapefruit.

"It's no problem." She set plates in front of us. "I like to look out for the youth. The punk-rock, runaway youth."

I couldn't tell if she was making fun of us. I guessed it didn't matter. After we ate, she went back into her room and closed the door. Plaintive guitar began to seep through the walls, and all three of us stood up at once.

Piper tipped her head and said, "Beach?"

Nina and I breathed *yes* in unison and then we were out the door, on the sand, in the water. We stayed within view of Naomi's house for most of the morning, following the shifting patches of shade as the clouds crossed the sky. Around noon we wandered around the curve of the beach and found a taco shop perched in the sand. We stuffed ourselves, sand and salt freckled across our skin, and watched the waves.

It was just starting to get toward dusk when we got back to Naomi's. She was standing on the porch, leaning on the railing, and I could see the glowing tip of her cigarette at a distance. She was wearing a denim shirt and a pair of cutoff sweatpants, one bare foot pressed against the opposite shin. I had a rush of emotion looking up at her as we approached. How much time had she had with Marikh? Enough time to love her. Enough time to make some kind of a life together. Envy and pity washed through me, the combination putting me off-balance. We followed her into the house without speaking.

"In case you want to call your parents." She put a cordless phone on the kitchen counter in front of us.

"It's long distance." Nina pushed the phone back to her.

"I don't care," Naomi said.

"I think we're good." Nina got up and went into the living room. "But thanks."

Naomi looked from me to Piper, clearly wanting to press the issue, but she let it go. She made us more eggs for dinner and disappeared again.

"I think she's mad at us," Piper whispered as we situated ourselves on the floor.

"So?" Nina whispered back. "It's none of her business."

"She's been really nice to us."

"That doesn't mean we have to tell her anything."

"I guess so."

"Better to keep it simple. We'll be out of here soon."

The hush of their voices and the sound of the ocean washed

over me, and I sank slowly down into sleep.

I opened my eyes and I was in the Sugar Bowl, the empty ravine stretching all around me. Lisey was sitting on the ground in front of me. She looked up at me and her lips moved. The words took a moment to reach me, and once they did they stayed a few seconds behind her lips, like a poorly dubbed movie.

"You have to find me, Clem."

"What do you mean?" My voice had a tinny, recorded quality, like I was speaking into cupped hands.

"The ash covered me up. You have to find me so I'm not lost."

She pointed a thin, trembling finger. "You left me."

Lisey's mouth moved, whispering to herself, to the Bowl, to Old Town. Her eyes fluttered but didn't open; her lips moved faster and faster. I leaned forward to listen and as I did, her eyes snapped open. Her mouth snapped open. She made a sound that was not a scream but something hollower, something that sounded like it was coming from farther away than her own body, a muffled recording of a faraway scream, and suddenly the sound burst into her, out of her, and she was screaming at full volume. I recoiled, scrambling away from her, and Lisey screamed and screamed and screamed. Her eyes were wide and blank and her mouth was a black circle in the middle of her too-pale face. Her fingers were plunged into the earth of the Bowl, her whole body trembling, and then the sound stopped. It cut off as though a door had been slammed, abruptly, and Lisey's mouth was still open but her eyes rolled back in her head. Then she was on the ground. She looked like a fish that had been hooked, writhing, mouth gaping soundlessly, hands scrabbling, and the blanks of her eyes were so white. She arched backward; a horrible empty whooshing sound came howling out of her and she went limp. I dropped to her side and then, without warning, she was gone.

Lisey, I cried silently, looking wildly around the gray-white emptiness of the Sugar Bowl. *Lisey, please. Please come back, we need you. Where are you?* There was a dull, throbbing ache behind my left eye. I started digging, ash coating my hands and filling my lungs, certain that at any moment I was going to uncover Lisey's face and she would be staring at me with blank dead eyes. A crow fluttered down through me, its feet disappearing into the ash. It cawed and ruffled its wings, and another swooped down to join it. I pulled my hands out of the earth.

Is that you, Lisey? I asked the crows. A third spiraled down. That meant something, I knew, but not what. A snatch of some long-ago rhyme pattered across my brain, *three for a girl, three for a girl three for a funeral four for a—?* The crows pecked at the ash, cawing and clicking at each other, and then they plunged their beaks down, deep down into it, and when they raised their heads they were dripping with blood. It bubbled up from the holes in the ground, spreading and pooling underneath me, bright and sinister and beautiful against the pale gray. The first crow looked at me, into me, through the blood in its eyes. There was a perfect drop suspended on its crimsoned beak, glowing like a jewel, and the crow opened its blood-covered mouth and the jewel fell and winked red in the light and the crow said—

I gasped and jerked upright. Someone was screaming and it wasn't me. Lights came on in Naomi's room, then the living room, and I saw that it was Piper. She was still lying down, eyes open and rolled back into her head. Naomi was yelling—not screaming, she was yelling words at Nina, and I could see them talking to each other, moving around us, and Piper didn't stop screaming, and then Naomi stepped forward and threw a glass of water into her face. Piper bolted up off the floor, arms flailing, and Nina dropped to her knees and grabbed her, holding her until she stopped thrashing. I blinked tears out of my eyes and shook my head, trying to reorient myself.

"What the fuck?" Naomi was wild-eyed, breathing hard, clutching the empty glass with both hands in front of her like it was a shield. Her chin trembled as she looked at each of us in turn. "You're leaving as soon as the sun comes up."

She walked back into her room. I heard the door lock and rattle as she tested it. I didn't blame her.

THIRTY-FOUR

Naomi looked frayed and tired when she roused us a few hours later, but her eyes had lost the glitter of fear.

"It's nothing personal," she said as she shoved granola bars and bananas into a plastic grocery bag. "It's just, you know, clearly there's more going on here than just some fuckin' teenage hijinks, and I'm just not down for it, I'm sorry—"

"It's okay," I said. "We're sorry."

I wished there was anything more to say.

She gave us directions to the hostel and a note to give her friend, and then she closed the door on us. I stood there for a moment before I touched my fingertips to it, just lightly, and turned away.

We'd been driving for about an hour when Piper finally spoke. Her voice was cracked and rusty, hoarse from screaming. "Did you dream about Lisey?"

My foot twitched on the gas and the car lurched forward, making a strained coughing sound.

"Did you?" I met her eyes in the rearview mirror and saw her nod.

I could feel Nina looking at me. "What happened?" she asked, so quietly I almost didn't hear her.

"She told me we have to find her," I said, nausea rolling through me. Piper inhaled sharply and I braked.

"Sorry," Piper said. "She—she told me we shouldn't go back."

"What the fuck?" I whispered.

"Nina, did you dream at all?" Piper asked.

"It was just static," she answered. "Snow. No sound."

"Ash," I realized. My knuckles were white on the steering wheel. I forced myself to loosen my grip as I pulled the car back into traffic.

The hostel was closer and nicer than I'd expected, a small white building with big windows and a sun-soaked interior. We were given a room with three other girls, who spoke to each other in German and ignored us. We threw our backpacks onto cots, left the hostel, and walked down the street, each lost in our own thoughts. We wound through the tree-lined neighborhood and every time I noticed how beautiful it was I felt another little stab of grief.

A strange underwater feeling chased us throughout that day. The sun filtered down in ripples, in waves, in radiating circles around us. We bought popsicles. We found a tiny café and sat in the shade and took small sips of cold, sweet green tea. We hardly spoke at all. Time drifted past us and we were ghosts.

"I guess now we wait," Nina said as we folded ourselves into the tiny bunk bed that afternoon. "We have to give ourselves time to, I don't know, work the mine out of our systems. Like a splinter."

"Lisey would say that some splinters actually go the wrong way and end up in the heart," I said.

I heard a muffled sob from Piper, curled onto the lower bunk of the bed next to ours.

"She'd also say, *Don't catastrophize, Clem; it's bad for morale*,"

Nina said.

I wasn't tired, but there wasn't room to sit up on the beds. I had no choice but to lie down. I watched the light move across the bottom of Nina's bunk above me as the sun set, listening to the German girls murmur to each other, listening to the soft rush of blood in my ears.

"Clem," Lisey said.

I turned and she was sitting next to me on the merry-go-round, glowing in the sun.

"Lise." I couldn't move. I was frozen with happiness and fear, and a bizarre certainty that if I moved too quickly she'd burst apart like startled birds and be gone. She was holding a glass bottle of mineral water, and she held it out to me. I took it as I would from something dangerous. It was wonderfully cold, fizzy and faintly salty, the mouth of the bottle sticky for some reason. I pressed my lips together as I handed it back. "What are you doing here?"

"I was wrong." She drummed her fingernails against the glass. "I thought it would let us leave."

"We did," I said.

"*You* did," she murmured as she took a sip. "I'm still here."

I shook my head. "Wait. What?"

"I thought I'd be gone," she said. "I thought it would be satisfied."

She gave her funny little one-shouldered shrug, the way she had the day I'd met her, the way she had every day since then. I missed her so badly it hurt.

"I don't know. Maybe this is always what being dead is like. Maybe no matter where you die you just hang around."

I put my hand on her leg. Her skin was cool and smooth and

not right, the texture of it just shy of real.

"I'm cold," she said, a touch of apology in her voice.

"It's not that bad," I said.

She put her hand on mine. "How's California?"

"It's okay," I said.

Her grip on me tightened.

"I can't tell if it's working, though." I rapped my knuckles on the merry-go-round. "If we're here, that means it's not, right?"

Her hand was growing warmer, and my fingers were beginning to ache. I tried to shift so I could pull my hand away but she clutched it tighter, and then tighter still. I felt something in my knuckles pop and crack, and I cried out in horror and pain. She smiled at me and her mouth was full of blood.

"Listen to me," she hissed, blood bubbling from her lips and spilling down her chin. She blinked and her eyes were flat black beads, pupil-less, shiny. Crow's eyes. I screamed and tried to pull my hand out of her grip, feeling the bones splinter and bristle under my skin. She leaned in close.

"The covenant," she whispered. "Come back before it's broken for good."

"What do you mean?" My voice was weak with fear.

"Blood was the first language." Her voice had a strange timbre that wasn't her own. "The first thing that humans understood. When they made a promise, they spilled blood to bind themselves together. To make a covenant."

"Like we did," I whispered.

"I thought I could bargain," she said, the words heavy with sorrow and rage. "I thought if I let it have me, it would leave you alone."

"Lisey, what—"

"It's been with me since I was little." She gripped my hand even tighter. "In my head. Talking. Trying to make me do things. Trying to make me hurt you." The fathomless black eyes flicked down to my mangled hand and back to my face, but she didn't loosen her grip. "I fought as long as I could. When we started talking about leaving it got so hard."

"You said it would let us leave," I whispered.

"I thought it would!" she howled. "I didn't know I'd still *be here!*"

With each word she crushed my hand tighter, moved closer, and before I could answer she spoke again, her lips painting mine with blood.

"You have to come back," she hissed. "When you break a covenant, you pay in blood."

Suddenly we weren't on the merry-go-round anymore. We were standing at the entrance to the mine, the ash heavy around us, sticking to the blood on our skin. She was still holding my mangled hand, squeezing it ever tighter. My blood started to seep out from between her fingers.

"I'm so sorry," she whispered. "I miss you so much."

Then she grabbed my shoulder and pushed me into the mine.

I thrashed awake, smashing my head into the underside of Nina's bunk and falling onto my back immediately. My cheeks were wet and the word *blood* flashed across my mind before I realized I was sobbing. I put a hand to my forehead, rubbing at the welt that was already rising. There was a red flicker in my periphery and I turned to see Nina's upside-down face.

"You okay?" she asked.

"No," I said. "Bad dream."

Her eyelashes flickered. "Me too." She pulled her head back up. A moment later she swung down onto the floor.

"Where's Piper?" she asked, looking at her empty bunk.

"I don't know," I said.

We trotted out into the common room, trying not to panic, and asked the tired-looking security woman if she'd seen Piper.

"She walked by not too long ago." Her tone was just short of scolding. "No shoes or anything. This is a drug-free facility, you know—"

We were already out the door, tossing apologies over our shoulders, and then we were on the street. The sun was just beginning to rise.

"Which way?" Nina asked. There was a knotty tangle of fear in my stomach.

"East," I said bleakly, and I saw understanding in her eyes.

We moved quickly, one of us on each side of the street, calling out as loudly as we dared at that hour. We'd been walking for maybe fifteen minutes when we heard a yell. Our eyes met and we bolted toward the sound.

The house was on a corner, surrounded by grass and golden wheat, glowing in the dim light. There was a woman in slacks and a dress shirt, wet through and plastered to her skin, kneeling on the ground above something small and crumpled. Her shoulders heaved as she moved, pistoning her arms up and down. A man ran out of the house yelling into a phone, and I realized that the crumpled thing was Piper, and that she was dead.

I ran toward the woman and saw she was next to a shallow pond, and I knew what had happened. I screamed and flung myself to the ground beside her. The woman didn't stop pumping her arms. Piper's body compressed underneath her like a paper bird, and then she coughed and spat green water up and into the woman's face. The woman laughed, a short, surprised, grateful laugh, and sat back on her heels, keeping one hand on Piper. Piper's eyes fluttered open and she looked first at the woman, then at me. Her face was a mask of fear and confusion.

"What happened?" She took a breath in and gasped, her hand going to her chest.

"You might have a cracked rib or two," the woman said. "But you're alive. You walked into the water feature."

"The what?"

The woman waved her hand. "It's an irrigation thing. Instead of sprinklers. I don't—it doesn't matter."

Piper's eyes moved back to me. "I was asleep, Clem. I was dreaming."

A wave of nausea rolled through me. *She would have drowned just like Mellie.* We hadn't escaped anything. I held out my hand to her and she took it, pulling herself up as gingerly as she could. The woman stood along with her, watching.

"Thank you," Piper said to her. "You saved me."

The woman nodded. "My husband called an ambulance."

I blanched at the thought. I didn't know how a hospital would react to three unaccompanied minors from out of state, but I could guess. Nina slipped her hand into mine and squeezed, a short one that meant *it's fine.*

"You have to keep an eye on her," the woman said, turning to us. She looked back at Piper. "Are you on any medication for this?"

"It's never happened before," Piper said quietly.

"Well, you better look into it. If you'd been five minutes later, I'd be at work right now and you'd be dead in the front yard while Steven's still at the table drinking his coffee."

"The water woke me up," she said.

"And then you inhaled it," the woman snapped. "Where did you come from?"

"The hostel," I said. "We're just visiting—"

The ambulance swung around the corner. The woman got to her feet and waved, big over-the-head swoops like she was landing a plane. The paramedics hopped out and hustled toward us, wheeling a stretcher.

"I'm not going to the hospital," Piper said.

One of the paramedics gave her a placating smile. "Well, we'll get you checked out and we'll see—"

"I'm not going." Her voice was thin but firm. "Just do what you can here."

The other, younger-looking paramedic blinked a few times and said, "Uh, okay. Just come over here then, I guess."

She sat on the back step of the ambulance and they listened to her heart, watched her chest expand and contract, and shined a little flashlight at her eyes. The older one placed his hand flat on her chest, right below her sternum, and a little crease appeared between his eyebrows as she breathed. He saw me staring and motioned for us to come over.

"She's got at least one cracked rib," he said as we approached. "We need to take an X-ray."

"You can't make me go," Piper said firmly. "And it's not like you can set a broken rib. All you can do is confirm it, right?"

He nodded reluctantly, taking her wrist to time her pulse.

"So tell me what to do for a cracked rib and I'll do it."

He waited until he was finished counting, lips moving slightly, and then put her hand down and sighed.

"I'll give you a bandage and show you how to wrap it. But I have to *strongly* advise that I think you need to be seen by a doctor—"

"I understand," Piper said gently. "I'm refusing."

He nodded and climbed past her into the ambulance, extending a hand to pull her up.

"We'll be right back," he said to me and Nina, swinging the door shut.

The woman trotted over to us. "Are you riding with her? I can follow you there."

"She's not going," Nina said. She was doing the voice she did with unfamiliar adults, higher and more lilting than her regular tone. It made you think of babysitters, honor students. It was very useful. I watched a crow land in the little pond and begin bathing itself, ducking its head and shaking its wings out.

"We'll take her to her doctor once we get back home. She doesn't do well with strangers, so as long as everything's okay to drive, we're just going to stick to our schedule."

The woman pursed her lips and frowned. Another crow joined the first.

"Where did you say you were from?"

"We're staying at the hostel," I said, still watching the birds. "Just in town for a few days. We're heading back to—"

Fuck, what was the name of Naomi's town?

"San Diego," Nina lied. "Leaving tomorrow."

The ambulance door opened and Piper climbed down, holding herself straight and still. She breathed shallowly as she moved toward us.

"Thank you for saving me," she said to the woman. "I can't hug you, but—"

She held out her hand to shake. The woman looked suspicious, convinced that we were hiding something from her, but she put her hand in Piper's and shook.

"Well, good luck, girls." The corners of her mouth pulled down. "And you're welcome," she added to Piper.

We turned and walked back down the street the way we'd come. I heard the paramedic through the open window as they drove past.

"—clear on a patient refusal—"

I waved. He saw me in the rearview, but he didn't wave back. When I sneaked a look over my shoulder the crows were gone, but the woman was still standing there in the street, her wet clothes dripping onto the pavement. We were almost back to the hostel before any of us spoke.

"We have to—"

"I think—"

"What—"

We laughed awkwardly, nervously.

Nina looked at me. "You go."

My heart was battering against my ribs, but my voice was steady. "We have to go back." I felt hollow and sick. "Lisey was trying to warn me."

"What do you mean?" Nina asked. "Wait. Hang on." She ducked into the first coffee shop she saw and we followed.

"You sit," Nina said, pointing at a table. We sat in silence while she ordered, paid with cash, and got the change in quarters. She walked back to us with one gigantic cup of hot cocoa that she placed in the very center of the table.

"Okay," she said, her eyes scared and somber. "What the fuck?"

"I think Lisey fell into the mine on purpose." I pushed it out in one long breath. "I think she did it so we could leave."

Nina put her hands over her mouth.

"She said she's heard it her whole life," I continued. "Trying to get her to go in, to take us with her. When we started talking about leaving . . ."

I spread my hands.

"She knew it wouldn't let us," Piper said. A tear ran down her face and plinked onto the table. "Not unless she gave it something it wanted."

"Is that why we're still seeing her?" Nina said. *"Them?"*

She jerked her thumb over her shoulder at the crows already gathering outside the window of the coffee shop.

"Yeah," I said. "She didn't count on it keeping her . . . not alive, I guess, but . . . present. She thought she'd go into the mine to buy us immunity, but—" I held up my hand, palm up so the red weal across it was visible. "We made a covenant, and we made it in blood. The only way to break it is with more blood. She thought her death would count as the payment for breaking the covenant, and the three of us would be safe. But she's not gone—not the way she would be in a normal place—and so we're still tied to her, still blood-bound. And if we don't go back—if the covenant breaks for real—"

"We pay in blood," Piper said bitterly. "It's using her to get us back."

"More or less," I said, looking down at my hands. "Look what happened to you, Pipes. You've never once walked in your sleep, and the first time you did, you almost drowned in a foot of water. Things haven't gotten better, even though we're as far away as we've ever been."

"She wouldn't hurt us," Nina said.

"I don't think she's the one in charge." Those black eyes flashed across my mind.

"When I was sleepwalking," Piper said, "I dreamed about the crows. I was walking in Old Town, looking for Lisey, and the crows were watching me. They kept flying and landing, flying and landing, keeping up with me but never getting close. They were always just behind me, above me in the trees somewhere. I could hear them. I don't know if they were . . ."

She paused, moving her hand to scratch at the paper sleeve on the cup.

"I don't know if they were helping me or hunting me," she said at last. "I don't know if they wanted me to find her or if they knew I was going to the mine and they wanted me to die there."

I shuddered. I pulled the cup out of the sleeve and took a too-big gulp, burned my mouth, my throat, a painful, grounding ache opening below my breastbone.

"She pushed me into the mine," I said, watching Piper pull the sleeve toward her and begin shredding it in earnest. "That's when I woke up."

Both of us shifted our focus to Nina. She tucked her hair behind her ears, smoothing it down, the Nina equivalent of sitting on your hands if they were shaking.

"I dreamed about her, too," she said. "I dreamed she was in the mine, in there alive, and I saw her climb up out of the ground. She climbed up and started following us, walking by the side of the road with blood pouring down her face, and when I opened my eyes—"

She shook her head once, sharply, like she was trying to fling the thought away.

"When I opened my eyes I could have sworn—for a split second I could have sworn I saw her perched above me in the hostel, like she was sitting on the side of the bed looking down at me, only her neck was turned funny and her eyes were so cold—"

She reached for the cocoa and put it to her lips, eyes shut tight as she drank.

"She looked so angry," she said at last, putting the cup down.

We were all silent for a moment.

"We have to go back," I said.

THIRTY-FIVE

The hostel lady was nice enough, once we told her Piper had been sleepwalking. She checked us out without comment, even gave us a plastic bag full of fruit and some prepackaged muffins. We found a gas station, filled the tank, bought gallon jugs of water. It had been twelve days since we'd left. We still had money; we could have stayed longer if the mine had let us. If our plan had worked, if we had Lisey with us. The unfairness of it was almost more than I could bear.

The drive back seemed too short, every hour bringing us deeper into the shadow of the Basin. I kept catching myself going fifteen or twenty miles below the speed limit, trying to delay the inevitable, only noticing when cars started to pass us with their horns blaring. We kept the music loud, didn't talk much. There wasn't anything to say.

Nina was asleep in the back seat, and I was looking out the passenger window. Piper took her hand off the wheel and turned the radio down. The sudden silence was a vacuum, sucking at my eardrums. I turned to look at her.

"What if it's a trick?" she asked. Her voice was so small. "What if it's not her?"

"Pipes—"

"What if she died the first time we went in there?" she whispered. Her lips barely moved. "When we all blacked out? What if she died then and became part of the mine and she's just been trying to lure us—"

"She *saved* us," I said. "When we were caught in the light down there. That was her."

"What if she's always been part of it?"

Piper's hands were clamped on the wheel like she was drowning and it was a life preserver. She was breathing like she'd been sprinting.

"What if when she was little and she almost fell in, what if she *did* fall in and died and she's *always* been a ghost since before you even *knew* her and that's why she couldn't leave with us—"

"Piper," I said, sharper than I meant to. "What the hell?"

"I'm scared, Clem!" Her voice wobbled and cracked, getting louder as she continued. "I'm so fucking scared. I don't want to go back there. I don't want to go back into that fucking mine, I don't want to be anywhere *near* it, I don't even want to get back within city limits. If it's a smart predator—which I think it is—this is what it would use as bait."

The idea slid into my mind with so little resistance it must have already been there, tucked away in some dark corner, waiting to spring. Lisey was haunting us. That was undeniable, no matter how you felt about the term. But to what end? She'd done everything in her power to get us away from the Basin, and now she wanted us back. The only reason that made sense was that we were in more danger staying away than we were in town . . . or that she wasn't Lisey anymore.

"I—" I said. My chest ached. "I guess I don't know." I pressed my forehead against the cool glass of the window.

"That's why we have to go." The words were scratchy,

heavy with sleep. I turned to see Nina lifting her face from the windowsill, rubbing at the marks it had left on her cheek. "I can't believe I'm the one saying this," she said. "But it doesn't matter. Whether Lisey's been dead for two weeks or for the entire time we've known her, she's still Lisey. And even if the mine is using her somehow, manipulating her, she's still trapped there. So either we go back and figure out a way to free her, or"—a muscle in her cheek twitched as she clenched her jaw—"or we stay with her."

I felt a lump form in my throat. "You're right. Whatever she is, she's ours. We're responsible for her."

"I know," Piper said, blotting her eyes on her shoulder without letting go of the wheel. "Fuck."

"But what are we going to *do?*" I asked.

Nina sat all the way up, putting her chin on the edge of Piper's seat. "We're going to finish what we started. We're going to kill it and set her free. Maybe set everyone free."

"How?" Piper asked, her voice full of doubt—and hope.

"I actually have some thoughts about that," Nina said. "Do you remember all the signs we passed on the way here for Wally's Reptile Extravaganza, or whatever it was called?"

"Vaguely," I said, "but I *strongly* vote no—"

"Shh," she said. "Did you see what else was on the signs?"

"I was transfixed by the giant snapping alligator jaws," I said.

Piper was grinding her teeth so hard I could hear it. "The point."

"We can't get a bomb," Nina said. "But you know what we can get?"

"If you say alligators I will drive this car off the fucking road," Piper said.

"Fireworks," Nina said. "As many as we can fit in this car."

"Fireworks."

I stared at her. My neck was starting to ache from being twisted around, and it was making my head hurt. I almost thought I'd misheard her.

"Fireworks, like—" I made a little motion with my hand, like I was flicking water off my fingertips. *"Fireworks* fireworks?"

"Yes," she said. "Remember when Danny Nelson put that thing in—"

"In Seth Keyes's car!" I finished as the memory rushed back. "What was that, a cherry bomb?"

"I think so," Nina said. "The Bangarang. I remember because he kept telling me. With lots of eye contact."

"I mean, the car was burned to shit inside but it wasn't, like, obliterated," I said. "How—"

"Fireworks have all the *ingredients* of a bomb." Nina scooted even closer toward us. "We can take them apart. We can use them to make something actually dangerous."

"How? We don't know anything about—"

I realized the answer a split second before we said it at the same time: "Danny Nelson."

She grimaced. "I know it's not ideal, but you know I can talk him into it."

"Even if he weren't desperate to bone you, he loves to fuck with his dad," I said, warming to the idea. "And I honestly think he's a little scared of the mine. He'd probably be on board."

Piper finally spoke. "We might still have airplane fuel. I don't know if my dad would have brought it in the move, but if he did, we could use that, too."

"Shit, yes, we could," Nina said. "Clem, where's the map?

Where are we right now?"

I fished it out of the footwell and handed it to her. She slumped back into her seat and unfolded it so far I couldn't see her behind it. The paper rattled as she traced a finger across it.

"If it's where I remember, we should be there tomorrow," she said. "I think it was right before the pink motel."

"That sounds right," I said.

A rabbit loped alongside the road. I turned to watch it as we passed, and a hawk swept down out of the sky and seized it in a plume of dust. I faced forward again, shaken. I hoped the others hadn't seen.

"What if we die?" Piper's voice was low, her hands shaky on the wheel.

"We won't," Nina said.

"But—"

"We won't."

"It'll fight us," Piper said. "The mine."

"Then we'll fight," I said. "The four of us."

Her chin trembled as she nodded. She pressed the accelerator into the floor and the car leaped toward the horizon. Up ahead I saw a crow soaring, winging its way toward home.

THIRTY-SIX

We moved through the woods like we were sleepwalking, in silence, in single file without meaning to, backpacks slung over our shoulders. Nina carried her mom's old hard-side suitcase; Piper had a milk jug of stale plane fuel stretching her crocheted shopping bag. I had three of Danny Nelson's homemade M-80s in the front pocket of my overalls. It didn't feel real; every time I blinked I expected to wake up in the passenger seat. Ash swirled around our feet as we walked, and the memory of the Pacific washed over me fuzzily. Like a dream, a mirage, the feel of warm sand beneath my toes. Had I ever breathed truly clean air? I imagined my lungs full of ash, piled like snowdrifts. Maybe there was some way I could scoop it out, scatter it away from me on the wind. I scratched at my sternum, thinking about curling my fingers through skin, through bone, into the dark wet space of breath. *Dig it out, let it go.*

"I wonder if it knows." Piper's voice was swallowed by the ash almost immediately. I stopped walking as she turned to look at us and felt Nina bump gently into my back. "I think it does."

"Stop that," Nina said, trying to nudge me forward.

I shook my head slowly, seafoam curling away behind my eyes until my mind was nothing but an empty spit of land that looked like bone. My thoughts were cloudy, and something about the feeling was familiar. I thought about that cold, dead light at the bottom of the mine, that single bright eye peering up at us from deep below the ground.

"She's right," I said. "It knows."

"*Stop*," Nina said. "No giving up before we're even there."

"I'm not giving up," I answered, reaching for her hand. "But I feel it waiting for us."

Something brushed my cheek, fast and soft like the back of a wing. I jerked my head up and looked around, but I didn't see anything.

"Good," Piper said fiercely. "I'm glad it knows. I want it *scared*."

I took her hand with my free one and squeezed it, hoping she could feel how much I loved her. She squeezed back and pulled away.

"I want my dad to know," she whispered. "I know he's gone, I just . . . if there's any part of him that's left in there, I want him to know I came back. I want him to know that he told us how to kill it, that it didn't win." She bit her lip. "Or at least—at least that we fought it to the end."

Nina leaned her head on Piper's shoulder. Piper's eyelashes flickered as she glanced at her. "I know you said we won't, but I really think we might die."

Nina sighed. "We might, I guess. We're putting a lot of faith in discount fireworks and Danny Nelson knowing anything about anything."

"What if we get stuck here?"

"Then it'll be just like we're alive." Nina butted Piper's neck gently before straightening up. "But maybe we'll have Lisey back."

"There's really only two options." I looked from Nina to Piper. "Either we destroy it, or we never get away from it. So we have to at least *try* to destroy it."

Piper nodded, something hardening in her eyes. "Yeah." She hoisted her bag higher on her shoulder and nodded again, smaller, almost to herself. "Yeah. We can try."

We put the end of the detonating cord on the ground next to the mineshaft, tucked firmly under a rock so it wouldn't fall in behind us. Nina crouched, rolled the spool over the edge, kept the cord pinned to the earth with her fingertips until we heard the dull thump as it met the ground. She looked up at us.

"Now or never," she said. Then she pushed herself to her feet, cupped my face with both hands, and kissed me hard. I let myself lean into her for a moment before ducking my head to catch my breath.

Piper lifted her eyebrows, a tiny smile twitching one side of her mouth. She tilted her head toward the hole. "Lisey," she called. "You owe me five bucks."

Our laughter was real, but it had a too-sharp, too-bright edge as it rattled against the trees. The silence that followed it was worse.

"Well, if no one's gonna kiss *me*, I guess I'll go—"

Nina threw her arms around Piper and kissed her cheek. "You can still go first," she said. "But remember how much we love you."

Piper put her hands on Nina's shoulders, held her out at arm's length, and looked at her. "I can't believe you goons are my best friends." She turned to me and I hugged her, burying my face in her neck. "You brought me in," she said, her voice vibrating against my skin. "You found me."

"We found each other," I whispered, blinking back tears.

She released me and I stepped back. She yanked her backpack straps tighter and then knelt at the mouth of the mine. She looked up at us and smiled—a real one, wide and dangerous, that brilliant, daring Carlisle grin. Her eyes glistened. "Love you."

Love you, I mouthed. She slid over the edge, and the darkness closed around her. I listened to the soft sounds of her descent as I tied all the bags together, letting the forty extra feet of rope coil on the ground next to me. I straightened up when Piper's voice drifted out of the mine.

"Come on!"

Nina looked at me sidelong, brushing her hair out of her face with the back of her hand, leaving a smudge of ash on her cheek. "I love you, you know."

A tiny, startled exhale burst from my lips. I stared at her, heart beating hard against my ribs, and then I felt a spike of rage so strong it sent white sparkles shooting across my field of vision. This couldn't be how it was. How it *ended*. It wasn't *fair*. I pressed my hands to my mouth, suddenly convinced I was going to scream or cry or both. Pain sank teeth into me and I shook with it, felt my bones reverberate with it, and then—as quickly as it came—it was gone, and in its place was one thought.

Moon Basin had our history. I would not let it have our future. It was as simple as that.

She hooked my pinky with hers and tugged, lifted an eyebrow. I threaded our fingers together and looked up at her. The rage had cooled and hardened like forged steel, folded into something dangerous. All I felt now was calm.

"I know," I said, and she smiled. A little breeze spun up around us, picking up dead leaves and ash and whirling them around, and I felt that weird brushing sensation again. I touched my face.

"I felt it too," she said. "If I were a different person, I would say it's Lisey."

After a moment she hiked her backpack over her shoulder and leaned forward. She brushed the lightest kiss across my lips and then she was descending, her hair burning red down the tunnel like a dying flare.

I sat next to the hole in the ground. "Lise," I said. *Too quiet.* I cleared my throat. "Lisey."

Nothing answered. I wrapped the rope around my arm, above the elbow, and slid the bundle of explosives over the edge. I paid the rope out gently, lowering the bags until I felt it go slack. I sat back on my heels and dug my fingers into the earth.

"I don't know if you're still here," I said, closing my eyes. "I think you are. If you are—and you're still, I don't know, if you're still *you*—can you help us? Can you keep us safe like when you pushed me out of the light?"

The sound of wings filled the air around me, so loud it felt physical, feathers against my face and arms and hands, and I wanted to reach out and catch one—

There was a sound like an inhale and then everything was quiet. I opened my eyes. I was alone.

I got to my feet, scanning the woods around me. I heard the rustle of wings, the clicking of beaks, eager, hungry little sounds that made the hair on my neck stand up. I felt beady eyes all over me.

"You told me to come back!" I called into the trees. "We came back!" I turned in time to see a crow flutter up out of the mineshaft and settle on the ground in front of me. I stared at it.

"Good omen or bad omen, Lisey?" I murmured, settling into a crouch as slowly as possible. The crow tilted its head and screeched at me. I extended my hand, palm up. The crow hopped toward me, then back, then forward again. It ruffled its wings and made a sound like a cough somewhere deep in its chest. I waited, my arm starting to ache, and after a moment it coughed again. I watched as it threw its head back, almost like it was eating something, its beak stabbing at the sky as its neck jerked. Then it went still, lowered its head, and gently placed the point of its beak in the center of my palm. It hopped back and screeched again, bright eyes tracking my movement as I brought my hand to my face and saw what it had given me.

A single white eyelash.

The crow launched itself off the ground in a swirl of ash and feathers, flapped up into the trees, and was gone. I stared after it, feeling precarious and unbalanced, then carefully pinched the eyelash between two fingers. I closed my eyes, thought, *Thumb*, and then opened my eyes and my hand. The eyelash clung to the tip of my thumb.

"One wish, right?" I brought my thumb to my lips and blew, closing my eyes so I wouldn't see where it landed.

I wished.

Then I shuffled to the edge of the hole in the ground and swung my legs down. The ash seemed thicker now, big flakes drifting past me into the dark.

"Okay, Lise," I said softly. I took a deep breath.

I followed my friends into the mine for the last time.

Paranormal America, Episode 100
Unused Footage

(The lens cap is removed to reveal SIOBHAN SINCLAIR, hair in a wild tangle around her face, trying to talk to the camera and walk backward at the same time.)

SINCLAIR: We got here as soon as we could. We received a call from—a local source—

(She narrowly avoids putting her foot into a shallow hole.)

SINCLAIR: —advising us that the Moon Basin mine was collapsing. No one knows what happened, but as you can see behind me—

(The camera pans out shakily, revealing a dark, jagged gash in the earth. Ash pours down the sloping, ever-widening sides as the sinkhole expands.)

SINCLAIR: As our loyal watchers know, this little town was the first place where the *Paranormal America* crew made their mark on the world of paranormal investigation. It's hard to believe that was almost a decade ago. It is with heavy hearts that we return to witness this, the end of an era. The Moon Basin mine is no more. The town's history will forever be divided into a before and after, and who knows whether the town's supernatural occurrences will continue in the after? *(She moves closer to the sinkhole.)*

SINCLAIR: No details are known yet, but we will remain on the scene, reporting as the story develops.

STEVEN MORELAND, *from off-screen*: You know this is all going to air in one episode, right?

SINCLAIR: What else am I supposed to say, Steven? We're not leaving until we know what happened. We might as well get some B-roll—

(Her foot slips out from under her in a flurry of ash and she begins to teeter toward the sinkhole. Her arms flail and she drops to one knee, the ground still crumbling under her.)

MORELAND: Ah, shit—

(The camera is lowered slowly, gently, to the ground, and then a pair of feet jogs into frame where SINCLAIR is scrabbling at the side of the hole.)

SINCLAIR: Delete that. I can get out myself. Go delete that right now so I can watch you do it.

(The feet move out of frame. The camera ascends once more, panning over SINCLAIR, who is now lying halfway out of the sinkhole with only one shoe on. As she writhes out of the hole, MORELAND chuckles. There is a clicking sound, as if he is tapping something against the casing of the camera.)

MORELAND: All gone. Don't even worry about it.

(The camera swings; a blurry shot of the sky, and then darkness.)

(A flicker. The picture returns. Four girls stand at the edge of the sinkhole, heads bent together. Their hands are joined, hair shining even in the ash-clouded sunlight as the wind ripples around them. Perhaps it is a trick of the light, or an imperfection in the tape, but they appear not quite solid, shimmering as if seen through a heat wave. The humming present in most footage taken in the Basin is absent. Instead there is only the sound of leaves rustling, although there are no trees present in the shot. One of the girls looks up as the camera zooms in on her, pulling a strand of hair away from her face. She opens her mouth to speak.)

ACKNOWLEDGMENTS

I wrote the first paragraph of the first draft of this book when I was eighteen years old. If your path crossed mine at any point during the last eleven years, you're a part of this. There are so many of you, and I love you all so much, and if I fail to mention you here it is only because writing acknowledgments is somehow more difficult than writing a book (although slightly less difficult than remembering how to spell "acknowledgments" right on the first try).

Rena Rossner, first and foremost: None of this would be possible if you hadn't taken a chance on me. You are the best agent I could have dreamed of, and I am so blessed to have you in my corner. You are fierce and tireless and talented, and your insight has made me and this book better in so many ways. You kick so much ass.

Ashley Hearn: my first editor. You have such a place in my heart, forever, for bringing me into the Page Street family. To have been able to work with someone like you, who really loves this book and understands it—I can't believe I could be so lucky. You are the reason this book exists in the world, as the best version of itself that it could be, and I am forever grateful to you for your voice and your passion and for believing in me.

Lauren Knowles: I got dropped in your lap and you didn't even hesitate, just got to work, and you have been so lovely and insightful and patient with me. I am very, very glad to have you as my second-ever editor.

Page Street Publishing: Tamara Grasty, Jenna Fagan, Meg Baskis, Lizzy Mason, Lauren Cepero, Kylie Alexander. All of you helped make this book a real thing, a real tangible thing, and I cannot tell you how much it means to have this dream of mine come true. You did that! Thank you!

Emma Yost: How does it feel to see your name in print, beautiful mama? You have kept me sane and alive long enough to get at least one book into the world, and that's why it's got your name on it. You inspire me every single day, you are my best friend, you are the other half of my heart. I am so grateful to call you my bat sister. I love you forever. Tell Davey I said hi.

Lio Min: I could not have done this without you, full stop. You have become such an important person in my life, and the fact that writing is what brought us together feels very appropriate. You are such a talented writer, and so sharp in the way that you express and interpret things, and it never ceases to amaze me that you like my work. I can't wait to see your book in print. Please also give my thanks to Onion Min, my demon overlord.

Mandie Williams: If we hadn't met, I don't know that I would be here. You inspired me, and you made me realize that this is an achievable, tangible thing, and you put me on this path, whether or not you know it. You are a gorgeous writer, you are impossibly cool, you are a dream of a friend.

Corbin DeWitt, Elisabeth Sanders, Kenzie Moore, Mariam Sleiman, Tess McGeer: God, I love you guys so much. We've been together-while-apart for years, through some really weird and bad shit, and I can't tell you how much it means that at the end of the day, or in the middle of the night, or any time at all,

I can reach out and you'll be there. I was lucky to find you all, and I am lucky to have you still. Corbin: You are my favorite living writer, and your food photos almost make me want to eat meat. Elisabeth: You drove across the desert to meet me and we drank vodka from tiny skulls and I have rarely felt so perfectly, brightly connected to a person. You are sharp and funny and you look so good in hats. Kenzie: Your strength and resilience are evident in everything you do, and I am so grateful to have been part of something you created, and to have become your friend. You are a truly good witch. Mariam: You are smart and judicious and you're the only person I want to talk about God with. Thank you for Lebanese breakfast and recipes and book recs, and if you do ever move here, you have a place to stay. Tess: You made me love Taylor Swift, and you let me text you the entire time I was watching *The Vampire Diaries*, and you write about sports in a way that makes me care about them. I can't wait to see your work on a big screen. I LOVE YOU ALL SO MUCH. Thank you for everything.

Jamie Hathaway: I still have the selfie you sent me when you finished reading the first version of this book. You are so good and kind and supportive and you have helped me through too many late-night crises, and I can never thank you enough. I can't wait to see you at the Iditarod.

Isabel Cole: I will never forget what you told me when you first read this. You said I really think you have done something here, and that was the first moment I thought that it could be something real. You are one of my favorite writers, and for you to see potential in me gave me hope. And—perhaps most important—you gave me One Direction. My gratitude and my love are endless.

J-Jams: You are my favorite hype girl. You are one of the best people I know, you are selfless and supportive, and you deserve every happiness that comes to you. Thank you for believing in me enough for both of us.

Sam Fox-Hartin: I wouldn't be who I am without your friendship. Thank you for new music, good jokes, one very promising unfinished vampire screenplay, and for keeping me upright.

Liz Parker: You are rapidly becoming one of my dearest writer-friends, and I am so grateful to have you. Your critique has been game-changing, as have our late-night brainstorms. I love that we can be sounding boards for each other. I can't wait to read your new work!

Katharine Tree, Stacey Filak, and the rest of the Renegades: Thank you for all the ways you have helped me, large and small, during this process. It is a blessing to be surrounded by so much talent and support, and I value each one of you so much.

Juli Barbato: You are a pleasure to work with, and your dogs are beautiful. I hope you get out of the desert and back to the ocean soon, and I am so grateful for all the work you've done on this book.

Hendrik Jasnoch: You gave me my first real platform and I will never, ever forget that. Thank you for giving me a chance, supporting me and keeping in touch, and I swear, I swear to you now that the book is done I'm gonna do some writing for you the next time an occasion rolls around.

Erica White, Beth Gier, Mimi Yu, Ryan Yost, Anna Prendella, Max, Britt Thornburley, Sadie Spalding, Sophia Clara, for advice and support and friendship and putting your eyes on this mess at least once, thank you.

Mason: Thank you for swords and shields and being brave

when I'm not, and for being there for me when I'm freaking out, even if all you do is say, Don't freak out. It's pretty helpful. I promise now that the book is out I will catch up on all the TV I was supposed to be watching. You are a very good brother, and I love you a lot.

Emily: I love you so much. You keep me grounded and safe and you believe in me; you support me, you inspire me with your own work and dedication. You are beautiful and funny and talented and I am so blessed by your love. Thank you for literally everything in my life, from pierogis at ten p.m. to puzzles every day of quarantine. I am better because I am with you; you are my comfort and my darling and I love you. Thank you for keeping me afloat.

Sadie: You got me through grad school, you got me through the last seven years of my life. I wrote this book almost entirely with your butt in my face and your paws on my keyboard and I miss you like crazy, my love.

Fern, Kif, Leelu, Citrine: You can't read. I hate you all so much. I can't believe you live in my home. I would and will gladly die for you.

One Direction, MCR, and Haribo: The things you have created have gotten me through some of the darkest moments of this process and, honestly, of my life. Thank you.

And finally, most important, Mom and Dad. You gave me my first words; you were my first and best fans. Thank you for reading everything I wrote, saving it, *laminating* it in some cases, and encouraging me beyond all reason to keep doing this thing I love. Thank you for believing in me, supporting me, and giving me a safe place to land. I'm proud to be your daughter and I love you both so, so much. Sorry about all the swearing.

ABOUT THE AUTHOR

Alison Ames lives in Colorado with a lot of animals and her almost-wife. She loves birds, comics, and the rule of three. *To Break a Covenant* is her debut novel. Find her on social media @2furiosa, and if you know (or are) Harry Styles, she insists you do so.